BLOOD RED

Books by Sherri Leigh James

BLOOD RED

LADY AND THE DON
SAGA OF A LADY

GIRL WITH A PAST

BLOOD RED

A Novel

SHERRI LEIGH JAMES

Introducing Cissy Huntington,
Interior Designer to the Rich and Famous

BLACK HAWK PRESS

Black Hawk Press Trade Paperback Edition
Black Hawk Press
P.O. Box 57737
Sherman Oaks, CA 91413
BLACK HAWK PRESS and the colophon are trademarks
of Black Hawk Press, Inc.

Library of Congress Control Number: 2018966058
Trade Paperback Edition ISBN: 9780999858257
eBook Edition ISBN: 9780999858240

www.SherriLeighJames.com

To all my friends in the world of interior design.

A gentle mixture of furniture expresses life and continuity,
but it must be a delicious mixture that flows and mixes well.
It is a bit like mixing a salad.
I am better at mixing rooms than salads.

Design Rule #7 for the "English Country House" Style
~ Nancy Lancaster, Socialite Interior Designer ~

Doctor Martin's
Beverly Hills Estate
Main House
Floor Plans

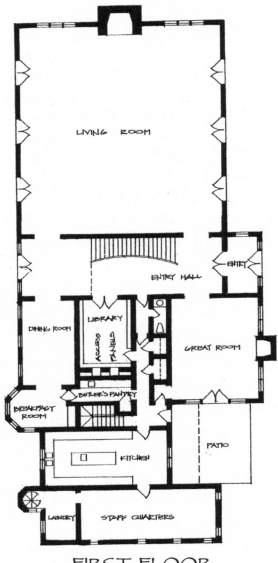

FIRST FLOOR

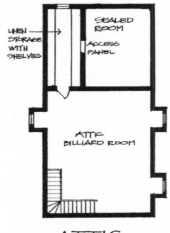

ATTIC

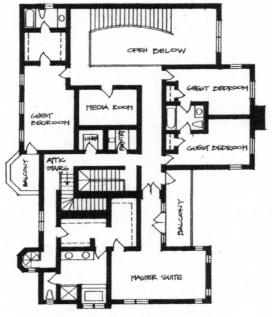

SECOND FLOOR

Prologue

The doctor was early for the appointment with his interior designer. Plenty of time to walk through the rooms to check the progress. The house was coming along.

Living room—definitely impressive. Damn! The fireplace surround and mantel with its elaborate carving was worth waiting for its arrival from Scotland. Fucking thing even had a hidden compartment.

It was going to be one hell of a housewarming party. This place was going to knock the socks off his friends, clients, and especially his snooty neighbors.

What's that noise? Somebody was in the library. He'd seen the electricians and painters loading their vehicles and the day laborers waiting to be picked up near the front gate as he entered the estate. What asshole was still here?

They better not be fucking up those red leather walls. Or the walnut paneling. Damn, it sounded like someone was opening the hidden panels.

He hurried through the entry hall and pushed open the library paneled doors that stood ajar.

"You! What the hell are you doing in here?"

The panel doors to the secret compartments were open.

"You moron, you can't be seen here. Leave now."

He walked into the room and checked to see if any damage had been done to his walnut linenfold wainscoting or his red leather walls. "Security saw you," he said as he ran his hand over the ultra-smooth wood.

"No."

"Don't be a fool, of course, they did. Remember the cameras." The doctor stomped his foot. "Get out now."

"I'm not going until we have a new understanding— you've totally fucked the one we had," the person answered. "I'm not going to stand for any more of your bullshit. And I'm sure as hell not taking any more orders from you." The person who had been rifling through the secret compartments reached into one, withdrew a wood box, and slammed the door shut. When the linenfold door bounced open without latching, the person hit it with the box.

"What the hell do you think you are doing, you savage!" The doctor pushed past the person and examined the open compartments to see if his treasures had been disturbed. "Bloody hell. What have you done?"

"I'll show you *savage*, you pretentious asshole."

"What's with the gun?" the doctored stammered. "Fuck. Don't point that thing at me, you fool. It's loaded." The doctor tried to grab the gun. "That's mine!

2

Chapter 1

Had I known how the events of the day would unfold, I wouldn't have bothered to change out of my sweats. Hell, I would have stayed in my pajamas—and in my bed. As it was, I zipped up the black and white tweed suit skirt.

"Mom, you aren't going to wear *that*!" Emma threw herself across the chaise lounge in my dressing room.

"I know it's last season's, but it is Chanel." I swiveled my feet in the thick silk carpet to check my reflection in the three-way mirror. Not too bad—for a woman with a twenty-two-year-old daughter.

"Oh, Mom, it's way too much for L.A. Put on some jeans—or at least, pants that aren't so-o matchy-poo."

"Darling, I am not wearing jeans to a business meeting."

But I grabbed a pair of black slacks, the interior designer's uniform, and slipped out of the bouclé skirt.

Emma took the skirt from my hand and hung it up before I could reconsider.

"Are you going to Dr. Martin's?"

"Uh-huh." I applied a fresh coat of lip-gloss.

"Does he let you come in the front door of his office?"

"I'm meeting him at the house. Did he tell you to use the back door?"

"Ye-ah. Like I'm the help, 'cause I'm the design assistant? What's with that? I'm not allowed to wait in his reception room anymore?"

"Sweetheart, it's only because he's tired of his patients demanding a nose that looks exactly like yours . . . which he can't deliver."

"Yeah, he told me that if he could do noses that look like mine, it would make him even richer than the liposuction. Has he ever shown you those horrible, disgusting before and after pictures of his lipo patients? Sick."

I smoothed my blonde hair and smiled, "Now I am confused. I thought that sick meant good . . . as in bad is even better than good, or how saying you're down with something means you're up for it."

My beautiful blonde daughter rolled her big blue eyes. "Oh, Mama, you are so *cute*."

I ignored "cute" even though it sounded suspiciously condescending. "I'm afraid he did insist that I look at those albums of pictures," I said. "I couldn't decide which was scarier—the before cellulite or the after bruises. The photos of face-lifts creep me out too. Even worse, I thought maybe he was leading up to suggesting we trade services."

"And just what would he suck out of you?"

"I was afraid he was going to want to suck fat out of my ass to put in my lips!"

"Eew, gross!"

"Fortunately, before I had to deal with that, his nurse interrupted to say that Kirstie Ally and Sally Abbey had arrived."

"They must be two of his biggest customers, especially Sally . . . quite literally." Emma giggled. "I thought I would miss out on seeing the famous people in the waiting room, but I'm down with going in the back way. That's where the really big stars go in. When I took the antique rugs over there the other day, I saw Sally and her trainer."

I smiled. "Have to run now, sweetheart. The doctor has some problem with the hardwood floor installation. And I need to collect some money from him."

"Mom, I'm sorry you have to put up with assholes like him."

"It could be so much worse. Having to work for a living isn't so bad. I do love design work."

Keeping busy was distracting. Who needs that damn husband of mine?

"I did all the returns and pickups at the Pacific Design Center," Emma said as she pulled a fabric sample of blood red mohair out of her pocket. "And I found a sweet William Morris fabric for the media room." She held up both samples. "Look good together, right?"

"Ooh, very nice. You're right, perfect for that room." I leaned over and gave her a quick hug. "You are the best assistant I've ever had!"

Emma flashed a smile. "If there's nothing else you need today, I'll take Lulu for her walk."

At the sound of her name, our labradoodle stood up

and fluffed her chocolate brown curls with a quick shake.

The three of us exited the house through the courtyard and down the terra cotta tile steps. Lulu and Emma took off down the street, and I got in my Prius.

Chapter 2

I drove faster than I should have down Western and fought the traffic on Sunset Strip. Escaping the slow stream of tourists, I turned up Coldwater into the Beverly Hills side of the canyon.

I needed to make up a bit of time.

Chatting with Emma was, of course, much more important than being prompt. I still regretted the time I had spent traveling while she and my son, Skip, were growing up. It had been important to their father that I travel with him, but once they started school, the children seldom accompanied us. They grew up sooner than I would ever have imagined. Emma was now a college graduate and Skip a Cal student.

I checked the time. Dr. Martin would not appreciate me making him wait. Even when I arrived first, he was likely to check with security to see if I'd been on time. It's the, "don't you know who I am," and "how dare you treat me with so little respect," thing common among the secretly insecure.

I sped up a little.

Turning onto the road leading to his house, I noticed a large, black SUV with dark tinted windows parked on the shoulder. It was the kind of so-called inconspicuous vehicle commonly used by celebs to avoid attracting attention, but everybody in LA knew that ploy.

The driver's side window was partially down. It looked very much like Nathan Carrington with his baseball cap pulled down low. Strange to have a star of his caliber driving himself. What was he doing there?

I pulled up to the guard booth at the entrance of the six-acre, walled estate.

"Is he here yet?"

"Oh yeah," said the uniformed muscle in the booth. "He may be at the tennis court, but all my cameras are all fu . . . messed up from the electricians reworking wiring, so I'm not too sure."

"I'll just head for the main house." I added, "Perhaps you would call his staff to let him know that's where I'll be?"

The guard nodded and waved me through.

I was never too clear just why Dr. Martin had as much security, if not more, than my biggest celebrity clients or friends. It was obvious why superstar celebs had to have security: how else could they keep the rag mags from snapping photos constantly, or protect their family from over eager fans? Or, even worse, guard their children against kidnappers? But the doctor had no children, no family (except a few ex-wives), no over eager fans, and he was only known in rarified, rich circles . . . . What was with all the security?

I was a bit creeped out by the audio/video hidden in most of the rooms of his house. I mean, who was going to listen to or watch all that footage of twenty different cameras in the rooms for both the doctor's use and the servants' quarters?

And why was he planning to spy on the servants who were not yet hired? He hadn't met them yet, but he clearly did not trust them, whoever they might be.

As I headed down the private drive outlined by a hedge of English roses beneath a lofty canopy of sycamore trees, I caught a glimpse of rolling lawns. I lowered my window to enjoy the fruity fragrance that filled the air from the hundreds of roses. Typical of the made-to-order furnishings we purchased for the doctor, the roses had been bred to order in the UK to attain the deep blood red of the blossoms that covered every bush.

My worry cut short my enjoyment. What could possibly be wrong with the damn floors?

I had hired the very best installers. I'd used them for our own floors over the years, and I had never had a complaint. Even my husband, Jamie, who was as "Way-Too-Fucking-Picky" as they come, didn't find fault with them.

Of course, Dr. Martin, was WTFP to the max.

I often thought he was just looking for excuses to get me over to his house, but what could I do? Skip's tuition bill was already overdue. If he wanted attention, I'd give it to him.

I loved his beautiful Tudor style house. It had been built in the 1920's, when construction methods still allowed for fine craftsmanship and charm. With its authentic half-timbering and herringbone brick façade, leaded glass windows and multiple twisted brick chimneys, the place oozed quaintness.

Now though, the circular drive in front of the house was full of new construction materials, cartons of wood flooring, and piles of sawdust with end-cuts debris. But no trucks or vans. I wondered where everyone was. There were no sounds of electric tools: no shots of electric nail guns, no whine of sanders. Was I that late? It was only a few minutes after 3:00 p.m. Damn, the workmen must have scurried out early.

I walked through the entry. Thank the gods he didn't want to redo this lovely floor with its beautiful inlay pattern. I'd liked the living room floor as well, but he had insisted on completely new rather than refinished. Therefore, we were laying new antiqued dark oak floor in eleven rooms, plus halls. Even in the media room where the acoustics demanded that the entire floor be covered with carpet.

But who am I to complain? After all, the more work we did, the more money I made. I guess I had lived with "Old Money" too long. Neither my husband's family, nor mine, would so much as consider replacing perfectly good, but old, floor with new floor that would be distressed to look old.

In the creamy yellow living room, I stopped to admire

the eighteen-feet tall, dark mahogany fireplace mantel and surround taken from a Scottish Manor. Despite elaborate carving, the mantel was thoroughly masculine right down to a perfect replica of a growling bear's head in the center of a medallion. I had been thrilled to discover it at Charles & Charles Antiques and grateful that they held it for me while we rebuilt the room to accommodate it.

The doctor wasn't in the living room, so I wandered around through the entry hall and into the great room hallway searching for what could possibly be the matter with the floors.

Honestly, I was a bit distracted by my enjoyment of the sight of the antique pine paneling that had been hauled to California from an 18th century manor house in the British Isles. It, like the terra cotta chimney pots on the seven chimneys, the blue and white tile in the powder room, the cobalt blue and blood red stained-glass window, the bronze chandelier, and the red Aga stove in the kitchen, had also been "looted" from merry old England.

For the Anglophile doctor, it had to be British and old. Like many nouveau riche, it seemed he was covering up the stigma of new money by burying himself in authentic antiques. I doubted he was fooling anyone who cared.

I called out to the doctor, but no one answered. I continued my inspection.

I was looking forward to seeing the paint in the library again; I had devised a technique to apply over the paint which included hand rubbing with several coats of wax to create a soft sheen and depth in the blood red color, so that it resembled sumptuous leather. I was happy with the way in which the color set off the richness of the walnut paneling and crown moldings. The doctor had actually smiled when he saw the color. The floors should be the perfect addition.

But first I must check on the powder room before its new threshold was permanently installed. The transition between the hardwood floors in the hallway and the antique stone floors in the powder room required a new stone threshold. But it needed to resemble the reclaimed stone flooring that had been delivered from an estate in the Cotswolds. Finding a new piece of stone that matched the pale gold hue and texture of the Cotswold stone had proven to be challenging. I turned left off the entry hall into the narrow hall outside the powder room and was pleased to see that it blended nicely with the stone floor.

I continued down the narrow hall, passed the coat closet and shoved against the servant's door to the library. The door was supposed to swing into the room to facilitate service from the kitchen but would not open.

Stuck.

I tried again. No luck.

"Damn." Flooring materials, or some such thing, must have been left against the door on the other side.

I walked down the hall to the butler's pantry. The doctor was pretentious enough that he probably would actually have a butler.

Beyond the butler's pantry, I admired the progress of the woodwork in the dining room. What a pleasure to have one's designs executed to perfection.

The entry hall was also coming along nicely. With a flourish, I opened the double library doors—what the hell?

I froze.

Construction materials were not blocking the door.

A bloody body held the door closed.

With great trepidation, I tiptoed to the body and reached down to check it for signs of life.

The body was still warm, but not breathing.

I tried to find a pulse on the blood covered neck.

Nothing. I fought off the squeamishness that threatened to overwhelm me as I moved my fingers through the blood hoping to feel some sign of life. Still nothing.

I pushed back the sleeve of the soft virgin wool suit trying to find a pulse in his wrist. Again nothing.

Checking for pulse had never been my forte and perhaps I was missing a faint beat. But if there was any chance that the doctor might survive the gaping wound to his head—I needed to get help. And fast.

"Help, help! I need help in the library." I screamed. "The doctor has been shot!"

Chapter 3

I stared. No movement. He still wasn't breathing. Was he dead?

What the hell was the use of security guards with all their cameras and microphones if they don't respond when needed?

"Call an ambulance! And send help over here fast." I yelled as loud as I could.

I knew enough to realize that head wounds bleed profusely, but his face and neck were shrouded with blood. I forced myself to look closer at a circle were the blood was darker.

It was a hole in his forehead. When I tried again to find a pulse on his neck, his head turned a little to the side. Oh damn, the back of his head was gone. My next scream was involuntary.

He was on his side lying in a giant pool of blood. Red spatters dripped down the rich walnut paneling.

Surely a microphone in this part of the house was picking up my cries. Where was the security? I reached across the growing crimson lake to touch his neck again. Still warm, but no hint of a pulse.

I straightened and brushed against an open door-panel normally hidden by linen-fold woodcarving.

No one responded to my screams. I fumbled for my cell. No service!

I ran into the entry, out the front door, trying to get a signal.

My hands were shaking violently. I struggled to hold onto the phone.

"Shit, shit, shit!" 9 . . . I poked the keys, 1, 1. Two rings followed by, "If this is an emergency, please stay on the line."

Oh, my God, they've put me on hold.

I ran up the drive, phone still to my ear.

Just as I arrived at the guard booth, someone, a real person, came on the phone. "911. What is your emergency?"

I was so out of breath, I could barely speak. "I . . . think . . . he . . . is dead!" I huffed.

"Who's dead, ma'am?" asked the voice on the phone.

"The doctor . . . in the library, . . . in a pool of blood. He isn't breathing." I spoke loud enough that the guard in the security booth heard me. He stepped back into the hut and pushed a button. Alarm bells rang, sirens went off all over the place.

Men with guns drawn flew out from every direction.

I threw my hands in the air. "Hey guys! You know me!"

"Ma'am! Ma'am! What is your location?" demanded the voice on the phone.

Chapter 4

I showed the security guys the doctor's body on the library floor. Not only were there blood spatters on the walnut paneling, I saw drips barely visible on the red "leather" walls. I gagged and the two security guards allowed me to return to the warmth of my car to await the police. One of the security guards watched me from the edge of the parking area; the other watched from the porch of the main house.

A Beverly Hills Fire Department ambulance arrived. Two paramedics hurried into the house and shook their heads as they exited almost immediately.

My phone dinged an incoming text from Emma. *"Mom, flooring guy trying to reach you."*

"I'll call him later service spotty here," I texted back.

"How's meeting going? Does the doc love the red walls?"

"Not too well"

"What's up? Is doc being a dick?"

"Not exactly"

"What's going on?"

How should I answer that without freaking her out?
"Shooting here"
　"Film crew?"
　"Crime"
　"R u safe?"
I looked at the cluster of security guards strutting around the front steps of the main house. *"Lots of security here,"* I answered.
　"Same f-ups allowed shooting, come home"
　"I'm ok, will call later"
　"R u sure u r ok?"

Chapter 5

Twenty minutes after I found the body, the police arrived and insisted I move to the wood paneled entry hall. I sat on a step of the grand staircase. One of the uniformed officers ordered me to stay put. With both the entry doors open to the chill, I was glad I had on the black slacks rather than the little Chanel skirt.

Two officers strung a yellow tape around the vestibule porch at the entry of the house. They placed a plastic tub of blue surgical booties just outside the vestibule and each person put on a pair before they entered the house.

One of the officers silently wrapped plastic bags over both my hands and handed me a sheet of paper and a pen for me to fill out a form with my name, address and phone number. Their names were written at the top of the page.

I struggled to print my name, CISSY HUNTINGTON in block letters and sign my name with the bags on both hands. "What's this?"

"A security log," the officer answered.

I looked at him, shrugged and raised my hand in a questioning gesture.

"A sign-in sheet. Gotta be signed by all visitors to the

crime scene." He walked away.

I shivered on the cold step for an hour, watching police, forensics people, and medical examiners put on booties and walk in and out.

I calmed down a bit, but I wished the clear liquid in my water bottle was a martini. I wondered what the officers would say if I asked to get my pashmina from my car.

Finally, someone I took to be a crime scene investigator came over to me. "I'm going to check your hands for gunpowder residue. Hold still."

He carefully removed the bags and wiped each of my hands with moist swabs that he then placed in evidence bags. He used a felt tip pen to write my name, the date, and which hand had been swabbed on each bag. He then took a filter paper and wiped down my jacket. That paper was also placed in a labeled evidence bag.

"Can I go now?" I asked as he bundled the bags into a plastic container.

"No." He walked away.

In the back of the entry hall, I heard him conferring with a tall, dark man I assumed to be a homicide detective, based on his suit and his in-charge attitude.

"It's really unlikely she was the shooter unless she stood on a ladder. The angle of entry and the forward blood splatter pattern indicate a much taller person," the CSI told the detective.

"Good to check her anyway. You never know," the detective said.

A few minutes later, two men pushed a gurney with the

doctor in a body bag through the hall and out the front door. The man I figured to be a medical examiner followed the wheeled stretcher out to the crushed granite drive.

I caught a glimpse of a coroner's wagon through the entry hall door and the vestibule arch.

I was cold and hungry. Worse, now that I had calmed down a bit, I found it difficult not to think about the shambles my life was in. My usual method of avoiding anxiety was to keep busy, thus being forced to sit still and idle was torture.

"Now can I leave?" I called out to no one in particular.

A barrage of "No!" answered me from multiple directions.

The crime scene investigator and his photographer assistant were now checking out the two front entries. The assistant took numerous photos from every conceivable angle, including climbing over me to get to the top of the stairs and shoot the entire area.

Meanwhile, a female CSI sketched the room. A third man took notes as two CSIs called out a description of the area.

"Please stand up," the photographer said as he brushed past me on the stairs. He took close up photos of my chest, my arms, my legs, my head, and then full-body shots, front and back.

The female CSI turned out all the lights and closed the doors to the entry hall.

It was nice to have some relief from the cold winter wind that blew in the door, up the stairs and chilled my toes. Too bad I hadn't changed my Jimmy Choo sandals when I switched my skirt for the pants.

The sun was low in the sky; it was not yet fully night outside, but the hall was dark. A shadowy figure shone a laser light on the doorframe and door, both of which glowed with hundreds of hand and fingerprints, bringing forth a chorus of groans from all of the investigators in the area. The photographer set to work shooting every inch of the room.

Next, one of the investigators sprayed a path in the floor from the library to the back doors.

"What's he spraying?" I asked.

"Luminol. It reacts with blood to produce a glow," answered the note taker.

I saw tiny spots glowing near the library doors and a few specks leading to the doors that opened off the back of the hall onto the terrace. Amazing. I had no idea almost microscopic specks of blood would highlight the trail of a killer.

The male CSI then sprayed from the library to the front door. A wide path of tiny particles of luminance appeared immediately.

Wait. Was there more than one shooter? Why two paths? Maybe the killer changed his mind as to the best exit? Could it have been because I was coming in the front entry? Damn, that was a scary thought.

From where I sat on the stairs, I could make out the pattern of the treads of a work boot. The steps were far apart. Surely that stride length would indicate a tall person.

The photographer took several pictures of the glowing pattern.

Next the spray was turned on me. My Chanel jacket didn't glow, nor did my pants, but the toes of my Jimmy Choos were bright with lumens. Yuck.

"Does this stuff wash off?" I asked but the sprayer merely shrugged.

The camera turned on me.

"Did you think I had blood on my clothes?" I asked.

Again, the note taker clued me in. "They're looking for blowback blood. You know, back spatter."

I didn't know. "Why?" I asked.

"You aren't tall enough to be the shooter, but you could have been standing next to the gunman," the note taker explained. "But so far, there's no sign of you being in the room at the moment the shots were fired."

The investigator wasn't taking any chances. "Stand up." He sprayed the back of me. Apparently, my back didn't glow, as the photographer wasn't asked to take any shots.

I wondered what that spray was doing to my clothes. Would dry cleaning remove this white residue?

I sat in the dark as the rest of the hall was sprayed. Several more photos were snapped and then the note taker flipped the lights back on.

Before I could even adjust my eyes to the brightness, one of the CSI's was removing my sandals.

"What are you doing to my Jimmy Choos?" I cried as he painted the sole of one of the shoes with ink. "Please be careful not to get that black stuff on the top of the shoes."

But it was too late. The slathered-on ink rode up to the top of the sole and onto the inner lining of my precious sandal, one of the pairs I had hoped would last me a long time.

Apparently, CSIs have no respect for fine footwear. Probably had no idea these shoes were a major investment.

Next, he pressed the sole of my shoe against a sheet of paper, transferring the pattern.

In response to my plaintive moans, the note taker once again explained what the CSIs were doing. "They have to be able to exclude your footprints and those of anyone else whose presence at the scene is already known."

While the shoe slayer took my other shoe, the woman investigator destroyed my manicure by rubbing each of my ten fingers in a pad of black ink to take my fingerprints.

She handed me one wipe to clean up the mess. All I accomplished with that single wipe was to turn both my hands gray.

"Can I leave? Or at least can I get my pashmina out of my car?" Now that the front door was open again, I shivered in the winter Santa Anas blowing cool air off the desert.

"Stay right where you are," said the tall, dark-haired hunk, presumably the detective. He walked out of the library and close enough to me that I could see his dark chocolate eyes were beautiful—but not friendly.

Chapter 6

"Who are you?" I asked.

"Manny Rodriquez, Homicide Detective Rodriquez, Beverly Hills PD." He turned away and walked back into the library.

I watched two men carry a section of the library paneling out the door. It was splattered in blood and had a bullet lodged in the center of the raised panel. I thought that must be the "forward spatter."

I assumed they would cut the bullet out of the panel at their lab. Judging from the ragged edges of the piece, little care had been taken to remove that one-of-a-kind panel. Replacing it would be a bitch. The library I had once loved would never hold the same charm.

The crew working in the library complained, "These damn walls are the same color as fresh blood. We'll never find it all unless we spray every inch."

I checked the time on my phone. It had already been three hours, and I was obviously not going to leave any time soon. I called home to tell Emma I would be late for dinner.

Addie Mae answered the phone; "You aren't having dinner with that sleazy old man, are you? You still a married woman. . . . At least, we think so."

"No, he's dead."

"Wha-a-hat? Mr. Huntington?"

"No, the doctor."

"So, why can't you come home for dinner? I got to leave, I can't wait here all night." Addie Mae doesn't waste any sympathy or concern on anyone she doesn't know well.

"Just go ahead! Let me talk to Emma, she can clean up."

"Oh, I know how she cleans up. We be having ants by morning." Addie Mae had been my mother's housekeeper and had been taking care of me as long as I could remember.

When my young parents left the guesthouse on my grandparents' estate, and moved into their own home, my grandfather sent Addie Mae along to ensure that I was well cared for.

Addie May didn't like the neighborhood we lived in during those first few years. She refused to let me play with the neighbors' children. She called them white trash. Occasionally, she would take me back to my grandparents' neighborhood where children she approved of populated the park. She'd been bossing me around ever since.

"Please Addie Mae, let me talk to Emma."

"Hey, Mom. Are you okay?"

"Sweetheart, please feed yourself and put the leftovers in the fridge. I'm going to be here a bit longer."

"Mom, did someone die?"

"The doctor."

"What! OMG. How?"

"He was shot. I found him, so I guess I have to answer questions. I can't leave yet."

At least that is what I assumed. Actually, no one had paid the slightest attention to me since I was sprayed with luminol.

"Un-freaking-believable. Do they think you had something to do with this?"

"No, I'm sure they don't think that."

I wondered if that was true.

I turned to see the thirty-something, dark-eyed hottie who had introduced himself as Detective Rodriquez standing behind me, listening to our conversation.

"Sweetheart, please go ahead with dinner, and I'll see you later. Love you, bye."

"Husband?" asked the detective.

"Daughter."

"What can you tell me about this?"

"I had an appointment with him at three o'clock. I showed up no more than five minutes after. I looked around at the project, the floors, and there he was . . . behind the door to the library. Of course, I had to go around from the butler's pantry entrance to open the other doors in order to see him."

"Did you see any one else here?"

"Just the guard at the gate." I said. Then I remembered the dark SUV. "On my way in, I did see a dark SUV parked on the shoulder just around the corner before the gate."

"Anyone in it?"

"A driver."

"Can you describe him?"

"He had on a dark baseball cap pulled down low. He was slumped down in the seat. I kinda thought the person looked a bit like Nathan Carrington. Pretty unlikely a mega star would be sitting out there, huh?"

"Do you own a gun?"

"I don't know."

"What do you mean, you don't know?" He crossed his arms and scowled at me.

"I think my husband may have. I don't know where it is . . . . If he did own one . . . . Or if my father did, it could be in our house."

"Where is your husband?"

"I don't know."

"Call him and ask him about the gun."

"I can't."

"Can you leave him a voicemail? Talk to his secretary?"

"No."

The detective's dark eyes focused on my face like a laser. "Is he a jealous man?"

I sighed. "I haven't seen him in six months. He walked out on us—our children and me—the same day he declared bankruptcy without having said one word to me about it."

His dark eyebrows knitted, he squinted at me. "Where are you from?"

"I live in Los Feliz now. I was born in San Francisco."

"You have an accent."

"I do not have an accent. You and everybody else who came here from various places have accents!" I snapped at him, then took a deep breath. "I'm sorry, I'm a bit on edge. I don't know about my accent. Until I moved to LA, I was never told I had an accent. I've lived in California all my life."

"Maybe your parents were from England?"

"My parents, and my grandparents, and most of my great grandparents were all born in California."

"Wow, a native! Don't meet many of those around here!"

"Look, Detective, I really don't know much about this man. I'm an interior designer. He is—was—one of my clients."

"I'm sure you know more than I do. How does he afford these fancy digs?"

"He was a wildly successful cosmetic surgeon with a Beverly Hills practice. His clientele list reads like the Who's Who of Hollywood. He introduced liposuction to this country. He said he brought it here from Switzerland about 30 years ago. I'm sure his staff can tell you much more than I can."

"Who else was here when you got here?"

"No one. I was surprised that all the workmen had cleared out so fast today. I know there were security guys here, but I only saw the one at the gate."

"Why so much security?"

I shook my head. "I've wondered the same thing my-self. Why don't you ask his security guys? They must know what they're paid to watch for." I hesitated. "He was shot, right?"

"It's traditional in investigations for the police to ask the questions," he said without a hint of a smile.

I rolled my eyes and gave him a "give me a break" look.

"Yes, he was shot."

"The workmen could only have been gone for a matter of minutes when I arrived. You would think they would've heard a gun. Well, . . . maybe not, with all the nail guns that must have been going here all day. That was one of the reasons we were meeting after three—so that the nail guns wouldn't be . . . I hate the sound of those things, especially when there are several going at once."

It finally hit me. Whoever had shot him may well have been in the house when I came in.

"But wait, there were men working in the library today. That floor isn't finished. They would have seen him lying there." I realized my panic had me blathering, but I didn't stop. "Oh, God! Does this mean he may have been shot right before I found him? The puddle of blood was huge!"

His brown eyes focused on the ceiling as he waited for me to calm down.

"Who was installing the floors?" he asked when I quieted.

I gave the detective the name of the floor installing

company. "But they wouldn't have had anything to do with this.

"Did you find the recording devices?" I asked.

The detective gave me a puzzled look. "Where?"

"There are cameras and sound recording, AV equipment in several rooms that I know of. The cameras and mikes had to be hidden in the walls or ceilings."

"In the room where you found the body?"

"Yes, in the library."

"Show me," he said as he offered me a hand-up from the step where I sat.

I tiptoed through the entry to the library, trying to avoid stepping in blood and doing further damage to my Jimmy Choos. The metallic smell from the large amount of blood in the enclosed library turned my stomach. I noticed a cupboard door hidden in the paneling—the one of those that had been open earlier—was closed. I wondered about the pile of jeweler's cases and the other boxes my quick glance had noticed in that opening.

The detective was studying my face, waiting for an answer.

I pointed to the paneling above the puddle of blood. "See that little black hole in the edge of that beaded molding?"

"That's a camera?"

"Not just a camera. It's also a microphone."

The detective grinned. "Are there any more of those in this room?"

"Not that I know of. I know of that one because I coordinated the installer with my wood workers," I said. "But, who knows if the shooter will be on the recording? It may not have been turned on yet. Or, he most likely had his back to it if he came in through the pantry door and shot the doctor."

The detective nodded his understanding. "Where is the recording equipment?"

I frowned and shook my head. "Presumably the security team knows?"

"Would anyone have reason to have a ladder in here today?" he asked.

"I doubt it. The painters polished the last coat of wax on the red paint yesterday."

"Show me the camera in the entry hall."

"It's in the chandelier," I said as we headed in that direction.

I pointed out the tiny camera that had been retrofitted in the antique light fixture.

"Please, I really need to get home." I said. I gave him my numbers and said bye, hoping he wouldn't ask me to stay any longer. To my relief, he said, "We'll be in touch."

As I drove home I thought about who would have had any reason to shoot the doctor. He had little personal life that I could see. Not surprising, since he was not a pleasant man. I had often wondered why he was so insecure. Everything seemed to revolve around his very successful practice. He liked to socialize with his "patients". I never thought of them as patients. Somehow, with elective surgery, it doesn't seem like "patient" describes the recipient. It seems more like customers buying themselves a new nose, a young face or a slim body.

I remembered again the pile of cases and boxes hidden in the library paneling. Some of the jewelry cases were open. Perhaps the doctor interrupted a burglary?

What a day. I cranked up the heat and rubbed the back of my neck as I drove.

Despite the brave face I tried to put on for the sake of my children, I constantly had to buoy my own spirits since Jamie had left. The emotional pain was harder to deal with than the financial difficulties. At least there was something I could do about the finances.

By the time my husband's success with real estate development had mushroomed into an empire, we had all grown accustomed to a lifestyle that very few could afford. Now we had cut back enormously. Gone were the well-staffed multiple houses in prime locations all over the planet. And gone were the jets to get there.

I had returned to work as an interior designer in LA to take advantage of my friendships with all the celebrities I'd met on the constant round of charity balls and fund-raisers that were required by Jamie's business.

And now this. My only client was dead and his payments weren't current. Emma and I had invested so much time working on both the doctor's office and his estate that I hadn't taken the time to find any other work. And now, what would have been my best work, was a murder scene with the library's beautiful red walls masking the blood.

Murder put my problems in perspective. The thought that the killer may have still been in the house when I arrived was chilling. Maybe I was lucky to still be alive.

I was left with the nagging feeling that there was something about all of this that I should have told the detective, but I couldn't quite get hold of it. Maybe it would come to me when I wasn't hungry and exhausted.

Chapter 7

I woke up the next morning worried about my big problem: I really did need that money from Dr. Martin's project. I should have made sure he stayed current with his payments.

I had to get over my social training forbidding the discussion of money. On the other hand, I could take advantage of my mother's example and collect this money the same way I would fundraise for charity. *That* I knew how to do.

When I got back from the crime scene the night before, I called Carl's flooring company while I downed the strong gin and tonic that Emma had waiting for me. I explained to Carl what had happened, relaying that Detective Rodriquez had asked that the crew show up at the usual time the next morning. The detective had plenty of questions for them.

Now over my first cup of coffee, I dug out my letter of agreement with the doctor. Thank God, his attorney's name was on the letterhead. I called to demand an appointment for later that morning.

I must have been a bit sharp with the secretary because

Emma poked her head in my bedroom door.

"Mom," she said, "maybe you want to take today off? We could go for a hike. Get some distance on all this. What do ya think?"

"I'm fine, and I can hardly afford a day off."

"You don't sound so fine. You sound kinda tense." She came over to where I sat at my desk and massaged my shoulders. "That must have been fucking shocking . . . finding a dead body."

"Oh, God." I burst into tears within seconds of her contact. Her sympathy crushed my resolve.

Emma wrapped her arms around my shoulders and patted my back. "I'm sorry, Mama. I should have said something last night."

The ring of the phone followed by Skip's voice on the answering machine interrupted my good cry.

"Mom, are you okay? Emma, are you guys still there? Or did you go for a hike?"

I picked up the phone. "You two have been discussing me again?" I asked my son.

"You're really good at this denial stuff, Mom. Like how you never talk about Dad. Emma was worried," Skip explained.

"It's okay. I'm glad I have you two to worry about me."

I was grateful to have wonderful, grown children who were no longer teens—meaning I was no longer the stupidest person ever, though I evidently, still needed looking out for.

Emma picked up an extension and the three of us had a nice chat, until I noticed the time. I was due at the office of the doctor's attorney in an hour. I rushed to get dressed in my black Armani suit and out of the house.

Traffic wasn't too bad, and I arrived at the attorney's offices on the 34th floor of a downtown LA high-rise with a few minutes to spare.

I have been in many extremely posh offices—God knows my husband always insisted on impressive offices—but this one really won the prize. Paneled in amber toned pearwood, carpeted with super thick, hand-knotted, golden brown silk rugs on rich walnut floors, and lit by outrageous Murano gold glass chandeliers: the reception was almost tasteful. For LA.

I recognized the design concept a few of my past clients had asked for. It clearly stated, "Don't fuck with me, I have got more than enough resources to best you any time."

The doctor's attorney didn't keep me waiting more than a few minutes: just long enough to get the full effect of the décor.

I refused to let some wood, glass, and silk intimidate me even if it was well done. I'd done better.

Just months before, I'd made the major error of allowing my husband's attorneys and accountants tell me what I could and couldn't do in regards to his bankruptcy and asset forfeiture. Later, when the shock wore off, I realized I should have hired my own lawyers. I wasn't going to make the mistake of ladylike compliance again.

I looked at the list of the firm's attorneys inscribed in a stone plaque on the wall and spotted the one I had come to see. Beyla Karloff Jr. Familiar name, seemed famous but not as an attorney. Beyla Karloff Jr., oh yeah, his father was that old movie star. Beyla Karloff had been in lots of scary movies.

"Mrs. Huntington, what can I do for you?" He didn't look scary. He looked like a perfectly groomed, pleasant faced gentleman in his 50's. Armani suit, Italian shoes, solid colored beige silk tie, very short gray hair. All in all, an attractive man. But a lawyer, nevertheless.

"As you may recall, I have been overseeing some work on the Beverly Hills house of Dr. Robert Martin." I settled myself in the taupe silk covered guest chair in his corner office.

"Yes, I'm aware of your arrangement with the doctor."

My mother's voice with her fundraising advice ran in my head: "Come straight to the point dear, don't waste a businessman's time with social niceties." Aloud I said, "The doctor was behind on his payments."

He sat down behind an enormous Biedermeier desk and placed his fingers over the black edge of the satiny pearwood top. "There is a bit of awkwardness with the doctor's estate." He picked up an ebony handled letter opener and ran his hand along the gold blade. "But I'm sure we can get your fees covered quite soon."

That didn't sound good. The barely audible sigh that had prefaced his statement made me think he'd heard this before. "What exactly do you mean by a 'bit of awkwardness'?"

"Let's just say that the Doctor's estate was not what one would have assumed."

Oh God, not again. Had I gotten myself involved with another "rich" person who was not actually rich? Was no one in California what he or she seemed?

"Look, I've got my lawyers onto the liens and so forth," I lied, "but I prefer that we work this out between us. And if the estate is that impoverished, I doubt you want to invest a lot of time in these matters either."

"His heir arrives at LAX this afternoon. I will have to consult with her prior to making any agreements with you." He hesitated while he appeared to study the impressive view out his wall of windows.

"What do you mean 'prior'?" I felt the heat of anger creep across my face. "I already have an agreement."

"Don't get excited, we'll work this out." His voice was calm, but the way he rubbed his hands together told me he was nervous. Probably thought a hysterical woman was about to lose it right there in the stillness of his posh office and embarrass him in front of his colleagues.

"We need to work this out right now!" I was starting to get the knack of being a "tough" businesswoman. This might be better than polite fundraising.

"His niece, and only heir, is coming in from Wichita this afternoon to be involved in the funeral arrangements. After I have a chance to go over this with her, we'll get with you. How does Thursday afternoon sound?"

"It sounds terrible! This has to be resolved today." I

pounded my fist on the antique desktop. "I need to know that the bills that have been and are being run up will be covered. Should I stop the workmen?" I did my best to keep a pissed off look on my face, despite the fact that I was starting to see that this "tough" act could be fun.

"Look," he said, "Miss Wallerski's flight is due in at 1:45. I've sent a car for her. If you were to come back at say, six o'clock . . . does that sound better?"

"I'll be here." I gave him my sternest look as I stood up.

As I passed the reception desk, I heard Mr. Karloff's secretary say to the receptionist, "Oh shit! I forgot to arrange for a car for Susan Wallerski, and now the service doesn't have one available."

Allying the heiress might help my cause, I thought. I turned around and volunteered to help the poor girl out.

"You know, I'm headed out that direction, and I have to come back here later today. . . . Maybe I could pick her up."

The hesitation in the secretary's eyes was obvious. She studied my face for a full thirty seconds, then shook her head. "Thank you, but I'll try another service."

"I know you don't know me, but I'm going to be working with Ms. Wallerski. She's inheriting me along with her uncle's estate. It'll give us a chance to get acquainted."

Again, she looked at me without speaking for several seconds. "I better check with Mr. Karloff." The secretary picked up the receiver of her phone.

"If you do that, you'll have to tell him you forgot," the

receptionist reminded her.

"Shit!" The secretary set the phone receiver back in the cradle.

"Really, it'll be okay. I'll pick her up and he'll never know."

"Okay." Karloff's secretary glanced down the hall towards his office and then handed me a slip of paper. "Here's her cell number. She's coming in on United, Flight 1117 at 1:45."

I got down to the subterranean parking and realized two things. One, I had failed to get a parking validation. Damn, twelve dollars for less than an hour! I had to learn to think of these things. New habits were needed.

And two, I had less than an hour to get to the airport. Possible, but only if the traffic wasn't bad.

I would be missing the worst rush hour, but the thing is LA doesn't actually have a rush hour, or even hours, anymore. I have been caught in traffic jams at all times of the day or night.

I worried that I would miss her, but I called the airline and was pleased to hear that the flight had been delayed by thirty minutes.

Next, I called Susan's cell to leave a message for her to call me back when she turned on her phone after landing.

To my surprise, she answered the phone on the second ring. "Miss Wallerski, my name is Cissy Huntington. I'm, . . . ah . . . I was your uncle's interior designer. There was a slight mix up regarding the car that was to pick you up, so I volunteered."

"That's very kind of you, Ms. Huntington."

"Please call me, Cissy. If it's okay with you, I'll pick you up just outside baggage claim. Look for a grey Toyota Prius with dealer plates and a blonde driver. Hopefully I won't be caught in this traffic much longer."

Within twenty minutes I was helping her load her suitcase into the back of my car. I'd had no difficulty spotting her: she definitely resembled her uncle.

During the drive downtown, we had plenty of time to get acquainted as we sat in heavy traffic even in the car pool lane. I was charmed by how cute and animated she was. Physically, she may have been mid-thirties, a brunette, petite (the fashion euphemism for short), plump, feminine version of her uncle, but she lacked his reserve and snobbish pretension.

Apparently, she shared his fondness for the color red, although the blood red he preferred would have been more flattering on her than the orange shade of red of her coat that washed out her delicate coloring.

It turned out that Susan and I had mutual acquaintances—people from Wichita that I had met at Aspen. I've only been to Wichita once for a very short stay, but it is apparently an even smaller town than I realized. Susan knew everyone I knew from there.

"Were you and your uncle close?" I asked.

"I really didn't know him very well at all. Only met him a few times that I can remember. The most recent time was when he turned up at my mom's funeral after refusing to come while she was dying."

"I'm sorry."

"He and my mother were not close, but I thought he could've at least come to say good-bye," Susan continued. "He told me that bullshit line about wanting to remember her like she had been before she got sick. Plain old selfish, if you ask me. I could've used his help with all of the arrangements. It was really hard those last few weeks. I had to deal with it all by myself. Now I guess I'm going to have to handle his arrangements . . . . Oh, God, I'm sorry, I'm really goin' on. Suppose it's obvious that I didn't like him very much."

"Susan, please, I don't mind."

Then Susan didn't hesitate to get right into it with me. "My mom always said that her brother lived way beyond his means, so I'm not surprised to learn that there isn't much to his estate. I hope there's enough money to at least pay my expenses for this trip, I'm not exactly flush myself. Just got outsourced."

"Well, yes, and I hope there's enough to pay for the work we've been doing on the house. I guess we will soon see." I pointed to a sleek high-rise. "There's your lawyer's office."

Susan stretched her neck trying to see the building. I pulled into the underground garage.

Susan stared at the over-the-top, rich décor of the elevator.

"Wow, he didn't scrimp on his attorney!" she said with awe.

"I don't think he *scrimped* on anything. That may have

been the problem."

I led Susan directly into Karloff's office, the protesting receptionist chasing our heels.

Karloff stood, waved the receptionist away and pointed at his guest chairs. "Ladies, please have a seat."

He reached across the large antique desk to offer his hand to Susan. "Thank you for coming. It's good to meet face to face after all of our phone conversations."

Susan nodded her agreement, then studied her hands folded in her lap. In spite of the fact that she and Karloff had gotten acquainted via phone calls, she was obviously intimidated by the office and his physical presence.

Next, he looked at me. "Thank you, Mrs. Huntington for picking up Miss Wallerski. Now, if you would please excuse us." He motioned to the office door.

"I want some answers." I stubbornly held my seat. "You said we would work this out once Susan arrived. Well, here she is."

"Mr. Karloff, I don't mind if Cissy stays. It's the least I can do in return for her comin' after me." Susan looked at me and smiled.

He shuffled papers around on the black leather inset of his desk as though he were giving Susan a minute to think over her decision. "It's highly unusual." He looked up from the papers. "But if you're certain?"

He tried to look Susan in the face, but she stared at her feet. "I had Robert's accountant send over his latest profit & loss, his balance sheet, his financial statements."

More paper shuffling. "It is quite a mess actually, it is

going to take a while to determine if he has any real money by the time we pay off all the indebtedness." Karloff was appropriately uncomfortable.

"But the house, the estate . . ." I wasn't going to give up easily this time.

"Oh yes, he had assets—the house, cars, his practice. If we liquidate everything, we may come out ahead, but it is going to be close. Mrs. Huntington, you'll need to complete the work on the house to get it into marketable condition."

"And just how do we pay for that?" I looked him right between the eyes. "You bring current the past due invoices, pay a deposit against future expenses, and then we can discuss completing the work."

"What will it take to bring the invoices current?"

"Seventy-five thousand."

"And the deposit?"

"Another one hundred and fifty thousand."

"And to complete the work?"

"That will complete the work in progress. We should discuss what of the planned projects need to be done in order to sell the house. There are a few areas where previous projects have left behind a mess. Such as in the pool house, where the cabinets were rebuilt. That floor will need to be refinished." I said. "But the doctor and I wrote a list of things to be redone that probably wouldn't affect the sales price. That list covered items that he wanted to do for his personal enjoyment and amounts to an additional $750,000 worth of furnishings and improvements."

"Mrs. Huntington, please, can you just give me a day

or two to get on top of this? I will put our most competent staff on handling this as quickly as they can. I will instruct them to give bills in connection with the house project priority as is legally possible. Please keep the job moving forward. And if you could possibly put together a list of what you suggest we do to get the house marketable, I would very much appreciate it."

He seemed sincere, but I wasn't sure if I should trust him. "How soon can you get the police out of there so that the crew can get back to work?"

I'd go along for a couple days if that's what it took to collect my fees. "Once the crews go onto other jobs, it could be awhile to get back on their schedules."

"The police indicated they would be out in time for Susan to stay there tonight."

I said to Susan, "Come on, I'll take you over there and we can check it out."

"Ms. Wallerski, Susan, shall we talk tomorrow after you've had some rest?"

Beyla Karloff Jr. stood as we left his office. "I'll stop by to see you on my way into the office in the morning. I imagine you'll be up on Central time, right?"

Susan merely nodded.

Now that we were well past the dinner hour, traffic over to Bev Hills wasn't too bad. We made the trip in less than an hour.

Chapter 8

"Wow. How could he possibly afford this amazin' place if he was broke?" Susan craned her neck to look at the brick walls with their stone caps, the now-empty stone security shack with its gray slate roof, and the elaborate wrought iron gate that stood open.

"The answer is he couldn't. I imagine there are a surprising number of people who can't actually afford their lifestyles around here. Even the seemingly mega rich can be living from paycheck to paycheck, only it may be from dividend or royalty or residual check to check."

I maneuvered the car down the long, winding drive through the tunnel of enormous sycamore trees.

No sign of anyone: no workmen, no security, no police. They'd cleared out fast enough.

"This puts it all in a whole new light. It's just such an outrageous level of . . . What do you call it?"

"Façade?" I suggested.

"Yeah. This place is huge. Oh, . . . I had no idea." Susan slumped back in the seat.

I gave her the driving tour of the estate. "Behind that row of redwoods is the tennis court and tennis shack. If you peek between those oaks over there you can get a glimpse of the pool, and the pool house." I pointed out a brick and stone house with a gray slate roof and a Tudor arched veranda facing the pool.

I slowly drove by the main house, the entrance to which was covered in yellow tape. "That's the main house. Prior to being a crime scene, it was a construction site. There's no furniture in most of the rooms."

I pulled the car into a small parking area hidden behind two redwood trees. "Here's the guesthouse. You'll want to stay here while the workmen are crawling all over the main house."

We parked near the charming brick cottage with windows and doors framed in stone. I helped her carry her bags over stepping stones set in mounds of baby tears, through the rose-covered, stone archway in the stacked stone wall, and across the flagstone and brick terrace that ran the length of the cottage. We were welcomed by the powerful "old rose" fragrance of the Falstaff blood red roses climbing on the archway.

Susan walked through one of three sets of French doors that opened to the main room. I lit the pre-arranged wood in the fireplace while she dropped the bags she carried and stared at the room, her jaw on her chest. The guesthouse consisted of a large, luxuriously furnished bedroom and bath suite, and an even larger main room. A bar height red jasper countertop divided the compact kitchen from the living room.

I took Susan's bags into the bedroom furnished entirely in cream colored velvet bedding and seating set on ivory and cream silk rugs.

"I'm not going to mind this too much." Susan said with a smile. "This guesthouse is larger than the apartment I grew up in. And twice as big as the one I live in now. And a heck of a lot nicer."

While Susan checked the place out, I made sure there were clean sheets and towels in the linen cabinet and food in the fridge. The doctor had been living in the guesthouse while the work was being done on the main house, so I wasn't surprised that the fridge had some basics in it and the freezer was full of meals.

Susan pointed to the bouquet of six dozen Mr. Lincoln blood red roses on the coffee table. "It's not hard ta know what his favorite color was," she said with a smile.

"You can change the standing order with the florist to another color if you wish," I offered.

"How often are they delivered?

"I think every three days."

"Wow! They sure do match the countertop." She smiled. "I'm definitely not in Kansas anymore."

She opened the refrigerator door "There is wine in the fridge. Have a drink with me?"

"Sure, I'll make spritzers. Hand me that Pellegrino please."

Two large armchairs with fluffy, down-filled red cushions faced the fire. Once we sat down with our drinks and some crackers we'd scrounged from the kitchen, Susan popped the question.

"Who do you suppose shot him?"

Chapter 9

"I don't have the faintest idea," I answered.

Was that actually true? Maybe I had some theories running around in my head. Like maybe the doctor had engaged in a little blackmail?

Or perhaps he had walked in on a jewel thief. Or he had just plain pissed off the wrong person. But none of my ideas were something to mention. Especially not to his niece. Besides, what did I know about murder?

Nothing.

"He never talked about anyone but his patients and a couple of the neighbors. Honestly, he mostly just complained about the neighbors and their noisy parties. Presumably, because he wasn't invited. He had me scheduling the project around his plan to retaliate with a big party as soon as the house was complete."

I sipped my spritzer and relaxed in the warmth of the fire.

"Who would he invite?"

"He mentioned some of his patients and their friends."

"Who?" Susan held her feet up to the fire while she

sipped her wine.

"Big names, like Cassie Green, Tom Henry, Carole Smythe-Jones, Gretchen Van Vleck, all of those were his patients, but then there were the friends of patients that he hoped would come, like Tom Cruise, Nathan Carrington, John Travolta, Jack Trevor, Brad Pitt, Nikki Howe, Paris Hilton.

"Wow! Holy crap."

"I know there were more, but I don't know who they were. Many of them were concerned with keeping their business with the doctor private, thus the back entrance to the office. I saw Sally Abbey sneaking in that way once."

"What was she doin' there?"

"I assumed liposuction. There is certainly nothing to fix on that beautiful face, but her ass is growing famously huge. I think the guy with her was her personal trainer."

"I'm sure not in Kansas any more." Susan gulped her wine.

I tried to think of other patients. "Uhm, there is the one everyone in town knows about 'cause she claims he ruined her career. He was supposed to take a little bump off her nose, but instead he gave her the standard JAP nose. She ended up looking like everybody else in Beverly Hills. Worse, nobody, but nobody recognized her anymore. Therefore, all the work and time establishing her face and name was wasted."

Susan walked behind the counter that divided the kitchen from the main room and took the wine and the Pellegrino out of the fridge. She brought the two bottles over to the table between the chairs. We both refreshed our drinks. Susan skipped the Pellegrino.

I thought of another one. "Then there is that anchor woman who was pissed off that he let it slip that she had had her eyes done. I guess news people are supposed to be above that sort of thing. She's suing him."

"There goes some more of my inheritance." Susan giggled.

"I know he once had to put Tom Henry back together after a stunt went wrong. But I don't think that's a secret. These action figure actors are proud of doing their own stunts." I stretched my legs out on the ottoman and continued to drink and think. I was really comfortable around Susan and I thought the feeling was mutual.

"Oh, I thought of another one. I could swear I saw the former actress who now sells that "magic, anti-aging face cream" on TV. What is her name? Susie Taylor. Anyway, she is another one I saw coming in the back entrance."

"Guess that cream isn't so magical after all." Susan snickered. "But seriously, do you really think anyone would kill someone over cosmetic surgery?"

"Until you've been here for awhile, it's hard to fathom how important one's looks can be in this town. A lot of people's livelihoods depend to a large degree on how good they look."

"Wouldn't money be a better motive?" Susan took another gulp of her wine.

"Seems it must have been something other than money—now that we know he didn't actually have any.

Guess it wasn't you hoping to inherit a fortune?" I said with a smile.

Susan answered me with a faked smile.

"Do you know anyone else who might have thought they would gain money by his death?" I asked her.

"I don't think so. My mom died last year, and I don't have any other relatives. So, I guess he didn't have any either."

"You had no idea he lived like this?"

"My mom explained away his unwillingness to help her out by saying that he had to keep up a front, even though he really didn't have money. Had to look like he was successful in order to be successful." Susan sipped her wine and smiled to herself. "I wonder what she would have thought if she had seen this place."

I kept quiet and let her talk.

"I didn't know I was his heir 'til last night. For all I knew, he had illegitimate kids, or he'd left it to his ex-wife, uh, wives." Susan squirmed into the down cushions of her chair.

"Yeah, what's the story with them? None of them seem to be too friendly with him. I've never met a one. How many did he have?"

"Four, per what Mr. Karloff told me on the phone last night. No children with any of them. I'm pretty sure he said they have all remarried. Moved on to greener pastures."

We both laughed.

"Did he and your mother grow up in Wichita?"

"No, in Nebraska. In Lincoln. My grandparents died

when my mom was around 18. You know, after my mom died, I realized I really knew so little about her family, and nothin' about mine."

"What about your father?"

"My mom told me that he was killed in Iraq."

"And what about his family?"

"I never met any of his family. We never had any contact with them. I didn't even realize that was strange until I was an adult. When I asked Mom about them, she said it upset her too much to talk about."

"Have you ever tried to contact them?"

"No. While she was sick I tried to talk to her about it, but I hated to upset her and talking about his family really disturbed her. Actually, it upsets me too. Could we please drop it? My father's family has nothing to do with this murder." Susan studied the wine in her glass while she rubbed the stem up and down between her fingers.

"Oh yes, sure. I'm sorry. I guess you've never been to visit your uncle before."

"We visited him in San Francisco when I was really little. I barely remember it. He went to med school, did his internship and whatever else doctors do at the University of California Medical School in San Francisco. A couple of times he came to see us in Kansas. He did send my mom money sometimes, but not very much when you look at his lifestyle. I'm still shocked."

"I'm sure this has been quite a distressing experience for you."

"I really didn't know him well enough to be sad about

his death. I'm a bit shaky from the sudden shift in my life; this place is not what I expected at all. And, I guess, it is upsettin' to have your last living relative murdered. I'm goin' to feel better when they find out who did it."

"Well, I suppose that will happen soon enough. I'm sure the police will give his case sufficient attention to resolve it quickly." I waved away Susan's attempt to refill my glass. "No more wine for me, I still have to drive home."

"Susan, there's one more difficult subject we need to deal with." I studied her face. Thus far she had been pretty easy to read; even when she tried she couldn't seem to keep her feelings off her face. Susan was refreshingly ingenuous: she was so bad at lying it was endearing. "If you don't want to have this conversation right now, I understand." I paused, waiting for her agreement to continue.

"What?"

"I want us to be friends."

Susan nodded her agreement while she waited for what I would say next.

"I do need to collect the money from the estate that is owed to me. And owed to the workmen I have hired."

"Sure," Susan said.

"But I'm not looking to run up bills against the estate. I think it would be great for you to realize some gain from all of this. I'd even be willing to make an agreement with you regarding my future invoices; maybe some sort of percentage of the profits from the sale of the property."

Susan smiled with obvious relief. "Cissy, I told you,

until last night I never expected anything. Not that I wouldn't love to be rich! But I certainly wouldn't want . . . you know what I mean?"

"Okay then. Let's take a look at the house and discuss what we have to do to get it marketable. You and I are going to have to decide how far to go; I'm thinking we should just finish up the projects in progress. That'll get you back home faster."

"You know, I'm not in a hurry to go back."

"Really?"

"I don't have anything there to go back to," Susan murmured.

Chapter 10

After a quick walk through of the main house, Susan and I planned that the next morning we would meet with the various contractors and finalize our list of what needed to be done to the house prior to putting it on the market. Since getting the house sold looked like the way I was going to collect my fees for this project, I had a vested interest in getting it done as soon as possible.

On the drive home, I thought about how very lucky I was to have Emma, Skip, Addie Mae, my father, and even my father's wife in my life. How perfectly awful to have no family!

I hit Skip's number on my speed dial. "Hi, just wanted to see how you are doing?"

"I'm fine, Mom. How are you?"

"I'm good."

"Are you sure? Emma was really worried about you this morning. She actually insisted I leave a class to talk to her. Can you believe that?

Skip was referring to the fact that his sister always took school much more seriously than he did.

"I really am fine," I reassured my son. The tone of his voice and the fact that he was practically a jabber mouth in comparison to his usual reticence told me he had been scared.

"I, hmm, ah, had something, hmm, I wanted, err, to tell you." This sounded more like my son.

"What's that?" I managed to catch myself before I said sweetheart knowing that the term of endearment might embarrass him enough that I'd hear "ah, never mind" instead of whatever it was he had started to say.

"Well, you and Dad were right. This is a good school. And I'm glad I'm not back East now, under all the circumstances; Dad gone, and you and Emma and Addie in LA. This morning, . . . well, it was nice to know that I could get home in a few hours."

"Thank you for telling me. I'm glad you ended up at Berkeley, instead of Yale. It's good to know you aren't too far away."

Not to mention how in the hell would I have paid for Yale? I was having enough trouble paying Cal's tuition and housing.

"Do you like your teachers and the other students?"

"Yeah, Mom, there's some fucking great profs here. And you were right. If you make any effort to talk to them, they're receptive. I had a great discussion this afternoon with my econ professor about free trade. He was actually saying, in his lecture that he believed in free trade. Pissed me off. Afterwards, I walked up and asked him if he didn't see how hard so-called free trade was on the people in poor countries." Skip was on a roll. "And then he invited me to the faculty club, and we had a great talk."

His excitement took a whole load of guilt off me. I'd been feeling bad about the last-minute switch to Berkeley, but his enthusiasm handled any concern I'd had.

"That's great!"

"Mom, gotta go. Catch you later."

I entered the house through the kitchen and immediately gathered Emma and Addie Mae in a big hug. "I love you guys so much."

They said they loved me too, but I caught them silently mouthing something to each other.

"Okay, what?"

"We're just glad that you're dealing." Emma said.

"Yes, I guess I am. And a good night's sleep will fix me right up."

*   *   *

But when I arrived at Martin's estate the next morning, I found a pitched battle ensuing between the police, who were back in force looking for clues, and the workmen who had been barred from their job site for the second day in a row.

A line of several men waited next to a police van to be fingerprinted. Another short line of men waited to have prints made of their work boots.

"What the fuck—excuse my French—are we supposed to do, Mrs. Huntington? I'm gonna lose my crew. You know they can't go for days without work." Carl's face was a picture of frustration.

"Whoa Carl, chill! I'll work this out! Go over to the pool house. Those floors need attention. Give me a price on the fastest, cheapest way to whip them into shape. I'll get with Detective Rodriquez over there and see what the plan is."

Carl headed off, his mood only slightly improved.

I waltzed over, planted my body right in front of his tall, slim physique. "Detective, may I have a word?" I looked straight into his dark brown eyes. "Look, my people need to get back to work. How long are you going to be here?"

"Hard to say. Until we find what we're looking for." He slid to the side in an obvious effort to get me out of his face.

I knew that dance step. I followed. "And what might that be?

He stared at me as if to say, "Oh right, like I'm going to discuss police business with you." In fact, he just stared, but I got the message.

"Okay, look, we need to get this project moving again. Any problem with us working in the auxiliary buildings— the pool house, the guest house, the tennis shack?"

"Fine," he paused and held my eye. "Please, this is a crime scene. We have gone through those buildings, but there's always the chance that we might need to seal the entire property."

Bloody hell! How did I get into this one? I needed to

find another job. I felt the red rush to my face. And had he forgotten that Susan was staying in the guesthouse? I reminded myself to stay cool; pissing him off wouldn't help a thing. I had realized what I should tell him, well, show him.

"If you tell me what you're looking for, maybe I can help, I know this building as well as anyone." I was jabbering as fast as I could, hoping he wouldn't cut me off. "Interior designers tend to have intimate involvement with both their clients and their client's houses, maybe you've noticed, there are a few unusual passageways, servant's passages so that they can service without being intrusive. Have you found all of those? There are even a couple of secret panels that I discovered while studying anomalies in the architectural plans. When I found the doctor's body, there was one panel door open in the library. Did you guys look through the boxes and jewelry cases?"

The tone of his stare adjusted from "back off" to mild interest. I had his attention. Maybe I wasn't quite as meddlesome!

"Please, come in and show me what you're talking about." He waved his hand towards the entry door in a gallant gesture.

We entered through the vestibule and entry hall. To our right was the living room, French doors on both sides leading to the gardens. This room, like all the rooms on the ground floor, was completely devoid of any furniture, unless one counted the massive carved fireplace with built-in seats.

I walked him to the left down a short narrow servant's passage into the library—the same short, narrow hall I had tried to use before I found the body. In the library, I stepped over the tarp covering the blood on the floor and walked over to the shelves on the wall opposite the double doors. I studied the wall for just a few seconds, recalling where I had noticed the wall cavities on the plans. I reached between two of the bookshelves. I pressed a panel edge and opened a hidden panel in the wall.

Files came spilling out of the opening. Names across the index tabs, Sally Abbey, Gretchen Von Vleck, Jennifer Gray, Yvonne Carrington, Joan Rivers, and Cassie Green. I recognized those celeb names, but not the one labeled Dr. Steinman.

"Shit!" Detective Rodriquez exclaimed and grabbed up the files before I could read anymore of the names.

Shit was right.

"Uhm, is this what you are looking for?" I asked.

"It's a start."

Not real free with the information, this guy.

"Look, you really should tell me what you're looking for. I can help. You have to let me if you're going to shut my job site down. I have to finish this project so I don't go out of business.

He looked me up and down. I could see in his dark brown eyes that my designer rags and expensive jewelry didn't sell that I was needy and certainly didn't buy me any sympathy.

I tried another tactic. "These workmen don't get paid

unless they produce something."

I waved my hand at where Susan stood on the front porch, blocked from entering by the yellow tape. "And Susan is living in the guesthouse. She has no other place to stay. She's just lost her uncle, her only relative, and now you are going to kick her to the street?"

"Okay, here's the deal: there are patient's medical files that seemed to be missing from the office. Patients for whom there are billing files, but no patient files."

Aha! They are thinking along the same lines as I was last night, that this has got to be connected with his patients. I was willing to bet he was blackmailing them.

"What do you know about his practice?" He jerked the arm with the files to his side, out of my line of vision. Damn! He must have caught me trying to read the names on the index tabs. "I can't let you see these. Patient confidentiality, you know."

"Yes, and I don't imagine you are supposed to read them either."

"That may be. Which is why I'm taking them back to the office until I get a court order."

"Are those the missing files?"

Once again, he just stared at me. Because he was distracted by the newly found files; he forgot to ask me about the rest of the secret panels.

Chapter 11

Sitting in front of the fire in the guesthouse with our wine had become our nightly ritual and that night, after fortifying ourselves with a couple of glasses of Pinot Grigio, Susan and I decided to search the house.

While we waited for the police to clear out, our third partner in crime, Emma, joined us. I don't know what I could have been thinking: drawing my daughter into this crime spree, but, when I explained what we had in mind, she said she'd be right over and not to go anywhere without her.

The moment we were sure that every last cop had left for the night; we prepared to go back to the library to check out the other secret panel. My stated purpose for poking around the house was to find saleable items to raise the funds to finish the project and to pay my bills.

But truthfully, I was curious. I had high hopes that we would find more files. And if a few pages just happened to fall out, well, we couldn't help it if a few details crossed our line of vision before we turned them over to the police. It wouldn't be like we read them on purpose. Who could blame us? It would be an accident.

Right?

"Okay, girls, gloves on?" Should we find anything of interest, I didn't want to confuse the police by leaving our fingerprints.

"Check," Emma answered.

Susan pulled on her second glove. "Check."

"Flashlights operational?"

We each switched on our flashlight.

"Check," Susan said when her light shown on the French door of the guesthouse.

"Operational flashlight confirmed." Emma had the drill down.

"Flashlight test: positive result." I rolled up the floor plans of the main house and tucked them under my arm just in case I needed to refresh my memory.

The three of us set off across the garden. We broke into a run to escape the chilling winds that blew off the cold winter desert. The Santa Anas had intensified at dusk.

We flew through the French doors leading from the terrace to the rear entry hall. Emma pushed the doors against the wind while Susan latched the lock. I led the way into the library.

"Watch out for that pile of tools. And look, there's a bunch of electric tools over there, too." The workmen had left numerous stacks of saws, axes, sledgehammers and the like in the hall.

The electricians had not had access to the house to finish the job. Entire sections of the house were without power. The entry hall and the library must have been on the same circuit; none of the lights were working in those rooms.

I aimed my flashlight on the opening in the paneling. "There's the cupboard I opened for the detective. That's where the patients' files were."

I unrolled the house plans on the floor. We knelt beside them. Emma trained her flashlight on the plans while Susan held the curling edges down. "See this other space three feet to the right of the open cupboard? That's a duplicate." I pointed to a spot on the plans on the same wall of the library as the already opened cupboard, then compared the plans with the actual wall and walked directly to the spot where the panel hid the other one.

I impressed myself with how adeptly I located and opened the panel exposing the cupboard.

A pair of blue Tiffany boxes sat in front of several older jewelry cases. Moving faster than I had imagined she could, Susan grabbed the first two boxes. She stuck one box under her arm while she opened the other box and found a hinged jeweler's case. As awkward as it was to open the case while balancing the other two containers, Susan jerked away from Emma's offered assistance.

When she discovered that the first case was empty, she tossed it onto the floor and opened the second one. Empty. It too landed on the floor. Two smaller, navy blue velvet cases lined with satin were also vacant. The next item was a polished wooden box with intricate inlay of jade and gold.

"Crap," Susan said when it too proved to be bare. I

grabbed it before it was launched toward the floor.

One large, hand-tooled leather case remained. This box was lined in velvet. The shapes of two guns were sunk into the velvet, but the guns were missing.

"That's a disappointment." I comforted Susan with a hug.

"I'm sorry. I thought maybe . . ." Susan heaved a deep sigh.

Emma picked up the boxes and cases and returned them to the cupboard. We put the boxes in place and left the cupboard open for the police to find.

The wind wailed in the dark. Blown trees scraped the building and shutters banged against the timbering.

"It's really creepy in here. Maybe we should do this tomorrow. In the daylight." Susan shivered, pulling her sweater tighter around her neck.

In her usual no nonsense manner, Emma ignored Susan's suggestion. "Mom, where are these other passages?"

"Let's go back to the kitchen. They all start from either there, or the servant's quarters." Emma and I made a beeline for the kitchen.

"Wait, wait! For God's sake, if we have to do this tonight, let's stick together." Susan hurried to keep up with us.

In the butler's pantry that served as the passage to the dining room and the breakfast room, our flashlights shone on cupboards full of antique red on cream Spode china, Bohemian crystal stemware, William Yeoward cranberry red goblets, sterling silver flatware and tea service, as well as an espresso machine, coffeemaker, and the usual accoutrements to be found in a butler's pantry.

The house plans showed unexplained cavities behind the walls of the cabinets. We spent a few minutes poking around behind the shelves, but no secret doors popped open.

I directed my flashlight to the rows of blue, orange, silver, and white boxes that filled the lower cupboards. "Susan, you could probably return the things that've never been unpacked." I highlighted the stack of blue boxes. "Tiffany's." Next, I lit the orange boxes. "Hermes." And then the silver. "Geary's."

From the indifferent way she looked at me, I knew she had never priced items from any of those shops, but I knew the items we found would provide significant funds. Later. We could have that conversation later.

The winds kicked up.

Construction debris left in front of the house slammed against the building. The sound resonated through the empty rooms. Our voices echoed off the walls.

"Please stay close to me." Susan grabbed my arm.

I placed my hand over hers. "Sure."

From just outside the kitchen, a narrow staircase led to the second-floor hallway which passed by the linen closet and the small upstairs butler's pantry. A small door at the end of the hall opened to the wide hall leading to the master suite on the right and the guest bedrooms on the left. At the second-floor, a third staircase turned and continued to the attic. Fortunately, the lights on the newel posts worked, even though their flickers gave the scene the look of an old silent movie.

Emma ran up the second flight of stairs. "Whoa. Holy shit, what a view!"

Emma had reached the top floor. From the attic windows one could "see all the way to Catalina" as the LA realtor cliché went. When wind scrubbed the air, the city lights sparkled like billions of diamonds scattered over the landscape.

The attic had long ago been converted to a playroom. Dr. Martin, childless, had used the room for billiards and hanging some of a rather eclectic art collection. His taste in art seemed to range from Norman Rockwell posters to Salvador Dali prints. A few "in the style of" Impressionists were the only originals; nothing of as much value as the contents of the colorful boxes in the butler's pantry.

Meanwhile Susan and I were banging on all the paneling that lined both stairs, but no hidden cupboards opened.

"Wait! Did you hear that? Someone's walkin' down there?" Susan moved so close to me I couldn't lift my arm to bang.

I held still for a minute and listened. "I don't hear anything but the wind."

"I thought for sure I did. But not now," Susan said.

From the second-floor linen closet there was a narrow hall leading to the dressing room, allowing access for the valet to place clean clothes or lay out outfits in the master closet. A second set of winding stairs led to this hall from the servant's quarters. In the narrow hall we could see the top of an even narrower set of stairs.

"Where do those stairs go to?" Susan asked.

"To the servants' quarters."

"Do I have any of those?"

"Ha-ha." I gave her a look. "There haven't been any servants in these quarters while we've been working on the house. I think everyone who works on the estate just comes in to work their shift: the gardeners, security, and cleaners. Nobody lives in now."

"Well, we better check that out too. Or we could just leave that area for the police. Nothing valuable would be in there, right? Let's just do the rest of the house. But, could we please do it tomorrow? I know I heard somethin'. Really, I don't like how creepy it is here at night, in this big, old empty house." Susan shuddered.

"If the police aren't here tomorrow."

"Oh, that." Susan was at least momentarily discouraged from quitting.

"Mom! Susan! Get up here!" Emma yelled down the other set of stairs.

"This better not be about the view," Susan gasped as she climbed the stairs to the attic.

"Mom, what's behind that wall?" Emma pointed to the paneled wall covered by Impressionistic knockoff paintings, Rockwell posters and Dali to Jasper John prints of various sizes and quality.

The attic playroom did not run the full length of the house. There was a small closet on one side of the far end of the room. The walls of the closet were lined with shelves filled with linens.

I pulled out the floor plans. "Per these, it looks to be a portion of the attic that was never developed."

"Come in here. I want to show you something interesting." Emma took us into the linen storeroom and pointed to the outline of a large access panel behind the shelves on the wall to the right.

"Look, you can tell from where that window is at the end of the closet that there's a big space behind the panel."

"What? I don't get it," Susan said.

"You see where that window is? It indicates where the exterior wall is. Here, look at the house plans." I pointed to the space that was surrounded by outside walls, but inaccessible from inside the house.

Bed linens, towels, pillows, and blankets that Emma emptied off the shelves of the interior wall covered the closet floor. She had managed to nearly rip one of the shelves off the wall.

"Susan, help me with this."

With both Susan and Emma pulling at it, they got the shelf that ran through the center of the panel off the wall. But the panel wouldn't budge.

Emma banged on the wall with her fist. "It sounds funny. Like it's lined with like metal or something. Really solid, yet tinny."

"Why would somebody line an attic wall with metal?" Susan asked.

"Do you think it sounds like maybe lead-lined? As in,

to protect valuables?" I offered.

"Oh totally, like to keep it from burning?" Emma beat on the panel. "Maybe there's a safe inside there. Hella yes, sounds like a safe."

"Maybe it's a hidden treasure. Maybe I'm rich!" Susan jumped from foot to foot.

Emma looked for a tool she could use to pry the panel open. She picked up the piece of shelf and tried to wedge it behind the panel. I banged on every panel, every stile, and every piece of molding. Nothing happened. We continued to pound, prod, and poke until we were exhausted and sick of it.

Emma plopped on the pile of pillows. "I give, Mother. This is not happening. We can't get in there. And, by the way, where the hell did Susan, Miss let's-all-stick-together, it's-creepy-in-here, go off to?"

In my enthusiasm for pounding on walls, I had failed to notice that Susan had left us

A lull in the howling windstorm allowed me to hear footsteps coming up the stairs.

I turned to look. The flickering lights on the newel posts threw the giant, dark shadow of a groaning person on the stairwell carrying an axe and a chainsaw.

Chapter 12

"Oh my God!" Emma screamed.

Susan burst into the room and I began to breathe again. She held an axe over her shoulder and dragged a chainsaw in her other hand.

Shit! I hoped I wasn't wrong about Susan. Was she a killer?

"What the hell?" Emma said. "What are you doing?"

"It's my house," Susan said. She panted and dropped the saw.

"Yes. It is," Emma and I both agreed, relieved.

"I can knock in some walls if I want, right?" She asked us, a hint of doubt starting to develop in her passion for wall bashing.

Emma and I looked at each other and nodded in unison, "Right. They are your walls."

"Do you actually know how to operate a chain saw?" I inquired.

"Hmm, not really, but how hard could it be?

"Let's try the axe." Emma looked at Susan. "With your

permission?"

Susan handed the axe to Emma. "Go ahead, swing away."

Emma swung at the center of the access panel. In several minutes of attacking the door, she hadn't managed even a dent.

"Oh, let me at it." Susan grabbed the axe and launched a sweeping stroke.

"I think you'll have more luck if you hit on the wall next to the panel," I advised.

Susan hit the wall with a mighty blow. A crack. A second, wide swing had me ducking out of range, but widened the crack. Several more hits and Emma relieved Susan.

Emma's tennis lessons were finally good for something as she forehanded and over-handed the axe into the wall. At last there was a six-inch hole next to the access panel.

"Where is that flashlight? Give it to me," Emma demanded. She put her face and the light up to the hole. "Oh, my freaking God! Un-freaking-believable! Mom, what is that? Is that what I think?" Emma continued to hold the flashlight in the hole but stepped aside so that I could look.

Susan jumped in front of me. "Let me see!" She peered in the hole.

"It's just some crates, and a few paintings." Crestfallen, she stepped aside for me to look.

"It looks like . . . It can't be, but I think it is. It's got to be. Did you notice the coarse brushwork of the one in the foreground? The broad, vigorous, swirling brushstrokes?"

I held the flashlight and leaned back so that Emma could look through the hole.

"Look at the short broad strokes rotating around the yellow sun," I said. "Doesn't it remind you of *The White House at Night*, Emma? Remember we saw that painting in the Hermitage? In St. Petersburg?"

"Wow! Holy shit!" Emma peered through the hole.

"And our guide told us the story about it having been 'transferred from Germany' after World War II. It was one of the paintings hidden in the basement of the Hermitage for nearly half a century. That sun looks identical. It must have been one of the canvasses he painted in the last 70 days of his life. I could swear it's—"

Emma chimed in, "It's a Van Gogh."

"Move the light over to that smaller canvas. Check out the feathery brushstrokes of that nude . . . I'm thinking . . . Renoir."

The small room behind the hole appeared to be crammed full of canvasses, most of which were crated, but a few were unwrapped and plainly visible. In addition to the possible Van Gogh and Renoir, I could see a probable Pissarro and what most certainly had to be a Matisse.

"How do you guys know all this?" Susan asked from where she stood, hands on her hips, frowning at us.

"Mom majored in Art History, and she buys art for her clients, and she's dragged my brother and me through museums all over the planet," Emma answered.

Susan slumped against the wall and slid onto the floor. "Could I . . . could it be for real? Could I be rich?" she whispered.

"Mom, could they possibly be real?"

"I don't know where the hell they could've come from. Of course, they'd have to be authenticated. Good chance they're merely well-done copies. But they certainly look interesting from here. We'd have to get into that room."

Emma and I joined Susan on the floor.

"Fuck!" we all said in unison.

Chapter 13

"Mom, what's the matter?" Emma asked as we drove home. "Aren't you excited about the paintings?"

I hesitated to put a damper on Emma's excitement. Why not let her enjoy the moment?

"Sure. It's an exciting discovery."

"What's wrong then?"

I shrugged. "Just that the job is likely to be delayed again."

"So, what? At least now we'll probably get paid."

I shrugged again as I stopped the car at a stop sign and looked at the traffic lane before turning right.

"Mom, what are you not telling me?"

"Sweetheart, those paintings are either unlicensed copies, or stolen. Or both."

"You mean copies of stolen paintings?"

"Quite possibly."

"Why can't they be the doctor's rightful possessions?" Emma leaned forward to study my face.

"Hidden in the attic?"

"In a specially constructed vault," Emma said leaning

back against her seat, "to keep them safe during construction?"

"Why take chances with paintings that valuable? If they were legitimate, why not have them properly stored in climate controlled, secure art warehousing?" I shook my head. "And he never mentioned them in any discussions we had about art for the house."

"In addition to being a "Richard Cranium," Dr. Martin, was an art thief?" Emma grimaced.

"Or a buyer of stolen property." I pulled into our driveway, pressed the button opening the garage, and drove in. "We'll see what the experts say, but I'm not thinking this discovery is a good thing."

"But if these are actual masterpieces, wouldn't them being stolen be big news?"

"May not have been stolen recently. There are still more than 100,000 pieces of art that were stolen by the Nazis still unaccounted for."

Chapter 14

The next morning, I showed up at the house to find pretty much the same scene as the previous morning: workmen milling about, or sitting on the tailgates of their trucks, grumbling, smoking, drinking coffee. The entrance to the house was still covered with yellow tape.

Detective Rodriquez stood outside the entrance vestibule watching me park my car.

After the events of the previous night, Susan and I were particularly anxious for the police to get out of the house so that we could remove the paintings and have them authenticated.

We had discussed the situation and agreed that it wasn't any of their business to know about the paintings. It seemed it would only complicate matters to have the police involved. And then there was, well, we were just a bit shy about mentioning that we had been exploring the house, err, the crime scene.

Prior to leaving the attic the night before, we had moved a painting from the billiard/play room and hung it over our hole in the closet. The three of us hoped that no smart policeman would wonder at a painting hung in a closet.

My heart pounded as the smart detective waved me over to his side.

Some feelings resembling guilt lingered on the edge of my conscience, but until we knew more about the paintings, I hated to further delay work on the house by prolonging the police interest.

I took a deep breath and walked toward him. "Detective, how much longer?" I threw in a few taps of the pointed toe of my Manolo Blahniks to stress my impatience as I hid my shaking hands behind my back.

"Ah, Mrs. Huntington, I've got questions. How much do you know about his practice?"

"Not much. I did see some of his clients as I went in and out of his office. I know he felt it was important to decorate the exam rooms more elaborately than one would expect.

"Like what?"

"We used antique, hand-knotted silk rugs for the floors, covered the exam tables in gold Ultrasuede, and pink dupioni silk for the privacy curtains. The walls were upholstered in flattering shades of peach suede and then hung with good quality decorative paintings."

"Did he talk to you about his patients?" Detective Rodriquez was looking intently at my face.

I felt myself inwardly squirming and wondered if my discomfort showed on my face. I decided that if he asked me about the paintings, I wouldn't lie. On the other hand, I didn't need to offer information that I was certain had nothing to do with the murder.

"A little. He explained that he wanted his patients to feel comfortable in his office, and that his clientele was accustomed to finer things. I assumed that he wanted to keep the décor in line with the prices he charged. My thought was that he wanted to create the impression that they were getting the very best, thus he wanted the various elements to be the finest available. When I asked for his approval for items, 'Is that the best?' he would ask."

"Did he ever say anything else? Did he speak of any of them specifically?"

"Only when he mentioned who he would invite for the completion party, his various patients and their friends."

I changed the subject. "Were those files helpful?" I was curious, and I hoped he would give me some hint. But as happened before, he just looked at me.

I tried another ploy. "My guess is that he was black-mailing some of those people."

"What makes you think that?" Detective Rodriquez accepted a steaming cup of hot liquid from a police officer. He held it out to me. "Coffee?"

"No thanks." I shook my head. "I remember a story about an anchorwoman who is suing the doctor—or was—because the press found out about her surgery. She must have had some reason to believe he had something to do with it."

"What was her name?" He squinted as he sipped the steaming coffee and motioned to the bench in the entry vestibule. We both sat down on the grey faux bois bench.

"Gretchen von Vleck."

"What makes you think he would be able to get away with blackmail? Wouldn't that be terribly damaging to his reputation? Who would recommend a doctor who black-mailed?"

"Oh, I don't think he blackmailed everyone. The ones he would have blackmailed wouldn't have talked about their surgery to anybody. I'm guessing those files you found would have been the blackmail victims. That's why they were hidden at the house."

"What do you think happened with this Gretchen person?"

"I would guess that he had an idea that she wouldn't go for it. She's married to a very litigious attorney—he's famous for the lawsuits he pursues. I think the doctor knew that if he threatened to go public, she would sue rather than prosecute."

The detective studied my face with questions on his.

I could see I needed to spell it out.

"You see, publicity from a suit would actually serve his purposes. If he leaked the info to the right media source, the whole thing with her would just make the point to others that he was blackmailing that he could let the news out without any problem." I stood up. "I need to check out something in the pool house. Do you want to walk along?"

"Sure."

We started towards the pool house.

"Interesting theory on the anchor woman. A bit convoluted, but maybe. So, do you think she's a good suspect?"

"Oh no, definitely not. I doubt she's vengeful. The publicity didn't end up hurting her in the slightest. In fact, she got a hell of a lot of free promotion for her new show. She probably pursued the lawsuit to add to the hype."

"Who do you think *is* a good suspect?" He opened the gate to the pool area. I passed through the arbor arch and the gate. He followed.

"Thanks for asking."

Distracted by the heady scent of the red roses climbing on the arched trellising, I hesitated. "Of course, I'd take a close look at everybody whose files we found in that cupboard. Who among them didn't have an alibi?"

"We're checking them out."

"And I'm sure you're keeping in mind that if these people could afford elective cosmetic surgery, they could afford hit men, right?"

"It wasn't a professional job."

That stopped me in my tracks. "How do you know that?"

"I've said enough already. Trust me on this one." He smiled.

I wondered if he was too old for twenty-two-year-old Emma.

"I never trust anyone who says, 'trust me'." I returned the smile. "I need to see how the floors are coming in here."

I opened one of the French doors to the pool house.

"So, when did you say you were going to be out of the main house?"

Detective Rodriquez shook his head as he walked away.

"Hi! Hello, Carl. How are the floors coming?"

"Doing okay." Carl took off his cap and scratched his head. "I appreciate you coming up with something we could work on before I lost all my crew. I'm not sure why, but I've already lost a couple guys I usually pick up at the day laborer station."

Carl nodded at the detective exiting through the trellis.

"All these police around maybe made'em nervous. I sure could use that the one big strong guy who was really good with picking up the floor sanders, but he hasn't been around since the day of the murder."

"Hmm. You might want to mention him to Detective Rodriquez."

Chapter 15

"Mom, come with me to walk Lulu. Please."

Emma fastened the leash to the dog's collar.

I knew an invitation to walk meant Emma wanted to talk. Because my children are often more nitpicky regarding ethical issues than I am, I was afraid I was about to get a lecture about not informing the police about the paintings. I braced myself as we walked down the sidewalk.

But it was something else entirely that she had on her mind.

"Jeff's totally sweet, and cute enough."

I couldn't help but smile at her understatement about her boyfriend.

"Okay, hot as hell," she said with a grin. "And ambitious. But I don't know. Maybe I'm just not ready. He scares me. Maybe he likes me too much. Maybe I like him too much. How did you know Daddy was the one?"

"I didn't. He scared me too, and I ran the other way numerous times. There were too many other girls chasing after him. He was too rich and too good looking."

For just a few seconds, I wondered how different our lives would have been had I not let him catch me. "Neither quality was what I thought I wanted in a man. But he was also the only man that I would stay up all night with. Not just making love, but talking on and on, interspersed with sex—"

Emma held up her hand in a stop signal. "Whoa, Mom! Too much information."

"What, the sex part? Well, that was only part of it. I do think it's important that you find each other attractive, but also that you can communicate. That you have interests in common, that you are interested in what the other one has to say. That you laugh together."

"Did you know you were in love with Dad even though he scared you? Was it love at first sight?" Emma asked.

I couldn't hold back the laugh. I remembered the first time I had seen Jamie. He was completely unaware of me. "I was a lowly college freshman at UC Berkeley, and he was a fifth-year senior—the-big-man on campus. The fraternity pinning party was celebrating his engaged-to-be-engaged relationship with a senior who had been *the* debutante of her year.

"You were a debutante," Emma said.

"Not like that. My debut was very low key. Just a simple dinner dance at the club with a small group of girls I'd known all my life. 'Unpretentious' per your grand-mother. My grandmother thought the huge balls and elaborate seasons were only for the nouveau riche," I said,

"Years later, I did ask your father if he remembered meeting me the night of his pinning party. He claims he did, but his lies were pretty unconvincing."

"I bet he did. I've seen the pictures of you from those years. You were gorgeous. He had to have noticed. You were probably the reason he didn't actually marry her."

Oh, my romantic daughter. "I was a gawky seventeen-year old. They were *the* beautiful people. I was in total awe of both of them."

"And, so what happened next?"

"The next time I saw him was seven years later."

"Wow, that long?"

"Yes, I had graduated from college, done the requisite year in Europe, and finished design school. The design firm I worked for in San Francisco had transferred me to their Beverly Hills office to handle their," I held up my curved fingers to frame my words, " 'rich and famous' clientele."

"And by then you definitely were hot. And sophisticated!" said my biggest fan.

I smiled at my daughter. "I was never even close to how beautiful you are."

"Okay, okay." Emma brushed aside my hand on her hair and grabbed a firmer hold on Lulu's leash, pulling the dog away from the suspicious thing she was sniffing.

"Then what?"

"Jamie and his father came into the studio for a meeting with my boss one afternoon just after I arrived. "Big Jim", your grandfather, had proven false the maxim that big money never makes it past the third generation. Jim had invested the dwindling capital his great grandfather had accumulated the previous century in building California tract houses immediately following the war. As you know, that was a wildly successful business that your father made into an even more successful business. At least for awhile."

Emma grabbed my arm. "Mom, is that Sally Abbey? She lives around here, doesn't she? What happened to her ass? Fuckin' A, her ass shrunk big time, and it's perfect."

"Emma shhh! She'll hear you."

A man and a woman, each had a leg resting on a low wall while they reached for the toe of the raised foot. I couldn't be sure who was behind the curtain of long glossy mahogany locks until she stood upright to switch legs, re-tucked her hair into a sweatband, and in her famously husky voice said, "Why the fuck are you making me fucking do this?"

It was Sally. And the ever-present trainer. Both Emma and I had seen the two of them at Doctor Martin's offices. They were stretching their legs on the low stucco wall in front of Kirstie Alley's house. Leashes of two miniature pinchers were attached to the gatepost.

Sally turned around, saw me and flung her superbly sculpted body at me with a huge hug.

"Hi Sally. You're looking great!"

"Thank you," said the tall muscular man I thought to be her trainer. Obviously taking credit for her newly slim body, he continued, "I have been studying the human body for many years and I now know all the secrets to a beautiful body. I can shape anyone into a goddess." His hazel eyes looked Emma and me up and down.

Okay, I'm not perfect, but Emma with her combination of long, slender limbs and feminine chest certainly did not need his "expertise." He evidently agreed with my assessment of Emma and wasn't going to bother with me. He turned his attention back to Sally.

"Cissy, this is Steve, my personal trainer."

"This is my daughter, Emma."

"Oh yeah, I've seen you walking the dog." Sally extended her hand to Emma.

"Wow, you look kick ass!" Emma has never been shy.

"We're working on a fab new weight loss program. Steve's developed a diet exercise program that fucking works. Isn't he great?" Sally showed off her slender body with a pirouette.

The red door to the butter cream stucco house opened, and Kirstie came out to say hello. "Whoa, Sally, you look like, wow!"

"You look pretty damn good yourself. Are you back on Jenny Craig?"

"It's not as quick as Steve's program." Kirstie smiled at Sally. "But you know, they say if you take it off too fast, it's hard to keep it off."

Steve looked Kirstie up and down much like he had done Emma and me moments before. "I don't agree with that. In my years of experience as a professional athlete and a personal trainer I've learned there's no such thing as 'too fast.' I could get you fit faster than you can imagine. I have a long list of actors I have gotten into shape nearly overnight when the script demanded it."

"Funny, I've never heard of you." It was obvious that Kirstie didn't like Steve's bragging tone, or his offer of assistance. The way he looked at her as though she were a slab of meat had to have been annoying.

Steve continued as if he hadn't heard Kirstie. "I have gotten women even heavier than you into shape in a matter of weeks."

"Ya, well, I've gotten pricks even stupider than you to shape up, but I wouldn't touch you if it were a ten-foot pole," Kirstie cracked.

Sally doubled over with laughter and high-fived Kirstie.

Steve glared at both of them.

Oh whoa, cat claws. I could see the eye scratching wasn't far off. And I couldn't avoid staring at the new brown hair plugs at the front of Steve's scalp. I decided to break up this little neighborly gabfest before anyone said something they would regret.

Sally's miniature pinchers strained at their leashes, yipping at Lulu, who looked down her nose at them.

"Oh look, Lulu is anxious to continue her walk. Good to see all of you. Bye, bye."

"Can I walk with you?" Sally asked unexpectedly.

"Uh, the dogs . . ." Sally handed the leashes to Steve, who looked none too happy.

We set off down the walk. Sally was making conversation about pretty much nothing, and then, "I heard that one of your clients was shot. A Doctor Martin?"

I wasn't sure what to do with the fact that Sally seemed to be pretending that she didn't know the doctor, yet surely, she knew both Emma and I saw her coming into his office. Now what's with that?

"Yes, he was."

"Do the police know who shot him?"

"It doesn't seem like they do." Aha, she's pumping me for info.

"Were you doing his house?" Sally asked.

"And his office," offered Emma pointedly.

"I'd like you to do my house. Would you like to see it?"

"Absolutely."

A tall, slender woman with a familiar face and dark blonde hair walked past us. We all politely said, "hello, how are you?" as neighbors out for a walk do.

"Who's that?" Emma asked. "She looks so familiar."

"That's Nathan Carrington's sister." Sally provided.

"*The* Nathan Carrington?" Emma asked. "Wow. Yeah. She looks just like him!"

Steve tried to walk with us, but there wasn't room for four of us to walk abreast. The leashes from the three dogs entangled, and the two mini-terrors persisted in growling at Lulu. Often, he ended up walking in the street gutter until parked cars forced him to walk behind us. Soon grunts of frustration were emanating from the rear of our march.

Emma handed Lulu's leash to me and dropped back to walk with him. God knew, we needed a new client. I could hear Steve behind us droning on about his illustrious career as a professional athlete.

Kirstie was right. If he was so damn good, why hadn't we ever heard of him?

"Fuck, Sally. Enough socializing," Steve said with a glare. "We have a lot of work to do and not much time left before that shoot starts. Do you wanta look like a blimp? Or what?"

Perhaps Emma hadn't sufficiently shown her appreciation for his brilliance.

Steve shoved next to Sally and got too close to Lulu. Three leashes got entwined, three dogs nipped at each other and ran in a circle using Steve as their maypole. I have to admit I hoped he'd fall face first, but he was stronger than the four-legged animals.

"Lulu, sit." Emma untangled our dog's leash from the mini's. "Mom, we need to get home."

Sally and I made a date to get together in two days to look at her house. We said our good-byes including lots of hugging.

Emma and I headed home.

"I had no idea you knew her so well, Mom. What's with all the huge hugs?"

"That's just a Hollywood thing. Now that you have been formally introduced, the next time you meet you'll get hugs, and maybe kisses too."

"She does look beautiful. She's lost a lot of weight. What a body! But that trainer guy totally didn't like her hanging with you."

"We were interrupting their exercise routine."

"I think it was more like he was jealous," Emma said. "I was kinda hoping he'd fall on his face. Is that awful?"

We shared a laugh when I admitted to having the same hope.

"Maybe it was jealousy."

Did that explain the fear in his eyes?

"He's not for real going to pretend that she lost that weight on some 'new' program he devised, is he? We all saw each other at the doctor's, the doctor who specialized in liposuction."

Lulu strained at her leash and dragged Emma across a lawn towards a cat.

"Chill, dog!" Emma yanked back.

"That might explain why all of a sudden she wants to hire us. So, we'll keep our mouths shut. She'll probably have us sign one of those confidentiality agreements, an NDA, and hope that then we won't be able to tell anyone we saw her at the doctor's office."

"Wow, that's devious. Mom, like sometimes you freaking amaze me with these theories you have as to what people are really up to."

"Emma, there is a lot of beauty in the world, and most people are basically good. But don't ignore the evil." I lunged at her playfully with both my hands held like claws. "Or, it will get you."

Chapter 16

Susan planned to hold the memorial service in the garden of the estate, but a January rain forced us indoors. Showers began minutes before the scheduled service, and Susan was at a loss for what to do.

Emma carried the easel with the photo of Dr. Martin into the guesthouse. I threw open the wall of French doors that ran the front length of the guesthouse and invited the very few attendees out of the wet.

A fire blazing in the stone fireplace gave a warm glow to the vanilla-colored walls of the guesthouse living room; the mulled wine gave a warm glow to the chilled, damp guests.

"It's totally a good thing you decided not to have an actual funeral, since the police still haven't released the body," Emma assured Susan.

"With no money, a fancy funeral was out of the question. I'll have him cremated as soon as his body is released," Susan whispered.

I didn't see any of the patients that I had seen in the

office. The room easily held Dr. Steinman, only three of Dr. Martin's eleven office staff, four elderly women with very stiff and unrecognizable faces, the hired minister who had never met the doctor, Susan, Emma, and myself. Not a single ex-wife to my knowledge. Detective Rodriquez observed the guests from inside the doorway to the bedroom.

The surprise guest was Yvonne Carrington. I heard her ask Susan if she had something hot to drink without alcohol in it. Susan poured her a cup of tea.

Emma whispered to me, "I didn't know Yvonne knew Dr. Martin. I never saw her or her brother at the office. Did you?"

"No, but we wouldn't have necessarily seen everyone." I nodded towards the four rigid faces. "I have never seen those four ladies, but it is pretty obvious that they've been there. You spent more time in his offices than I did, since you supervised the installations. Why did only three of his staff show up for this?"

"I don't think most of the women in his office liked him much. He was definitely an arrogant asshole to them." In response to my disapproving look, Emma continued. "What's with this don't-speak-ill-of-the-dead thing? Just 'cause he's dead doesn't change that he was a dick."

"Hush!" I said. "You're right, but this isn't the time or place."

The minister said a few consoling words that had more to do with soothing each guest as they thought of their own mortality than they had to do with Dr. Martin.

Susan stood next to the easel, waited for the attention of the guests, and gave a toast:

"I wouldn't live forever,
I wouldn't if I could,
But I needn't fret about it,
For I couldn't, if I would.
Good-bye Uncle Robert.
We wish you well wherever you may be."

We all drank from mugs of wine raised in a farewell toast to the large photo of the doctor.

Dr. Steinman, who turned out to be a cosmetic dentist, appeared reluctant to leave. He and Yvonne were apparently the only mourners who were close enough to the doctor to have an emotional reaction to the occasion. Everyone else, including Detective Rodriquez, left immediately after the ceremony.

There was one obvious thing that the two doctors had in common: Dr. Steinman dressed very much like Dr. Martin. The surgeon was, every time I saw him, completely dressed hat to shoe either in Burberry, Brooks Brothers, or Ralph Lauren. I guessed that he figured if he used the same designer for his entire ensemble he could be certain that it all went together.

Dr. Steinman was dressed entirely in grey and black by Ralph Lauren. His looks—partially balding wispy pale brown hair, Ralph Lauren horn-rimmed glasses, medium height and weight—were not remarkable. I wondered if he, like Dr. Martin, changed his eyeglasses to coordinate with his attire.

He asked Susan if she would show him the renovation work that was taking place inside the main house.

Feigning overwhelming grief, Susan asked if they could do so at a later date.

"This is a hard day for me. I'm sure you understand," she said with a weak smile.

I stepped up and offered my hand. "I'm Cissy Huntington."

"Hello, I'm Dr. David Steinman. The doctor, that is, Robert, and I had a number of mutual patients that we worked on together. I'm a cosmetic dentist." He checked out my smile as he said the latter.

"I'm an interior designer. I was overseeing the work on the house."

"So, I heard."

"I'd be happy to show you the house. The police have finished up in there so we finally have access to it again. Let's go."

The sudden shower had ended leaving the landscape fresh and sparkling. I exited a French door leading the way across the terrace.

"I appreciate you showing me. I need some sort of distraction from the sad business of the day. This has been a terrible shock," the doctor said.

He followed me across the terrace and through the rose-covered arch.

"Doctor Steinman. Your name is familiar. Have we

met?" I asked.

"I don't believe so. I'm sure I would remember meeting you," he answered. "Robert mentioned he had hired you. Bragged, actually, would be more accurate."

"Were you and Dr. Martin close?"

"We coordinated cases. And, yes, over time we became close."

The central entry hall that held the grand staircase had an entrance at either end of it. We entered off the terrace.

"I can see why Robert was pleased with these floors. They are lovely." He admired the floor in the entry that was the one floor we had not redone, but I decided to let it slide.

"Yes, they are nice. What would you like to see?"

Steinman glanced into the living room. I assumed he was admiring the massive carved fireplace. "Besides the floors, Robert mentioned paint colors. There was a red."

"In the library. We called it blood red, but considering the events of recent days, I'd better come up with a new name for that color." I led the way to the library hoping that someone had cleaned up the bloody mess.

The bloodstain was still covered by the tarp. I flipped on the light switch. Finally, the lights were working.

"I can see why he liked this color. It does look great with the wood." Steinman ran his hand over a panel. "Do you know about the secret panels in this room?"

"Secret panels?" Taken by surprise that he knew about the panels, playing dumb seemed the best tactic.

"Robert told me he had secret hiding places hidden behind panels. This is the library, right?" Steinman continued to run his hands over the paneling.

I nodded. "What else would you like to see?" I started to walk out of the room hoping he would follow me. The metallic smell of blood still lingered.

"What have the police found in here? Anything interesting?"

"The detective in charge is reluctant to tell us much of anything," I answered honestly. "Brrr, it's cold in here, isn't it?"

"What are you going to do with the antique billiard table? The one in the attic?" If she decides to sell any of the furnishings, please tell Susan I would be interested in that table. In fact, I would like to see it again." He started up the stairs and I hastened to catch up.

As we walked up the stairs, Dr. Steinman quizzed me about Susan. "I have to say, she took me completely by surprise. Robert had never mentioned her. One look at her, and the relationship is obvious. And here I was under the impression that he had no heirs." He rushed up the stairs. "In fact, I was expecting that his estate would be tied up for months during the battle of the ex-wives."

We'd reached the top of the attic stairs. I hoped there were no clues as to our recent activities in the area. A quick glance around reassured me.

Steinman walked over to the Queen Anne, cherry-wood billiard table, and rested his hand on the edge, but his gaze was not on the table. He looked around the room and, specifically, at the door to the closet. "Oh, yes, it is as nice as I remembered it."

He looked at me where I still stood at the top of the stairs holding onto the railing. "Sorry to drag you all the way up here. Thanks for putting up with my curiosity. Let's go." He started towards the stairs, but took a detour.

He was exaggeratedly casual about briefly stopping and opening the closet door, taking a peek inside. If I hadn't known what was just beyond that door, I would have thought nothing of it.

He hurried down the stairs and exited the house.

I followed as close behind as I could in high heels. Rain started to sprinkle as we walked back to the guest cottage.

"I'll just say good-bye to Susan. Thank you for the tour."

When we re-entered the cottage, I was surprised to see that Yvonne was still there. She was sitting on the hearth with her long black skirt tucked beneath her and sipping from a teacup. She and Emma were chatting comfortably.

When Emma saw me, she said, "Mom, you know that Yvonne lives near us? Isn't that great."

"That's nice. Hi, Yvonne, I'm Cissy."

"It's a pleasure to meet you. I've only been in my house for a few months and I've been traveling most of that time, so I haven't met many of my neighbors."

"Emma probably told you we haven't been there long ourselves." I poured myself a cup of tea and stood in front of the fire with it.

"Yes, she did."

"Were you and Dr. Martin friends for a long time?" I

101

asked.

"No, just for about a year." Her blue gray eyes filled with tears. "We met at a charity tennis tournament held here last year. Robert was very generous about lending his house out for charity events." Her voice broke as she said the last few words.

"I am sorry." I suddenly realized I was not being particularly thoughtful the way I was blurting out questions. I kept forgetting that there must have been people who did care for this man.

Emma spoke up. "Yvonne travels a lot because she works with her brother, Nathan Carrington. He is such a big star. I'm sure you know that, Mom."

"Yes, even your totally-out-of-it mother knows who he is. That must be really interesting, Yvonne."

"Yes. He keeps me busy." Yvonne had recovered her composure. "And you and Emma work together as interior designers. That sounds like it would be fun."

"It mostly is," I responded.

Yvonne put her cup on the table and then stood up. "I should go. It was nice to meet you. It's good to know that you live near me. See you around the neighborhood."

Emma picked up an umbrella and walked Yvonne to her car.

Once that last guest left, I took Susan aside. "I think we need to consult Beyla Karloff about the paintings. We can't pretend we didn't see them."

"I already called him. He's sendin' out an art expert in the morning. And the expert guy said that you were right, that we should leave them in . . . in . . . situ. In place like you said. Would you and Emma come and hold my hand?"

"Wouldn't miss it for the world. But what about the police?" I asked.

"Detective Rodriquez said they are completely outta here!"

"Halle-bloody-lujah!" Did they give you any clue as to what they found?" I hoped for some good news so we could put the murder behind us.

"Nope." Susan went into the kitchen to wash up.

Emma returned the umbrella to the stand and motioned me over to where she was carrying the easel and photo of the doctor into the bedroom closet.

"Mama, I was just noticing something interesting about family resemblances. You know how Yvonne Carrington looks almost identical to her brother Nathan. It's almost sad because where his looks make for a definite hottie, she is so . . . what's the word?"

"Rather plain," I furnished.

"Yes," continued Emma. "Look at that photo of Susan's mother on the table over there. She was beautiful, whereas her brother was, as you say, rather plain. Definitely not handsome. Now Susan looks very much like her uncle, in fact, much more than her mother looks like her brother. Susan is pretty in a cute way, but her mother was gorgeous."

"Yes, beautiful." I compared the two photos for another few seconds but I would have to think about that later. At that moment I was more concerned about the next morning and the possibility that the art might be worth enough to cover my unpaid invoices. I turned to my daughter to say, "Here's the big news. The art experts are coming tomorrow morning."

Chapter 17

We girls gathered in the linen storage closet bright and early the next morning.

We had taken Carl, the flooring man, into our confidence, and he had used a saws-all to cut around the access panel and provide an opening into the room. We were amazed to find that the room closely resembled a large, acclimatized safe. The walls were not as thick as a standard safe, but great care had been taken to control the temperature and the humidity in the room. We did not go in but waited in the closet for the art expert to arrive.

From the door, Susan and Emma counted crates, "fifty-one, fifty-two, fifty-three, fifty-four."

"Then there are the four that are unwrapped. That's fifty-eight altogether." Susan said. "Fifty-eight paintings."

"Provided there's one painting in each crate," I added.

From the small window in the closet, Susan spotted the car of the experts. "They're here."

She flew down the stairs to show them the way to the attic.

Susan got well ahead of the experts on the two flights

of stairs coming back up. She had hurried them so much that the two of the three experts who were elderly gentlemen were gasping for breath by the time they arrived at the top of the stairs.

One white-haired gentleman hung his arm over the railing to rest. Susan grabbed his other arm, herded the three into the closet and pointed to the entrance into the vault.

The men, still trying to catch their breath, wordlessly photographed the room and the crates. Not until everything was thoroughly documented did they touch one of the canvasses. The young man opened the crates with a tool out of the bag he had carried.

Carl said he'd better check on his workman and excused himself.

Susan was beside herself with impatience. She paced the floor, chewed her nails, and sighed melodramatically.

Emma and I sipped tea from the thermos that Addie Mae had packed with our picnic breakfast. Emma nibbled on a homemade biscuit.

"Susan, wouldn't you like to sit down and have a cup of tea?"

Susan gave me the you-must-be-crazy look and continued to pace. Ten steps north, ten steps south, each fifth step she peered into the safe.

The two white-haired gentlemen and one younger, bearded man occasionally murmured to each other; nothing that we could make out. Two of the men worked together. One of the pair held the crate upright while the second man very slowly, very carefully unwrapped the contents. The third man studied the unwrapped canvasses with a magnifying glass. Occasionally, one of them murmured a bit louder.

I thought to distract Susan with a conversation: I'd finally remembered to ask her something that had been flitting in and out of my mind ever since we found the canvasses. "Susan, do you happen to know if you are related to a Swiss man named Andre' Martin?"

"What? Who?"

"There was a man who lived in Zurich by the name of Andre' Martin. I remembered that Dr. Martin had spent time in Switzerland when he was working on the liposuction thing. I wondered if they could possibly have been related. Or at least knew each other."

"Never heard of him. Martin's a pretty common name. Why?"

"Well, I remembered reading that this Andre' had possession of a Matisse and a Courbet that the Nazis had stolen from a Parisian Jew, Robert Rosenberg."

"I'm not related to anyone like that." Susan couldn't take it any longer. She poked her head into the safe. "Well?"

The three heads turned to her. All three peered over the tops of their glasses in her direction.

"Well, what do you think?"

"These look to be authentic. There are some tests that should be done, but there's no reason to think they are anything other than what they appear to be," the man with the whitest hair said. The other two men nodded in agreement.

Susan screamed with delight. "How much are they worth?"

The three gentlemen looked at each other. One started to speak and then hesitated.

"Hundreds? Thousands? Millions? What magnitude are we talkin' here?" Susan asked.

"Oh, easily hundreds of millions." One of the three softly spoke. "If they can be authenticated."

More screaming. When she had exhausted her voice, she was interrupted by one of the experts.

"But it is also very likely that these are stolen property, indubitably looted I'd say, and, as such, will have to be returned to the rightful owners."

Dead silence. Susan collapsed to the floor and did not utter another word for several minutes.

Emma spoke up. "How could that be? They surely would have been missed. There would have been news, media coverage. It would've been a big deal."

"Oh, they have been missed." One of the older gentlemen came out of the safe to talk to us.

"You see during World War II, prior to the US entering the war, while we were still *neutral*, many of the objects of art looted by the Nazis from occupied Europe were shipped to the United States, especially to New York City, and sold to wealthy collectors. Of course, most of those collectors were not particularly proud of where and how they had acquired these objects of art. Especially once the US entered the war. It was embarrassing to admit that they had been financing the Nazis with these acquisitions."

"Wow! Have they been in this attic since then? Since 1939 or '40?" Emma's eyes sparkled with excitement.

A second expert exited the safe. "We don't know for a fact that that is where they came from, but it is one possible explanation. We will have to research records."

"They can't have been here since the 40's." I said. I thought about it another minute. "No, they definitely have not been here that long. The playroom was built in the 60's. The paintings couldn't have been here without the owners at the time knowing about them. If they knew about them, certainly they wouldn't have left them behind."

Emma looked at me. "And who built this special room for them with climate control and everything?"

"Probably my lovely uncle, huh? What a great guy he's turnin' out to have been. No wonder my mother wanted nothin' to do with him."

Emma looked at me again. "Do we think there could be any connection between these paintings and the shooting?"

"Good point Emma."

Me and my they-don't-need-to-know attitude. I got it all wrong.

Oh, bloody hell, they are going to shut down my job site again, I realized with a sinking stomach. How selfish I was being by trying to avoid the delay. In fact, I was an accomplice in keeping these precious paintings from their rightful owners. Owners and their families who had likely already suffered greatly. What was I thinking?

"We'd definitely better let the police know about these paintings, right away." I dug out the detective's card, dialed the number, and got his voicemail. "We've found some paintings in the attic at Dr. Martin's. Call the doctor's attorney, Mr. Karloff for more info."

Susan had been quiet for what was, for her, a long time. "Now that I'm not rich, do you think maybe I could have a temporary job with your design firm?"

I only hesitated for a second or two. "Of course." I gave her a quick hug. "Speaking of which, I had better get to work."

On our way home, Emma asked me, "Mom, how can we give Susan a job? All we have is one dead client."

"I'll have to take the job with Sally. I better get over there today for sure."

But it wasn't only the ability to pay Susan that I had misgivings about. Then again, I really did like her. Surely the lies she had told me didn't mean anything.

Chapter 18

I decided to walk over to Sally's. It gave me a chance to collect my thoughts. I didn't want to show up there in a panic, and I was definitely starting to feel panicky.

I was now supporting six of us: Susan, Emma, Skip, Addie Mae's two assistants, and me. Skip was going to get kicked out of college if I didn't pay his tuition and housing bills. And Emma was right; we had one dead client. If that stupid, asshole husband of mine ever turns up again, I might have to kill him.

How could he have left me in this position? If my father hadn't owned this house in Los Feliz, we could have been homeless. Okay—that might be an exaggeration. On the other hand, if I'd had enough sense to hire my own lawyer, I might have been able to save the money I had inherited from my mother's trust. I might have kept my own house. Then again, the maintenance on that monster would have killed me. As it was, I had sold everything that the bankruptcy court and the U.S. Marshals hadn't taken, including trading in my Porsche Carrera for the two hybrids. I only had a few heirloom pieces of jewelry left. I wasn't about to sell my grandmothers' jewelry, but I had sold everything that shithead Jamie had given me.

I really didn't want to have to ask my father for money, but I was running out of choices.

If only I hadn't been in shock when Jamie left and the Marshals arrived with their writs of seizure and talk of asset forfeiture. If only I had asked my father for advice sooner. If only, if only . . .

I could drown myself in the "what-ifs" and the self-pity. What the hell was I complaining about? My children had been fabulous about the whole thing, never once complaining about the abrupt change in their lifestyle. Addie Mae made it clear that she was well taken care of by my mother's estate and thus didn't need to be paid to take care of us. Refused to be paid, in fact. My father said he had no use for the house. I knew all the "right people" to start a design business. All in all, I was damn lucky.

I came out of my funk. It was a beautiful day. One of those sunny, but crisp, days with the softly lit scene encircled by a ring of snowcapped mountains with a perfect blue sky as a backdrop. In spite of my northern California prejudices against LA, I had to admit that in winter, there is no place better.

It was hard to stay down in such a beautiful environment. It was only money. I'd just have to get some more. After all, having a lot of money had never been what made me happy, so why should having less of it make me unhappy?

By the time I arrived at Sally's, I was feeling more like

myself.

I knocked on the door. While I waited on the wisteria-draped porch, I noticed the detail of the raised panel door with a wrought iron grill covering a small window. A pair of wrought iron sconces flanked the door. I recognized the California Spanish Colonial Revival style. The house would have good bones. This could be fun.

I heard the patter of little feet and prepared myself to be accosted by the two miniature pinchers. As expected, when the door opened, the dogs and Sally were all over me.

Steve scowled at me from behind Sally. He alone did not appear happy to see me.

The entry hall had terra cotta tile floor, a curved stair with an elaborate wrought iron railing, and doors opening to four other rooms. We began the tour through a graceful arched opening to the living room. Centered on the far wall was a fireplace surrounded by hand-carved limestone. French windows ran the length of the wall facing the street. French doors on the rear wall opened onto a loggia.

The room was furnished in a completely inappropriate frilly Victorian style with a pair of purple velvet sofas and four matching chairs.

"Sally, this is a fantastic room." I didn't comment on the furniture.

"Yeah, yeah, but the furniture sucks. It's left from my last house, I haven't gotten around to getting new. Which is why you are here."

We passed through the living room out to the arched loggia that ran the length of the back of the house. French doors set in an arch at the far end of the loggia opened into the family room.

"This porch is where we spend most of our time. We breakfast at that table." Sally pointed to a wrought iron table surrounded by ornate matching chairs. "We spend mornings at that table reading the calendar and entertainment sections. It would be great if the chairs were comfortable." Sally shoved the back of one of the delicate wrought iron chairs. "These fuckers blow."

The arches framed the view of the lush, green garden and sparkling swimming pool. Beyond the pool was a small, sand-colored stucco building with French doors opening out to the pool deck.

"Steve lives in the pool house. The exercise room is out there, too."

Speaking of Steve, I realized he had left us.

Hmm, they weren't sleeping in the same room. He was so possessive, I had wondered about their relationship.

It certainly wasn't unusual for celebs and their trainers, or for that matter their household staff, their stylists, their decorators, or their personal assistants to become best friends. Think about it. Who else were they going to be friends with? Are you going to ask every potential friend to sign a confidentiality agreement? Conveniently, your employees already had signed NDAs.

Then there is the fact that celebrities never knew why someone wanted to be their friend. Was it for bragging rights? With the shocking amounts of money, the scandal mags offered for info about celebrities, who could they trust? Thus, their best friends were the old ones, those friends prior to them being famous. Or family. Or other celebs. Or household staff.

Or their trainers.

We continued our tour through the family room and kitchen into the dining room.

Sally pointed to the walnut Eastlake dining table and the chairs upholstered in vibrant purple. "Again, not comfortable. We've never used this room, but I would like to have dinner parties when the house is more presentable."

The walk through the dining room took us back to the entry hall and then up the magnificent staircase. Upstairs were three guestrooms and a study in addition to the master suite. The master suite included a sitting room with a window seat, an oversized bathroom with a tub the size of a small pool, a dressing room off of which opened a large walk-in closet and a fur vault. The house did indeed have good bones. It would definitely be fun to decorate and furnish it.

"Do you have any ideas?" Sally asked.

"Plenty. I prefer to furnish in keeping with the style of the house, in this case the Spanish Colonial. Zorro meets Julia Morgan. What do you think?"

"I don't know Julia, but I like Zorro. Especially Isabella Allende's Zorro."

"We can go rustic—early California accent pieces and accessories with super comfortable, overstuffed, down-filled upholstered pieces. I'm not suggesting we go too authentic."

"I like comfortable. And I like rustic. Not formal, or too traditional, I got sick of the Victorian stuff really fast, although I still like purple. Casual sounds good." She considered for a minute. "I'd like some drama, too. Casual drama. Can we do that?"

"Absolutely. We'll go shopping and look at possibilities."

"Good plan."

I left Sally's with a promise of a hefty retainer, a new job, and so far, nobody had asked me to sign a confidentiality agreement.

Things were definitely looking up.

When I got back to the house, Addie Mae and her assistants had left for the day. I could hear Emma and her boyfriend, Jeff in the courtyard patio. Their voices were loud, not the slightest bit muffled by the sound of the fountain.

Since we'd moved into this house, we'd fallen into a routine of pre-dinner drinks in the courtyard. In the fall, when the weather had turned cooler, we lit the outdoor fireplace and continued to use the patio, even in the chilly winter weather.

After hearing the basic gist of the conversation, I debated the wisdom of making my presence known. I didn't want to embarrass them, nor did I want to cut short the discussion. I tiptoed into the kitchen and poured myself a glass of Cabernet Sauvignon from the bottle left on the countertop. Unfortunately, I could still hear every word they said.

"Pumpkin, I'm not going to wait forever." Jeff said.

"I told you, don't call me that."

"You never told me why not."

"My dad calls me that." Emma's voice broke, but she continued. "I agreed not to see anyone else. Isn't that enough?"

"I'm looking for someone to share a life with, I want to get started building that life, I want kids before we're too old to enjoy them."

"Oh, for fuck's sake! I'm only twenty-two. Stop sounding like my biological clock is running out."

"I'm older than you."

"By three years. BFD."

"I just want to know where we are headed."

"I can't tell you that."

"Why not?"

"Do you think I know?"

"Just what do you expect me to do?"

"I don't know, but I wish you would stop torturing me on the subject. I'm not much into these discussions."

I heard the sound of a chair sliding across the terra cotta tile. I prayed they didn't end off like that.

"Sweetheart, I don't mean to make you cry!"

She was crying! Oh, she was a goner. I peeked through the breakfast room French door out to the patio. They were standing up. Jeff was holding a sobbing Emma against his chest.

I snuck up the back staircase.

Chapter 19

I had to send a proposal to Sally's production company in order to collect the retainer. That night I worried that this might be the point at which I could be asked to sign the customary confidentiality agreement. By morning I had decided what to do about it.

I had just entered the library at the front of our house, which I used as an office, when a new auburn red Jaguar sedan pulled in the circular drive. I set my cup of coffee on the desk and went to answer the door.

"I couldn't bring myself to drive the doctor's—that is Uncle Robert's—Bentley to work. It seemed too over the top absurd."

I was glad to hear Susan appreciated the irony of her situation.

She continued. "I realize that you were just bein' kind in lettin' me have a job, but I am pretty good at all kinds of paper work. I can do bookkeepin', typin', anything like that."

"That's good because I suck at all those things." I

showed her into the library we used as our office.

"Make yourself at home please." I waved at the desk. "I have this standard form I use for proposals. You can get this proposal off to Sally Abbey's production company. It's called SAP." I handed her the card and the form that Sally had given to me. "Give them the bank info to transfer the retainer."

Susan quickly settled into the office. She rearranged the desk for work, removed piles of fabric and carpet samples, and set the laptop in the center of the desk. "Do you mind if I reorganize this room a bit after I get this proposal out?"

"Sure, have at it." That could be good. "Susan, are there police back at your place?"

"Oh yeah! The place is crawlin' with them. They showed up very soon after I called Mr. Karloff to tell him what the art experts said. And they never left last night either. I was kinda glad that they were around all night. To tell the truth, I've been nervous around there since we don't have security anymore. Maybe my imagination, but I don't think so. I really think I've been hearin' prowlers." Susan sighed. "And the police are everywhere now. They woke me up early this morning to ask permission to search the guesthouse. I heard them making a terrible racket over at the main house all night long. I hate to think what they were doing over there. I was afraid to look this morning. I just got out of there and came over here."

"I'll check it out. Did you see Carl or any of his guys?"

"I saw his truck down near the pool house."

119

"I'm going to head over there. I need to check on Carl, and I might as well see what's happening in the main house."

I wasn't surprised that Detective Rodriquez was not very friendly that morning. I guessed he was unhappy about us not mentioning the paintings right away. Fancy that.

"Detective, I have something I think I should tell you."

"Oh really? Something more important than several hundred-million in probably stolen paintings?"

Oh yeah, he wasn't happy or friendly. He studied the clump of dirt he was kicking.

I looked at the clump imagining that in his mind, it was my head. "Well, maybe not, but somehow I don't think the paintings are connected to the murder."

"Since you are the expert, what is it that you want to tell me?"

With all this build up, it really seemed insignificant, but I thought I should say it before it became a big deal to say it. I could imagine having to discuss it with multiple lawyers prior to saying anything.

"The thing is, both my daughter and I saw Sally Abbey and her trainer, Steve coming in the back way to Dr. Martin's office. Which is of no particular significance in itself, I know because I also saw Rita Dolan, Cassie Green, Tom Henry and several others come in that way. The thing is, then a few days ago, she acted as though she didn't know the doctor."

"So, you think Sally Abbey killed Dr. Martin?"

"No, oh God, no! I hope not. It just seemed a little

strange that she pretended not to know him, or at least didn't let on to it."

"Thank you very much Mrs. Huntington. The next time you have a thought about this case, be sure to share it with me."

Ignoring his sarcasm and my humiliation, I blundered on. "There's this other little thing that bothers me. Susan Wallerski, the doctor's niece didn't come into LAX on the flight that the doctor's lawyer had booked for her."

"What do you mean?" His head jerked up from the dirt clods he had been crushing.

"Well, she was supposed to be on the 1:45 flight, but it was late and she wasn't. She had to have come in earlier. You might want to check on that."

He made a note in his book.

"There are a few more passages that you may not have located. Do you want me to show them to you while I'm here?"

We entered the house, and I had a terrible shock. Nearly every wall had been stripped down to the plaster or studs. Gone was the beautiful antique paneling! I couldn't help it; I let out a cry of dismay.

"We tried to be careful as to how we went about this." Detective Rodriquez pointed to a stack of antique paneling in the living room. "We saved as much as we could."

Bloody Hell! He had destroyed the house upon whose sale my family's financial future was dependent.

"I guess there probably isn't much left to uncover, so to speak" My weak attempt at humor went unacknowledged.

"Show me where the passages are."

I walked him through the butler's pantry to the dining room, the breakfast room, and the library.

I led the way to the second floor, averting my eyes as much as possible from the horrendous damage that had been inflicted on the house. I showed him where the second-floor linen closet accessed the main hall and the master suite closet.

"There is this little hall to the master suite, well, there was." It was now cluttered with paneling that had been removed and was leaning against the walls.

I continued into the master dressing rooms and closet. "There are two hidden safes in the master closet."

Those were now exposed and open.

"The contents of those have been bagged and removed." The detective's attitude seemed to be softening just a tiny bit, probably in response to my obvious shock and horror, the tears that filled my eyes.

"This little staircase leads to the servants' quarters."

At the bottom of the circular stairs, there was a short, narrow hall off of which were a laundry room, a bathroom, two bedrooms, a Pullman style kitchen, and a small sitting room. The rooms contained old, cheap furniture and multi layers of dust. The dark layer of dust looked to me like fingerprint dust. But the walls were all intact. Of course, here in the servants' quarters, the walls had not been covered in fine paneling, but rather plaster and dingy Navajo White paint.

Gingerly, I opened a few cupboards.

"Be careful what you touch. We have thoroughly searched the cupboards, the cabinets, and the closets in this area, as well. There were no stolen paintings, no patients' files."

With a layer of real dust and then charcoal gray fingerprint dust everywhere, believe me, I was not anxious to touch anything.

"Did the fingerprinting turn up anything?"

No response from the Detective. Instead of answering me, he ran his hand over his short black hair and stared at the floor.

"How about the boot prints?" I studied his face to see if I could get a clue. But a view of his handsome face was my only reward. His poker-face expression gave away nothing.

"What are you looking for? More files? I could be more helpful if you told me what to look for?"

"Okay, a gun, a place that a person could have hidden a gun. Our theory is that someone entered the grounds with the workmen and then hid when they left. We don't have an explanation for how the murderer left the grounds without security seeing them. We have reviewed all of the tapes and failed to see anything or anyone leave the grounds other than when the workmen left."

"Do the cameras cover every inch of the grounds?" I decided not to think about the obvious corollary to that theory; that the murderer and I were on the grounds, if not in the house, at the same time.

123

"No, just points of potential entrance. Those were pretty much covered," he said. "The tree branches have been trimmed back to keep the wall exposed, except where the wall is too tall, or the branches too high that it had been decided that it wasn't possible for some one to get up there unseen. The wall completely encircles the property."

"When I entered the day of the murder, the guard said the cameras were messed up." I shot him a raised eyebrow.

He nodded. "The other area that is normally on camera is the front drive and the entrance to the main house. Due to the work the electricians were doing that day, the camera looking directly at the front door and the one at the kitchen door were off."

"Detective, I was wondering. If the murderer hadn't seen the cameras and the screens, how would they know where they would be visible?"

"A person could look at the screens in the guard house, or just look for the cameras. Most of the cameras are not that well hidden." His slender brown fingers tapped against his notepad. He was starting to lose patience.

"But how would someone know which cameras were not working?"

"They wouldn't. Unless they had personally disconnected them."

"With some of the cameras off due to the work the electricians were doing, another inoperative camera might not have been noticed. Right?"

The detective grunted his agreement.

"Just one more stupid question. So, the point is, the

cameras are set up to detect people coming in, not people leaving? Right?"

"Right."

"There is one other thing. When you check to see what flight Susan Wallerski actually came into LAX on, would you please tell me?" I thought maybe if I had the correct information I could confront her with it and convince her to come clean to the police.

His frown told me he had no intention of telling me anything.

Chapter 20

Alone in my car, I burst into tears at the thought of the severe damage to the interior of the house. It wasn't just the money involved; I cried for the architectural details, the antique paneling and moldings, all that beauty and history and craftsmanship, all of it irreplaceable.

When I arrived home, Susan was really into reorganizing the office. I worried about how Susan would react when I told her the destruction at the house, but she took it pretty well. Then again, I might have understated it slightly.

Susan and Emma had been awaiting my return so they could show off their accomplishments. Our little design firm was now occupying both the library and the adjoining study/sun porch. They had moved furniture from various parts of the house and set up the two rooms. The sun porch had become my office with a large table for all my samples. The library had a small writing table set up with Emma's laptop and telephone. The large desk in the library held the computer monitor, a calculator with a tape, and a multi-line phone. Next to the desk sat the old oak filing cabinet from the garage that the girls were busy filling with new files.

"Hey you two, well done." I smiled and hoped they wouldn't notice the tearstains on my face. "This is great!" And it was.

"I've got some bad news." Susan stopped filing long enough to deliver her news. "But first, Yvonne Carrington called. Here's her number. She said it was important."

"And the bad news?"

"Ye-a-ah, I faxed the proposal over to Sally's production company. Then I called to make sure it had arrived—you know, to see if they had any questions—but her bookkeeper got on the line to say that Sally does not pay for those kinds of services. She wants you to do it for free!"

"Bloody hell! I hate this shit! I'm supposed to take Sally shopping today. I'll call her."

I called Sally and made a date to meet at her house earlier than originally planned. "We need to talk," I told her. Then I went upstairs to wash and fix my face before I went to see her.

When I arrived, we went through the usual hugs and kisses, even with the dogs. Then I launched right into it.

"Sally, I have a rather touchy subject to discuss with you before we can shop. I know we don't have a lot of time before our lunch reservations, but I don't think we want to have this conversation at the Ivy."

"Don't worry about the reservations. Believe me,

they'll hold my table. But I'm fucking starving, so what is it?" Sally held both dogs in her arms exchanging kisses with them.

"Your business manager or bookkeeper, or someone at your production company apparently suggested that we do your house for free. I understand that movie stars and other celebs often are 'comped' certain things, for the publicity, but this is a large, time-consuming project, and frankly, I can't possibly afford to do that."

"Oh, God, those fucking idiots! I'm so embarrassed. I've instructed my production company to always ask if they can get something for free, but I never imagined they would ask you to do that." Her face was bright red. "Do you have a copy of the contract with you? I'll sign it right now."

I handed over the agreement. She flipped directly to the last page and with a quick glance at the bottom money figure, signed on the dotted line.

"Steve! Where the hell are you? Where is my fucking checkbook? I'm pretty sure I have one around here some-where." She was rummaging around in her Hermes bag. "Shit, Steve! STEVE!"

Steve sauntered into the room, handed her a check-book, and walked back out without saying a word.

Sally wrote out the check not for just the retainer, but for the full amount of the design fees. She handed it to me with the signed agreement. I was about to comment that I would like for her to actually read the letter of agreement when Steve came back into the room.

"How long will you be gone?" he said as he dropped something into her bag.

What was his problem? Did I imagine a growl in his voice?

"I'll let you know. We're going to lunch and then shopping."

While I drove us to the Ivy, Sally filled me in on what she had in mind for her house. Strangely, it sounded like something she had memorized out of a book, or maybe a design magazine, but I listened.

"Sally, do me a favor and read your copy of our agreement. I left one copy on your desk."

"Why?"

"I want you to understand how we are doing this. We'll be able to work together better," I said. "Do you often sign papers without reading them?"

"I usually just have my lawyers—"

"I don't want to deal with lawyers on this. I want to work with you."

"Maybe you could just explain to me the important points that I need to know?

I sighed. "The check you just signed was the estimated amount for hourly fees until you and I establish the design direction and exactly what we are going to do. Then I'll give you a flat fee price to complete the project that will include the items I purchase for you. At that point you can either agree to that. Or not."

"That sounds good."

"The point I want you to understand is the longer we

take to establish the design direction, the higher the hourly bill will be. Do you understand that?"

"Got it." Sally answered me just as we pulled up to the valet stand. "Let me know when you want more money."

We sat on the front patio of the Ivy right behind the shabby chic picket fence. Being seated at this front row of tables was presumably a status symbol, but it put us right where the always present tourists and paparazzi could get a close-up camera shot.

Now I understood why Sally had taken extra care to look her best today. She had made up her beautiful jade eyes and full lips. Instead of the spandex running shorts topped with loose fitting, sloppy sweat shirts she wore around the neighborhood, she had on tight fitting 7 For Mankind jeans, and a D&G jacket over a cut down to there silk blouse. Her fashionable ensemble contrasted to my conservative two-year-old black Armani wool pantsuit.

Apparently oblivious to being put on display, Sally studied the menu and said," Wow, look at all this good stuff to eat. I feel like really pigging out! Uhm, yum, chocolate soufflé. What a waste to have soufflé on the menu—like anybody who comes here does more than pick at a salad." She grinned at me. "What are you going to have?"

"A salad." I caught the disapproving look Sally shot me. "Hey, when you get to be my age, . . . but I'll share a chocolate soufflé with you!"

"Don't tell Steve! About the soufflé. Hey, whose phone is that? Why don't they answer it?"

"Sally, I think it's yours."

"Mine? Oh, yeah, it is." She pulled the phone out of her bag, but then she couldn't figure out how to answer it. She poked at the instruction to slide the arrow. "Hello, Hello . . . . Oh, shit. Oh well, they'll call back."

The waiter stood patiently watching Sally with obvious fascination. "What can I get you, Miss Abbey?"

The phone rang. "Shit, already." This time Sally managed to slide to answer the call.

"Yes, Steve, I'm ordering the salad. No, there isn't any bread on the table. Yes, I'm having iced tea. Later."

Once our orders were placed, including the chocolate soufflé, we continued our conversation about the house décor while Sally exchanged blown kisses with other guests whose names were big enough big to warrant front patio seating. Nathan Carrington and his sister Yvonne were heavily into a discussion with their matching dark blonde heads close together.

Cassie Green sat at a table on the opposite side of the gate with a gorgeous young man draped over her shoulders.

"Who is that with Cassie?" I asked, hoping I wasn't making a fool out of myself by not recognizing the latest mega-hottie.

"I'm guessing that's some guy her agent set her up with."

"Why do you think that?"

"One, she's up for a part with steamy fuck scenes; two, this is where you come to get publicity; three, she's a lesbo."

I cringed at Sally's insensitive choice of words. But at least I hadn't failed to recognize anyone important.

Sally's phone rang again. "Christ, Steve, we are in a restaurant! What do you want now?" She listened for a few seconds. "It just so happens I do know what the agreement says. Cissy and I've been over it." She hung up.

We devoured the soufflé. As she savored the last bite, Sally said, "We should've ordered two of these. What was I thinking?"

From the Ivy, it was a short half a block walk to Armani Casa. We waved to John Travolta as he exited Armani Casa and jumped into a car that had pulled up to the curb.

I told Sally about the day I had introduced John to Armani Casa. As we'd made our way to collect his vintage T-bird from the Ivy valet, John was spotted by a veritable herd of Japanese tourists with cameras in hand. In the stampede to get shots of John, I was caught in the uncontrolled headlong rush and nearly trampled. Like any loyal, self-sacrificing designer to the stars, I had signaled to John to go ahead without me.

"Are we going there next?" Sally asked as she prepared to leave the patio.

"Just as soon as I take care of the bill." I handed the waiter my credit card that I hoped would be good. Fortunately, it was, but by the time the transaction was complete, tourists and paparazzi had surrounded Sally. I skirted the crowd and waved at her to follow me to the corner, to Armani Casa.

When I entered Armani Casa, we overheard the salesman saying to the salesgirl, "and so I told him, 'No, not even for you sir, will we alter our designs."

He abruptly walked away from the salesgirl when Sally opened the door. "Ah, Miss Abbey, Mrs. Huntington, such a pleasure. What can I help you with today?"

"Just getting started on a project, so just looking today." While I spoke with him, Sally picked up an elegant crystal vase. I pointed in her direction. "How much is that vase?"

The salesman puffed up his chest as he said, "38,000."

"Dollars?" Sally quickly, but carefully set the vase down. She took a quick glance around the store. "Maybe Italian Modern isn't really appropriate for my house."

From Armani Casa, we drove the few blocks over to the Pacific Design Center. When the first six story building of the PDC, covered in royal blue glass, was completed back in the 70's, it was dubbed the Blue Whale, a name that stuck despite the addition of an equally large grass-green section, and another in blood red.

First, we stopped in at Pacific Hide & Leather to look at the leopard skins made from cowhides.

"I like drama." Sally rubbed her hands over the hides. "Can we have animal skins?"

"The unadorned cowhides would be more appropriate to our theme."

We speed walked the halls of a couple of the lower floors looking in the windows at possible furniture styles, until we came to a showroom with over sized upholstered pieces. Sally went inside and threw herself onto a puffy, down filled lounge chair.

"I do like the big overstuffed thing." She swung her legs onto the matching ottoman. "Perfect. Fuck yes. I need lots of these."

I asked Mabel, the saleswomen who had materialized far faster than usual when she saw Sally, to please give us tear-sheets and prices for the pieces Sally liked.

We headed upstairs to the Pindler showroom to find upholstery fabric.

Walking through the 5th floor atrium, we passed Aga John Oriental Rugs. Large, hand-knotted silk rugs in a rainbow of colors hung in floor to ceiling windows. I pulled Sally away from their entrance. "They're open later than the other showrooms. We'll come back."

I hurried to Pindler. The booming voice of one of my favorite people in the PDC welcomed me. "Well, Ms. Cissy, how the hell are ya?" said the jovial woman seated at the front desk. "And who is this you have with you? Why if it isn't Ms. Sally Abbey!"

In a flash, Jeanne, the Pindler showroom manager appeared from behind a wing of fabric samples. Far more reserved than either Sally or the woman at the front desk, Jeanne smiled at Sally. "How may I be of service?" she asked.

Jeanne and the rest of the girls were excited to meet Sally, and helpfully pulled out fabric samples.

Sally tested each fabric by rubbing it against her cheeks. "What's this called?" She held the sample out for inspection.

"That's a silk chenille. Do you like that color?" The sample was a deep purple.

"Oh, yeah!" Sally held the sample up to her face and turned to face me. "What do you think? Do I look okay in this color?"

"I can't imagine a color you wouldn't look good in, but yes, you look great. That particular purple is good with brown. And with yellow-green. Maybe we could use some lavender and mauve with it."

"I like the fabric on that wall, but that's not the right color is it?" Sally pointed to a framed sample from the latest collection.

"I bet there's a colorway that would work for us."

"Colorway?" Sally frowned.

"A combination of colors. Many patterned fabrics are made up in a few different colorways." I opened a fabric rack to show her the wing that held one pattern done in four different mixtures of colors.

Sally nodded.

Jeanne excused herself, but returned within minutes with the same type of fabric as the one on the wall in shades of purple. "Do you like this Ms. Abbey?"

"Ooh, yeah, it's yummy. But please call me Sally."

"Remember the Philippe Starck Ghost chair we were looking at earlier? In the window that we saw from the escalator, on the third floor? The one in the Louis XVI style, but made entirely in lavender translucent poly-carbonate?"

"The see through one?" Sally asked.

"That's the one. Can you imagine that chair in your dining room with this lovely lavender silk? See how it looks like pale lavender that would match that chair from one direction and then darker, almost an eggplant color from the other direction? Look what happens when you gather it." I demonstrated how the shadows were the eggplant and the ridges were lavender.

"That is so cool! I fucking love it!"

Sally grabbed the ringing phone out of her bag. "Goddamn phone! What now?" She listened with a scowl. "Look asshole, I told you I wanted this one day, just one fucking day." She listened again. "Okay, okay. I'll come home." She hung up without saying good-bye. "Cissy, I am so-o-o sorry, but I have to go home. Steve is pissed that I have been gone so long and missed every workout he had scheduled. I told him I wanted this one day off, but . . ."

Jeanne handed me a Pindler bag full of fabric samples and I gathered up my purse and tote with the tear-sheets I had dropped in the waiting area.

We were both quiet most of the way home. I finally decided to say what was on my mind. "Sally, I'm worried that Steve doesn't seem to like me very much."

"What makes you say that?"

"Just a feeling I get. I'm concerned it might effect our relationship, yours and mine that is."

"He's never said anything to me. I don't think he has a problem with you. He just worries about my weight. He hates for me to miss any workouts." Sally continued to stare out the passenger window.

"Is something wrong?" I asked.

"No. Well, fuck, yes. Just the usual . . . I'm sick of the shape of my body being all anyone cares about. I'm just a piece of meat." She pounded the dash with the side of her fist. "It doesn't matter how much I study, or how good my acting is getting, it's just my body. You should hear the way they—the agents, and casting directors, and the producers, and directors talk about my body. You'd think I'm deaf. Or, a cow." Sally turned her face back to the window." And it's all Steve ever wants to talk about. I'm fucking sick of it."

"But you're a wonderful actress. You have great comedic timing. Truly you're not a piece of meat. I'm sorry they make you feel that way."

We had arrived at Sally's house. "Thank you." Sally reached across the console to kiss my cheek. "For everything."

After I dropped off Sally, I couldn't stop thinking about how actors, even the men, but more so the women, are pressured to retain their looks. So damaging to one's sense of self-worth. I remembered the times, after the children started school, when I felt like I was strictly decoration—arm candy accompanying my husband to social occasions. And that was nothing in comparison to how Sally must feel.

I decided rather than staying home myself, I would pick up Susan and check out something that had been nibbling at the back of my mind. Something about those paintings. I had a vague recollection of seeing something in Dr. Martin's office.

Chapter 21

I collected Susan from my house and we drove to the doctor's offices on Canon in Beverly Hills.

"Are you going to sell the practice?" I asked.

"We're tryin' to. Mr. Karloff is shoppin' it around, but he explained to me that, as Robert was a sole pra . . . practitioner, and apparently lackin' much in the way of 'goodwill', it doesn't seem to be worth much. We'll get somethin' for the patient list. The staff there is puttin' things in order. The furnishings will be auctioned."

"What are we going to do with the house?"

"Yeah, that's discouragin'. What do you think?"

"I'm still suggesting that you sell it as-is. It would take months to get it back together and we've now lost all of the crew that was working on it. They have to have started other projects by now. We would have to get back on their schedules, and god knows how long that would take."

"Carl's guys are still working on the pool house floors. I saw them this morning." Susan said hopefully.

"Floors are not the problem. I'm sorry Susan. I can

empathize with how awful it is to be left with such a mess. It's not hard to imagine how unfair it must feel when you didn't even get to enjoy the good times." I looked at Susan, but she was studying the view out her window. I continued. "At least when my husband left me with his mess, I had some great memories to console me. We'd had quite a ride that lasted long enough for me to raise my children in luxury. And I have my children to motivate me to keep going." I patted her shoulder. "I'll help you as much as I can. We'll go over it with Karloff tomorrow. Okay?"

"Cissy, can we please just go down Rodeo Drive? Isn't it a few blocks over from the office?"

Susan didn't seem to be too concerned about the estate problems.

"Let's get to the office before all the staff leave."

Susan shrugged. "I just thought maybe the stores would close."

"Not until at least 8 o'clock. And the staff will leave soon."

She seemed reluctant to go to the office.

"Unless you have a key?"

"No, I don't." Susan admitted. "I don't have a key."

Was she avoiding the staff?

In response to her obvious disappointment, I said, "Tell you what, we'll head over to Rodeo Drive after we check out this thing at the office."

Susan brightened up immediately.

Maybe I was wrong. Maybe she was just drawn by the glamour of Rodeo Drive. Nevertheless, I held back and let her reach the bank of elevators first. I noted that she got into the correct elevator, the only one that went to the top floor, and she quickly pushed the button as soon as I entered. How did she know where the office was?

She'd been here before. What the hell?

Emma and I had laughed about the over-the-top decor Dr. Martin wanted for the exam rooms in his office. He had insisted on the best antique oriental rugs and oil paintings, even silk gowns for the patients. Emma had found some very appropriate and pretty little floral watercolors at the Rose Bowl Flea Market, but he was not satisfied.

Then one day he brought in this beautiful little painting in the style of Vermeer. "This is the quality I want," he had said.

Now I wondered, did that come from the attic stash? If so, it would prove that the doctor definitely knew about the paintings.

Most of the office staff had not made it to the memorial service, so they should have been meeting Susan for the first time. The women were not busy and more than happy to help us in anyway they could. But Susan nodded and hurried past them down the hall to the doctor's private office. Oh, dear.

It didn't take long to find the tiny painting that I had remembered. It hung in the largest exam room. The backdrop of navy blue suede wall covering intensified the colors of the oil paint.

Susan walked into the room, went straight over to the painting and removed it from the wall. "It looks vaguely familiar, what is it?" Susan held the tiny oil painting of a standing woman whose soft yellow and periwinkle blue clothing were washed by light streaming in from a deeply recessed window.

"The first time I saw it I assumed it was 'in the style' of Vermeer. But now I'm not sure. I mean, it could be a real Vermeer."

Susan shifted her grip so that she had a firm, but delicate hold on the frame.

"What do we do with it? I don't want to be responsible for it."

"I think we should leave it here. We can lock it in the private office and we'll have the art authenticators come here to collect it. That way they can look around the office to see if there are any other pieces here that are valuable."

Susan carefully handed me the painting before she continued to explore the offices.

I took the painting into the doctor's office and set it on the shelves of the Federal credenza behind his desk. While I was there, I glanced at the papers on his mahogany desk. Most of the desktop was clear, but red leather pending basket held a few papers. I snuck a quick look through the papers in the basket. Why would Dr. Martin have a copy of Susan Wallerski's birth certificate? Well, that seemed to confirm the idea I had been considering.

The receptionist startled me before I had a chance to further dig into the pile of papers. She poked her head around the door and said, "You just missed Dr. Steinman. He said he had loaned a book to Dr. Martin, but he couldn't find it in here. I told him to call you or Miss Wallerski. Maybe you saw it around the house?"

I collected Susan from where she was chatting with the nurses. Susan's initial uncharacteristic shyness had evaporated in the heat of the staff's curiosity. One of the nurses said, "That Detective Rodriquez is hot. Is he married?" As I walked down the hall towards them I heard giggles and sighs. Evidently the detective had interviewed all eleven of the staff.

"Did the detective give you any clue as to what they think?" I asked the cluster gathered by the reception desk.

"He came in here the first time to look at files, but I told him I thought he had to get a warrant for that," the receptionist explained. "He came back a few hours later with a warrant, his partner, and two crime scene investigators. They spent hours going through the files and comparing patient files with billing files. The investigators also took fingerprints and shoe prints from all of us."

A nurse jumped into the conversation. "And they got this awful dark gray dust, they called it "magnetically sensitive powder" all over the place. God awful mess to clean up."

"Yeah, but that wand they put it on with was cool," another nurse chimed in.

I repeated my question. "Did he give you any clue if they have any ideas as to who did it?"

"We couldn't get anything at all out of any of 'em."

"We all tried, too."

Well, at least I wasn't the only one left in the dark.

"Ready to go, Susan?"

Our chore out of the way, we headed for the shops on Rodeo Drive. We stopped at Sweet Beverly where I introduced Susan to soft serve pistachio gelato.

Susan took a bite of the gelato and sighed with satisfaction. "Wow, they even put pistachio bits on top." She took another bite. "I'm sure not in Kansas anymore!"

We savored each spoonful as we strolled down the street and onto Rodeo Drive.

"Do you know what the powder was that the police got all over the office?" Susan asked me.

"I would guess they were looking for fingerprints. They had wand things that they used on the flat surfaces at the house too."

"But why at the office?"

"I'm not sure." I thought about her question. "Maybe because of the files that were found in the house. They might have been checking to see if someone other than the doctor moved them. Otherwise I can't think of a reason."

Susan licked her plastic spoon.

Was she worried that the police found her fingerprints in the office?

"Are you concerned for a reason?" I asked.

"Oh, no, no." Susan shook her head.

I wasn't convinced.

We stopped in at Frette, so that Susan could feel the bed linens. "Twelve-hundred thread count, wow. I didn't even know what thread count was. And I had no idea sheets could feel like that."

We crossed the street and wandered through the rooms at Ralph Lauren. The two of us climbed up the curved staircase to the home furnishings department and toured through the themed model rooms. I waited patiently while Susan soaked in the ambience of the room that was done up in Anglophile navy, white, and hunter green; black watch plaids and Scottish tartans; and Edwardian dark mahogany antique furniture reproductions accentuated by bright silver accessories.

"These rooms are so luscious, so yummy, they make me drool. I could move into any one of them," Susan said,

Susan really wanted to do a bit more than window-shop at Marina Rinaldi. "Wow, expensive clothes for us fat people. How great is that!"

I appreciated her wishful looking.

As we exited Marina Rinaldi, she ran into a gentleman and his dog, profusely apologizing to him before realizing that he and his dog were statutes. "This place is amazing!"

"Let's cut over to the next street via Tiffany's. I'd like to show you the value of those blue boxes. And then we'll hit Geary's, and I think you just might get an idea why I think it would be worthwhile to return the items in the blue Tiffany's boxes, orange Hermes boxes, and all of those Geary's boxes."

Susan caught on as fast I thought she might. We had barely reached the top of the stairs in Geary's when she glanced at a price tag and then asked the sales woman, "How would I return some of your things that have never been removed from the box?"

145

"If they are special order items, they are not returnable. Otherwise, you can exchange them or we will mail you a check. Do you have receipts? Or were they gifts?"

"I'll see if I can find receipts," Susan said as she stared at the room filled with the sparkle of crystal vases and glassware, silver services, silverware, and china.

"Are you through drooling?" Even though I enjoyed watching Susan have fun, I had had enough conspicuous consumption spectatorship for one day.

"Yeah, let's go. I've got receipts to find."

"I'd like to stop at the house to look at a couple things. Would that be okay with you?"

The estate was less than a couple miles away. Now there was a policeman in the security shack, but he was dressed in the uniforms Dr. Martin's security had used.

"Mr. Karloff thought we would have to get the security back here despite the lack of funds to cover it, but fortunately the police wanted to stake the place out, so they worked out having policemen pretend to be the security."

"Well, now we know why he had so much security.

"It makes me feel a lot safer here. And Mr. Karloff says the cops figure that there have to have been other people involved with the stolen paintings. So, they are waiting for them to show up."

"Who do they suspect?"

"They haven't said."

"I'm curious about how someone got in here. And out of here. Will you walk the perimeter with me?"

I knew that the trees had all been trimmed to keep

people from climbing in, but, I assumed, without thought to them getting out. I had thought we would find a branch on the inside of the wall that would make it easy to get over. But Detective Rodriquez had been correct; there did not appear to be any such branch, or any other means of exiting over the wall.

"Let's see what can be seen from a camera. Let's go to the security booth and look at the camera angles."

I was disappointed to find that it seemed nearly impossible for anyone to have gotten past both the cameras and the security guys. "Has anyone ever asked the security that worked for Martin what his instructions to them were? What was he telling them to look out for?"

The policeman/security guard had no ideas.

"Cissy, don't you think the security was because of the paintings? That's what you said before."

"Certainly, the paintings warranted security. But they were well hidden. What else was he afraid of?"

As I drove Susan back to the car she had left at my house, I thought about asking her to tell me what really happened the day of the murder. I had been waiting for her to voluntarily tell me her secrets; after all, she might shed some light on the murder if she decided to come clean. She might have seen something, or someone. But I worried that our fledgling friendship wouldn't survive if she told me even more lies.

She asked, "Will you come with me to talk to Mr. Karloff about all this tomorrow? The three of us can make the decision about what to do with the house."

"You know what I think, don't you?"

"Sell it as-is?"

"Correct."

"Mr. Karloff thinks we would get more for it if it's in really good shape. Like maybe a couple million more."

"Has he looked at it lately? It's going to take close to a couple million to get it in "really good shape.""

It was then that I remembered what the security guard had said to me about the cameras being "messed up" the day that Dr. Martin died.

Chapter 22

"I tell you child, you got to find that husband of yours. Maybe somethin' bad happen to 'em."

"Addie Mae, if something bad hasn't happened, I'll see to it something does," I sassed her.

"You got to get your head outta da sand. That man has always needed you. I just know he be needin' you now."

"Oh, Addie, you know how much I love you." I wrapped my arms around Addie feeling how much she had shrunk from the strong, round, black dynamo of my memories. My parents had lived on my maternal grand-parent's estate until I was three. When they decided it was time to get a place of their own, Addie Mae came with us to ensure that we didn't die of starvation or live in filth. She was now old enough that she couldn't see dirt and frail enough that she couldn't do anything about it, if she had. But she supervised the day cleaners and still ran the household—and all of us too.

"And the other thing, I'm sure that Skip don't have enough clothes at school. Now that we can't afford for him to come this far every weekend, how's he get his laundry done?" Addie Mae continued to fuss at me, but now under her breath.

"Mom, are you ready to go? I already dropped off several bags of samples and tear sheets at Sally's. I need you to come and tell me if I got everything you need for this meeting."

Emma and I scooted down to Sally's house. "I have all the samples laid out in the loggia." Emma walked right in the front door she had left ajar and out to the loggia.

"Oh my God, Mother! Those tiny, freaking terrors she calls dogs have ripped up the samples!"

Sure enough, the two miniature pinchers were on top of the table having a tug-a-war with a sample of Cowtan & Tout lavender silk. Ripped up samples were strewn across the wrought iron table, the wicker sofas, the two chairs, and the ghastly indoor/outdoor carpet.

Sally hurried in from the opposite end of the loggia mere seconds after us. "Oh, I'm so sorry. Bad dogs, bad, bad dogs! Steve, where the fuck are you? I thought you were taking these little monsters for a fucking walk."

"I was going to take them out, but when I saw Emma coming and going, I thought I ought to stick around for this meeting," Steve said from the opposite doorway.

Emma stared daggers at Steve, but to my gratitude, refrained from speaking. As she set about straightening up the mess, Sally and I jumped in to help.

Steve leaned against a column and watched us work. "What's that purple stuff for anyway?"

We all ignored him. Once we had some semblance of order, we started going through the various samples and photos. Some we had picked up on the shopping day Steve had interrupted and the others Emma and I had collected.

Working together, we picked up each piece and decided which room it fit best. Some samples clearly didn't work anywhere.

"What the fuck were we thinking?" Sally and I shared a good laugh in response to a leopard skin pattern done in shades of purple. But the more we laughed, the more I could feel Steve bristling from where he stood leaning against a column with his arms folded.

"Okay, here's the pile for your bedroom. Emma please write the list of what we still need. Here's the curtain and bedcover fabric. Here's the carpet, and the sofa and fabric for it. We need a bedside lamp to go with this beautiful campaign chest that will be our bedside table. This bed is great. I don't know about this chandelier. I think we need the next size up."

"You need a lot of stuff cuz' most of that is crap," Steve said, "Sally, you are a movie star! The world's biggest female star! You need way better, way more expensive, really kick ass stuff!"

Sally looked at him in surprise. "Oh, I kinda like this lavender silk, and this carpet. Are you sure?"

Emma couldn't hold back any longer. "I thought you were the trainer—not the decorator. Just what is your job?"

"Someone has to look out for Sally's best interests."

"I don't know. I like this stuff. I think we're doing

151

okay." Sally continued to pick up and rub the various fabrics.

"These things aren't good enough. You need to have the best, the real stuff, real antiques, real smokin' killer stuff."

Emma stood up, walked over, so that she was right in Steve's face, and was about to unload when I spoke up, before it went nuclear.

"Let's call it a day. We'll leave these piles and you can look them over at your leisure. We'll talk tomorrow."

I rushed Emma out of the house.

When we got to the sidewalk, Emma held out her hand. "Look at this Mom." She had a small round metal button-like thing. "Did you and Sally have a reason to pick this up from the PDC?"

I took the object from her hand. "I don't have any idea what it is. Where did you get it?"

"It was in the bottom of your tote bag." Emma raised an eyebrow at me. "The one you took to the PDC the day you went with Sally."

"Do you know what it is?"

"I'm guessing, either a tracking device. Or a wireless mike. Or both."

"A microphone?"

As we entered our house, the cell phone in the bottom of my purse rang. By the time I dug it out, it had gone to voice mail.

"You *need* to call me. This is my cell number." It was Steve's voice on the speaker.

"Oh, I do, do I? What is with this guy?" I glared at the phone.

"Tell him," Emma said, "you *need* to eat shit and die."

Chapter 23

I dug out the card Detective Rodriquez gave me and called him.

"Ms. Huntington. How may I help you?"

"I'm not sure if there is any significance or connection to the doctor's murder, but a strange object turned up in my tote bag. My daughter thinks it might be a tracking device or a microphone."

"Did you have the bag with you at the doctor's house the day he was killed?"

"Uh, yes."

"Where is it now?"

"The bag and the object are right here on my desk."

"You're in Los Feliz?"

"Yes."

"Don't handle the bag or the object."

"But we already have." I sighed. "A lot."

"Give me your address. I'm not far from Los Feliz. I want to see this thing."

He must have been very close by as he knocked on our door ten minutes later.

"Detective Rodriquez, this is my daughter Emma." They shook hands. Emma offered him a drink, water or coffee, both of which he declined.

I walked him into my sunroom office and showed him the metal object and the tote on my table desk.

The detective leaned close to look at the object. He pulled plastic gloves from his pocket and picked up the button.

"When did you find this?"

"I found it this morning while I was unpacking samples and tear sheets at a client's house." Emma said.

"When was the last time that bag was emptied?"

Emma and I looked at each other and shrugged.

"I took a bottle of water out of it at the crime scene, but I didn't pay much attention to what else was in it."

"What is usually in that bag besides water?"

"A small bag of nuts, a digital camera, a notepad, and a pen. The camera in case my phone gets too low in charge to photograph furniture. I use the tote to carry samples and tear sheets I pick up in showrooms. And sometimes I toss in pieces of candy from showrooms."

"I think the two pieces of foil wrapped candy in the bottom of the bag kinda camouflaged the metal thing." Emma offered.

Detective Rodriquez nodded his understanding of her point. He turned to me, "Did you have samples in it when you took it to the doctor's estate?"

"No, but I was planning to pick up samples I had left with him."

"Was the tote in your possession the whole time you were at the doctor's that day?"

I thought back to that day. "I had my purse and the tote in my hand when I entered the house, but I set them both down on the stairs before I walked into the living room."

"Let's play it safe." Detective Rodriquez put the possible microphone back on the table desk and motioned for the three of us to move into the living room putting three doors and a hallway between the metal button and us.

I sat on a chair in front of the fireplace and waved the detective into the chair opposite mine. Emma pulled the double doors between the hall and the living room closed and landed on the sofa.

"Have you given any more thought to the possibility of someone being in the house when you went in?"

"I don't think I heard any sound—that I noticed anyway. I definitely didn't see anyone."

"It's possible that the murderer saw or heard you and thinks you saw or heard him. Have you experienced anything suspicious that might indicate someone has been following you?"

I shook my head.

"Any strange phone calls?"

"No, not that I know of. Not on my cell and Susan has been answering the office phone. She hasn't mentioned any."

"Do you know what that thing is?" Emma asked the detective.

"I'm thinking, tracking device, maybe a microphone.

Not my area of expertise. I'd like to take it with me to get it checked out."

"Of course. Please do."

"And the tote too?"

"Sure."

"If this is a mike, have you said anything to anyone that might indicate you know more about this murder than you've told me?"

I gave some thought to what, if anything, I'd said when I was anywhere near the tote. The tote had gone into the PDC with Sally and me, but we didn't discuss anything to do with the murder. Emma and I had it in the PDC, but we didn't discuss any aspect of the doctor's murder. The tote had been on my desk until Emma took it to Sally's this morning.

Neither my suspicions about Susan nor anything about the paintings had been said anywhere near the tote to my recall. In fact, I hadn't shared my concerns about Susan with anyone. I didn't think she had killed her uncle. She just wasn't telling us everything about her actions and her relationship with her uncle. Not relevant to the crime investigation.

I shook my head.

"If you think of anything . . . even if you aren't sure if it's relevant, you will call me, right?"

"Certainly."

"And, if anything suspicious occurs, don't hesitate to call 911 immediately—and then me."

Chapter 24

I went to Sally's to plead my case. Steve, who told me that he, not Sally would be working with me in the future, had intercepted all my earlier calls. I refused to have to deal with Sally via Steve. I had marched over to Sally's, banged on her door, and pushed past the housekeeper who opened it.

"Let's go shopping," I said to Sally as she entered the hall.

"Come out to the loggia and have some coffee. Steve's out there, we can talk this over."

When Sally and I sat down at the table, I smiled at Steve. He didn't return my smile, but rather continued to look sullen.

"Steve, I think the best way to deal with your disagreement with the direction that we were going with these designs would be to get your input from the onset. I would like you to help us formulate a design direction with which you are happy. Once that is established, we can take it from there because I know you are a very busy man." Yeah, I was blowing smoke up his ass. "If you'll just help us get started, Steve, we'll go shopping. You are coming with us. Can the two of you go tomorrow?"

"Whatever." Steve grumbled as Sally nodded her head.

"I'll be by for you bright and early . . . at 11:00 a.m."

True to my word, I was in their drive at eleven the next morning. Sally, clad in deep purple jeans covered by a metallic gold trench coat, came out first and got in the back seat behind the passenger seat leaving the front passenger seat for Steve. He plopped himself in a minute later and we took off.

"Good morning!" I greeted my passengers. "It's another beautiful day, isn't it?"

From the back, Sally agreed with my assessment of the day, but Steve continued his insistent sullenness. I tried to make conversation with him most of the drive to the Design Center but he wasn't having any part of it. I had thought that my concession to making him part of the process would soften his attitude toward me, but it wasn't working. He was still being Mr. Tough Guy. I ignored him and began discussing the design with Sally.

"I've been thinking about what would be appropriate for both your house and your movie star persona. We shouldn't ignore the beautiful Spanish Colonial architecture of your house. The house has some beautiful features, like the loggia with its outdoor fireplace, and the entry hall with the wrought iron staircase. And the architectural details throughout the house are great."

"The way I see it, we have three directions that would work well with the house and could be dramatic enough to represent 'the world's biggest female movie star'."

I glanced in my rearview mirror to see that Sally was attentive to my every word.

"What are they?" she asked.

"One, we further develop the Spanish Colonial into an early California style. We play up the wrought iron and add velvets, brocades, saddle leather, terra cotta pots, antique Persian rugs, a few really exquisite, finely-carved, Spanish-style antiques. Slightly rustic with a few imported-from-Spain-looking elements in jewel tones, including amethyst purple and jade green."

"I might like that. Kinda like Diane Keaton's place?"

I hesitated before I realized she wasn't thinking of Diane's current house. "Yes, kinda. But I was thinking more detailed, less rustic. I see your house as more glamorous. More colorful. Diane's place was very nice, but I think, a bit earthy for you."

I wasn't getting the enthusiastic response I knew we needed to carry us through the entire process of decorating this house.

"Here's another idea. We do a streamlined Spanish with clean-lined upholstered pieces and mostly solid, vibrant colors. Very little pattern. Dark wood in traditional pieces of furniture but sparsely detailed. Remember those chandeliers we saw the last time we went shopping that are simple wrought iron with the light bulbs hidden inside pillar candles so that the candles glow?"

"Oh, yeah, those were fucking cool."

Encouraged, I said. "It's a modern take on Spanish. That look can be a bit understated, but we could make it quite dramatic with intense colors such as magenta and eggplant, and some oversized pieces, like enormous pots with banana plants, wall clocks that are six feet in diameter, mirrors that are ten-feet-by-twelve-feet."

"That's a possibility. What do you think Steve?"

Steve seemed not to have been listening, but he said, "Maybe."

"What's the third idea?" asked Sally.

"We build on the time period when the house was built, the late nineteen twenties. We don't ignore the Spanish details, but we don't play them up either. We make the background as neutral as we can with mottled, cream-colored plaster walls and go for an ultra-glamorous silver screen look."

"Silver screen? Like Valentino or Harlow? Oh yeah, I think that's what I want! Show me what that would look like."

I pulled into the valet park at the Pacific Design Center. The three of us entered through the glass doors leading past displays, a small bookstore, and magnificent showrooms. I waved at Jim in Pacific Hide & Leather as we walked by.

I led Sally and Steve up to the 3rd floor of the blue building to the Schumacher showroom. There I showed them a handsome coffee table covered with faceted, bevel edged mirrors. "This would be one kind of piece we would use."

"That is fucking great! I love that!" Sally looked to Steve for a reaction.

He nodded his head without any enthusiasm, at which Sally shrugged her shoulders and said, "Well, I like it a lot. What else would we use?"

I showed her a bombé chest with a lovely patina silver finish, yards of ivory-colored chenille, cream-colored silk carpets, and crystal chandeliers.

Two hours later we stopped for lunch at Wolfgang's restaurant, Red/Seven, on the ground floor. As we slid into the minimalist booth, Sally enthused, "I'm so fucking excited, I love this direction."

I asked Steve, "What do you think?"

"It's okay."

"Just okay?"

I wanted to have the discussion as to Steve's opinions on this subject now, before we invested a lot of time in developing the designs, and while we were all together, so that Steve wouldn't start bad-mouthing my work to Sally as soon as I wasn't around.

"It could work," he hesitated, "if it's done well."

I looked Sally in the eye and said, "It *will* be done well."

Sally answered with a nod and a smile.

"Now, I think you should have a mirrored vanity. Your bedroom should be all done in shades of cream. The bed should be draped in silk, with an ermine throw across a chaise at the foot of the bed. Of course, it will be faux ermine."

We made a list of what to look for that day. Sally and I ate our lunches quickly so that we could get started shopping in earnest. Steve was dawdling, so Sally suggested that he finish his lunch at his leisure and then catch up with us. I was not sorry to lose his black cloud presence even if it was just for a few minutes.

"Steve doesn't seem too happy. Is he just being polite about this direction?" I asked her as we headed for the Kneedler-Fauchere showroom.

"No, I think he has some other things on his mind. I'm not sure exactly what all is bothering him, but its not what we're doing."

At Kneedler-Fauchere, I showed Sally a magnificent pair of crystal lamps. I explained how silver and pewter accessories looked great with the cream colors. We started pulling fabric samples for each room. We decided to use the cream color scheme with pale lavender touches throughout the house, including dramatic off-white carpets with a lavender accent color in each room. The exceptions would be that the living room and dining room would both have black accents, and the décor of Sally's bedroom suite would only be accentuated with mirror and silver.

The kitchen would have cranberry purple accents; the loggia, orchid accents, the library, eggplant purple, and so forth.

We pretty much had gotten most of the rooms worked

out when I got a call from Carl over at Dr. Martin's pool house.

"Mrs. Huntington, would you please stop by here today. I have some questions to ask you. It'll be really quick. But I would rather show you than try to describe it over the phone."

"Sally, would you mind if we were to stop by Dr. Martin's place before we head home? Carl promises it will only take a few minutes. We can stay here and shop until the showrooms close. Otherwise I have to drive clear to the other side of town and back with Carl waiting there the whole time."

"I don't mind at all. In fact, I'm curious to see the fucking place."

"Good. Thanks, Sally." I turned back to the phone. "Carl, we'll be over as soon as the shops close. I hope you don't mind waiting for awhile."

"No problem. That'll work for me. I've got stuff to do around here. I've got plenty of costs to work out for you," Carl said before saying goodbye.

"Let's head down to Aga John for area rugs. They have some beautiful wools with silk patterns in a tone-on-tone effect that will look great in your *boudoir*." The emphasis I put on the last word brought a smile to Sally's face.

As we walked by a tile shop on the way to Aga John, Sally spotted a honed marble that appealed to her. "Where could we use that? It's so yummy."

"How 'bout your bathroom counter?"

"Yes, way cool." Sally answered her ringing phone.

"Steve, we're headed to the carpet store on the fifth floor, Aga John. Meet you there."

Michael and Jerry, the two brothers who own Aga John, were pleased to meet Sally, who really turned on the charm. "Oh, you have such be-o-outi-ful rugs!"

By the time Steve arrived, Sally had looked at a dozen rugs. The men who were rolling them out for her appreciation were having the most fun they had that day as she went ape shit, jumping up and down and screaming that each rug was more beautiful than the last. We had moved on from wool with silk for the boudoir into Aubussons for the living room, Savonnieres for the dining room, and Kermans for the library.

"How in the world do you ever keep all these names straight?" Sally was really getting into rugs.

"Here's the simplicity of rugs. The different types are named for the location, be it a country, a province, a factory, or a tribal area where they are made. In different parts of the world different knotting or weaving techniques are used. Patterns are fairly consistent in a location. If you keep in mind the name of a rug is simply a matter of where it was made, it's less confusing," I explained.

Steve stressed that he was bored to death for the hour that he watched Sally look at rugs despite the staff's constant attentiveness in supplying him with cappuccinos and water. He lounged on a stack of rugs, playing games on his phone. Every few minutes he would swear at Sally. But his bored expression changed to alarm when Sally informed him of the next item on our agenda.

"Oh Steve, it's so fucking cool, I finally get to see Martin's estate. I have been so curious about that place and Cissy is going to take us by there next."

"What? What do you mean, 'take us by there'? What are you talking about?"

"Cissy needs to stop by there on the way home, and so we get to see the place. Maybe she'll even give us a tour?" Sally looked at me.

"Sure, I don't see why not," I said.

"Why does Cissy need to stop by there?" Steve asked in his typical gruff manner.

"Oh, she needs to look at something somebody wants to show her. Cissy, what's that guy's name?"

"Carl."

I thought I saw a flash of alarm in Steve's eyes before he caught me looking at him. "Hmm, Sally, we don't have time for that."

"What do you mean? I don't have anything else scheduled for today." Sally was much more interested in the rugs than in Steve's scheduling concerns.

"Well, I do. I have appointments." Steve said. "And you have a red-carpet next week! Do you want to look like shit and have all of the commentators rag on your fat ass?"

Sally glared at Steve, but then the next rug that was opened up for her viewing distracted her. "Oh, that is so fucking gorgeous! Cissy, we have to use that somewhere. Where could we use that?"

"Maybe in the media room?" I offered.

"We'll have to get new fabrics to go with, right?"

asked Sally.

"Yes, we'll want to pick up that Della Robbia blue in some of the throw pillows at least."

Steve stood up from where he had been sitting on a pile of rugs. "I'm going to Uber home," he announced.

"Really?" Sally asked. "What's this appointment?"

"Look, I just need to go. I'll discuss it with you later." He turned to Michael and asked, "How do I get out of here?"

"We will be happy to show you out. Mara, lead this gentleman to the main Melrose entrance."

Steve walked out the door without even a goodbye and turned the wrong direction to exit the Melrose Entrance. Mara hurried after him and guided him to the correct bank of elevators.

Sally looked at me and shrugged her shoulders. She immediately returned to enjoying the rugs. Mara brought Sally her skinny decaf latte, and she lounged on a pile of rugs and sipped.

We looked at rugs for another half hour. "Sally, we're keeping these people past their normal closing time. Let's continue this another time."

"Oh sure, I'm sorry, I didn't realize," Sally apologized.

"It's not a problem. We are happy to accommodate you in any way," Michael said without hesitation. I knew he meant it.

Sally planted a smacking kiss on his lips. He turned bright red. "You're very sweet, but we need to go anyway. Don't we need to meet your friend Carl, Cissy?"

"Yes, that we do. Michael, would you please send the rugs that Sally liked over to her house so we can try them in the rooms?"

"Absolutely, we will be very happy to do so immediately. Will there be someone there to take delivery?"

"My housekeeper'll be there." Sally pulled her phone out of her Hermes bag and called home. "Some rugs are being delivered in what? Probably an hour?"

Michael nodded.

"Yes, in an hour. Stack them up in the entry hall. Thanks." Sally gave Michael the address.

With that Sally and I headed for our appointment with Carl. We drove up to Sunset Blvd. and headed into Bev Hills.

Sally was impressed by the estate, but shocked by the damage that had been done to the interior of the main house. "My God! What fucking idiots did this?"

"Let's don't get into that. Do you want to look around while I find Carl? You'd give him a thrill if you were to meet him," I suggested.

"Sure, whatever."

Sally wandered into the living room where she was checking out the carved bear's head that was part of the center medallion in the mantel. "What a fucking amazing fireplace? Did you have that done?"

"No, I understand that Charles and Charles had that shipped over from Scotland. Pretty incredible, huh?"

"Un-fucking-believable!" Sally responded.

I called him and found out Carl was in the pool house.

"Let's walk over to the pool house and you can see the gardens on the way."

"This really is an amazing place. Do you think I should buy it?" Sally asked me as we made our way through the grounds past the charming guesthouse and into the pool area.

"Oh boy, I don't want to get into that. You saw how much damage there is in the main house." I gave it a moment's thought. "The house you have seems appropriately sized. Would you need something this big?"

"No, but did the doctor need something this big?"

"He was very anxious to impress people. You're the world's biggest female star. Who do you need to impress?"

"Damn right. Fucking A!"

We found Carl on the terrace outside the pool house. As predicted, Carl was overjoyed to meet Sally. "I can't tell you what a huge fan I am, Ms. Abbey."

"Please call me Sally."

"It's an honor."

Carl showed me the problems he was concerned with, and we worked out how he was going to deal with them. Then I showed Sally the rest of the estate, and we headed back to our own neighborhood.

"What a great day we've had! Thanks so much," Sally said when I dropped her at her house. "When do we go again?"

"Tomorrow?"

"It's a date."

But before I had driven the less than two blocks to my

169

house, Steve was calling my cell complaining that I was monopolizing Sally's time, and that she really had to take care of some other business the next day. He couldn't have been ruder.

Chapter 25

"Mom, you look great. Hella gorgeouso!" Emma stopped at the top of the stairs to appraise my black velvet tuxedo and diamond pendant earrings.

"Look at you! My darling daughter, I love this azure blue with your eyes." Emma had on a ruched velvet and lace camisole under a shrunken velvet jacket with her jeans. "Where are you and Jeff going tonight?"

I caught up with her and we walked down to the entry hall together.

"I don't know. He's going to surprise me." Emma headed into the living room to wait by the warmth of the fire.

"What fun! Tell him hi! I'm off." I went through the kitchen and laundry room to the garage where my Prius waited. I backed out to the street and headed for the Getty on the opposite end of town.

Early in our marriage, going to the type of social occasion to which I was en route was exciting fun. Later attending such events became a required chore. This night I forced myself to attend in the hope I would see potential clients. My father's annual donation to the Children's Home Society provided a pair of tickets to each of these fundraising events. I couldn't find an excuse not to use them and I admit I felt the stirrings of pleasant anticipation for an aesthetic evening.

I ignored the valets and pulled into the parking structure. As I waited for the tram, I looked up at the cluster of buildings, plazas, and gardens that comprise the Getty Center.

A college friend, who had been one of ten associate architects on the project, had let me in on the gossip about the design and construction process. The local conservancy groups had insisted that architect Richard Meier not build in his signature white metal exterior, but rather a hue that would blend with the natural colors of the hillside. Richard must have appreciated their interference while he sat at the quarry in Tuscany, under the shade of an umbrella, sipping his Compari and soda, as slabs of travertine marble were brought forth for his approval.

His enjoyment of the experience seemed to me to be apparent in the aesthetic end result. On this winter evening, I loved riding the tram as it glided up the hill to the Getty while the magic of the sparkling city unfolded below. The black ocean in the distance contrasted with the moonlit, roughhewn stone walls that reflected a soft gleam onto the gardens. From the reception site, music wafted over the stone plaza, the smell of the food enticed the appetite. Even the photographers failed to mar the scene by respectfully keeping their distance.

"Mrs. Huntington, you look even lovelier than usual tonight," said a stilted, somewhat familiar voice.

Oh, damn. The cosmetic dentist friend of Dr Martin's.

"Hello, Dr. Steinman! How are you this evening?"

"Please call me David. May I escort you in to the reception?" He formally offered me his arm. "The cocktail hour sounds to be well underway."

We strolled through the large room adjacent to the restaurant and overlooking the parterre gardens.

"Champagne?" offered the waiter circulating through the throng with his tray held aloft.

"Mrs. Huntington, don't take that cheap junk! Waiter, bring me a bottle of Cristal!"

I searched the room for a familiar face that would rescue me from this pretentious clown. I noticed several people that I had seen in Dr. Martin's office. Most of the attendees were checking out the offerings in the silent auction.

I spotted a lovely pair of antique sapphire and pearl earrings that had been donated by Cassie Green. They would've looked great on Emma. Oh, but the last bid, from Tom Hanks, was for seventy-five thousand. The earrings were perfect for Rita.

Kirstie Alley had donated a New York cab from the 1940's. Where the hell did she find that? I thought I recognized the last name on that list as that of a race car driver, and that bid was getting up there, too. Good! More money for the Children's Home and Rights Society. It had been my mother's favorite charity, and I knew they put the money to good use.

I averted my gaze from the auction tables to avoid further temptation. Even though I would have liked to add my support, my father's donation would have to suffice for the both of us. I no longer had extra disposable income.

Happily, I spotted one of my favorite, most entertaining acquaintances, who was also my newest client. I caught her eye and offered a subtle finger wave.

Sally Abbey yelled at me across the ballroom. "Get the fuck over here!"

"Excuse me, David. I really must speak with Sally." I rushed off to say hello to my very not-boring friend, brushing off Dr. Steinman's attempt to hold my arm.

My God, what did Sally have on? It looked to be a bronze metallic sheen fabric made into a very tight-fitting dress cut down to here and up to there, showing every aspect of her tall, voluptuous figure. Major cleavage! The bronze certainly set off her rich, bittersweet brown hair, creamy skin, and jade eyes. She looked every inch the movie star she was.

Sally threw her body full force into mine. I barely kept my feet. Without letting me go, she yanked down the front of my cami, "For fuck's sake, show off some of that!"

Sally's friend, sweet Nikki Howe, joined us. Nikki greeted me with a gentle hug and air kisses while she breathlessly whispered, "Darling, how very nice to see you! Sally is so-o excited to have you doing her house." She tossed her soft blonde hair and smiled up at me, her crystal blue eyes twinkling. Her Grecian-style dress was an ombre blue that started as deep blue at the floor-grazing hem and rose to a pale shade that matched her eyes.

The friendship of these two women proved the truth of opposites attract. Sally reminded me of a large, happy, sloppy dog that would enthusiastically jump up and lick your face, while Nikki put me in mind of a small, gently playful kitten that would greet you with the soft pat of her paw on your hand.

"So good to see you! I'm surprised to see you both unescorted tonight." Nikki was famously married to mega star, Jack Trevor, and Sally was seldom seen without Steve in tow.

"My husband is on location—as usual. And he worries about the Richard Craniums." Nikki explained as she threw her pale blue chiffon stole over her shoulder.

Sally translated for me, "Nikki means I promised her husband to keep the dickheads off her."

"You see, we're the A-list tonight." Nikki referred to the convention that required fund-raising events to have celebrities in attendance. That was supposed to attract the guests with the real money. Having been married to some-one who was supposedly attracted to a party by the promise of the presence of celebrities, I was doubtful it made any real difference. On the other hand, now that I needed the A-listers' patronage, I was grateful for the practice.

I moved on to make the rounds of the room, speaking with everyone that I knew, and introducing myself to those I didn't. I made a point to mention my design firm as often as I could. But many hugs, kisses, and don't-you-lookwonderfuls later, I realized Dr. Steinman was still on my heels.

"Mrs. Huntington, please." He handed me a flute of champagne. "Cheers." He raised his glass and clinked the edge of mine. "How is the remodeling on Martin's house coming?"

"It's not." I met his gaze with an icy smile. "The police shut down the job site long enough for us to lose our crew."

"What could be taking so long? Are they still processing the crime scene?"

"I wouldn't know."

I certainly wouldn't have told him anything I did know. I'd only been back in this interior design business a short time, but I knew that discretion was a very important part of the job. Especially with my clients. Not answering this pestering guy was good practice.

"Didn't I hear that his niece is working for you? Is that until the estate is settled?"

"You really ought to speak to Susan."

But no amount of reticence on my part discouraged his persistence. Finally, I said, "I really must go. No, no. I do not need an escort down the hill."

I rushed to the tram to make good my escape.

I stole a quick glance back to see if I had finally lost him. He was speaking to a woman I recognized as one of the directors in charge of acquisitions.

At the transition from the 405 freeway to the 101, I noticed that the car that had exited the parking structure when I did was also exiting to the 101. Was this the kind of

thing the detective meant? It made me a little uncomfortable when the same car exited on Vermont Avenue and
then turned onto Los Feliz Blvd. when I did. On the other
hand, plenty of patrons of the fundraiser probably lived in
Los Feliz. I turned up the hill and pulled into the garage.
The car continued past our driveway.

I was surprised to see Jeff's car in the drive when I got
back to the house. I came home early. I thought for sure
they would still be out. I let myself in the back entrance,
thinking I would avoid disturbing them. From the atrium
patio, I could hear Emma's giggle above the splash of the
fountain. It was nice to hear her sound happy. Looking
forward to my bed and book, I crept up the stairs.

I tiptoed through my dressing room, used the bathroom
as silently as humanly possible, and slipped into my bed. It
was then that I realized that my bedroom window overlooking the central courtyard was open.

"I could fix that for you, babe."

"Fix what?"

"That itch."

"I don't have an itch." Giggle.

"I can fix that, too."

Shit, I could hear every word, every moan. I escaped
back to the dressing room and slept on the chaise lounge.

At least somebody in this family was getting laid.

Chapter 26

I awoke to another one of those beautiful winter mornings unique to the irrigated desert that is LA. The low winter sun's soft heat warms pavement chilled by cool nights and creates deep shadows to contrast with the gentle light. I love to soak up this softer-than-summer sunshine by enjoying my Sunday morning coffee on the brick and tile patio.

I was dangling my feet in the cool water at the edge of the pool with Lulu's head on my lap, when I was struck with a sudden desire to create a Sunday brunch for Emma and Jeff. I stepped into the kitchen and mixed up a batch of scones, sliced up melon and prepped the ingredients for omelets. I squeezed fresh oranges while the coffeemaker did its thing. I set the table on the patio with blue willow china and fresh red geraniums snagged from the garden. As soon as I heard Emma's voice on the upstairs landing, I stuck the scones in the oven and poured omelet batter into the pan.

"Good morning, sweetheart," I greeted Emma as she poured herself a cup of coffee.

"Good morning, Mom. Did you have a good time last night? I didn't hear you come in."

"It was fine. Not quite as boring as I was afraid it might be. Where's Jeff?"

"He'll be right down." Emma caught a glimpse of the table in the patio. "Oh, how nice. Thanks, Mom."

Emma and Jeff carried the juice, melons and coffee to the table. I finished up the omelets and brought them and the scones to the table. Other than gratifying murmurs of enjoyment and appreciation, we ate in silence for several minutes. Finally, morning appetites satiated, we enjoyed the soft warmth of the sun on our skin, sunning ourselves like lizards.

Emma launched into a description of the dinner party they had left early last night.

I wasn't anxious to discuss any aspect of the night before that might embarrass them, so I quickly diverted the subject. "I've gotten the impression from Addie Mae that you think I am being negligent by not making more of an effort to find your dad."

"Mom, I don't want to ruin a beautiful day with that subject."

"Well, it occurs to me that we need to have this conversation eventually. Unless you would rather we didn't have it with Jeff here?" I looked at my daughter. I was convinced that her reluctance to commit to Jeff was related to her father's disappearance. Was she worried that she, or maybe Jeff, was incapable of fulfilling a commitment because her father had set a bad example?

"No, it's not that."

Emma stood up and began to clear the table. She carried a load of dishes into the kitchen.

"Ooh, I've ruined the moment."

Jeff spoke, "No, Cissy, we should have this conversation. I don't think I will ever get Emma to agree to marry me if we don't clear the air on this subject. She has issues with commitment that I'm sure have everything to do with her father's sudden disappearance and what she sees as abandonment of his family. I think she thinks that if her father could do that, I could do it too. But she refuses to discuss it."

"Emma, leave the dishes and come back out here," I ordered.

"In a minute, Mom."

"No. Now, sweetheart."

Emma came back to the table and took her seat.

"Now look, your father and I were together for 28 years. No matter how it ends, I will never regret the fact of starting it. I don't regret the years we spent together. And I am endlessly grateful for the gift of you and your brother. My regrets are more about what I did—and didn't do; the times I traveled with your father and missed out on parts of your childhood. If I had had any idea how quickly the time we had with the two of you as children was going to pass, I would have been much more careful to savor every minute of it. But that wasn't your father's fault."

Emma's big blue eyes filled with tears.

"Once I recovered from the sting of what I imagined to

be his rejection of me by leaving us, I realized that it was himself, not us that he ran away from. He couldn't face the mess he had made of his finances, and the effect that was going to have on our lives. Don't you see? It wasn't that he doesn't love us; it's because he loves us so much that he couldn't deal with it? I have to believe that he's okay, and someday he'll work up the courage to face us."

By now Emma and I both had rivers of tears streaming down our cheeks. Even Jeff's eyes were teary.

"In the meantime, we need to prove to ourselves, and to him, that we will be okay. That we can take care of ourselves. And that the money was not what made us successful as a family. When he does come back, I want him to see that we're flourishing without having to have enormous amounts of money."

Emma leaned over and wrapped her arms around my neck. "Mama, I love you so much!"

I wrapped my arms around her and squeezed. "I love you too."

We both turned toward Jeff at the sound of his sniffles. "Get over here!" Group hug.

Lulu barked at us as though she resented being excluded.

Chapter 27

Steve left his theater seat to get diet sodas for the three of us.

As he walked away, Sally turned towards me in the chair next to her. "Cissy, I'm sorry about Steve's rudeness the other day. He really does think he needs to take care of me. I've told him he doesn't need to protect me from you, but it's a habit with him. We've talked about it, and he is going to do better."

"I appreciate that, Sally. And I'll do my best to get along with him. But I'm concerned that if he continues to be negative about me, or our work, it's going to make our relationship difficult. Please promise me that you'll tell me about any problem that comes up so that we can work it out before it blows up our relationship."

What choice did I have? I had already made a huge dent in the money Sally gave me, so returning it was not an option. Of course, I would have preferred Steve apologize for himself, but I knew he was much too arrogant for that to happen.

We were ensconced in plush jade green mohair high

backed seats in a tiny theater just off Wilshire for a private showing of Sally's about-to-be-released film. Sally's Veronica Etro embroidered sweater jacket, worn over a layered, bright floral silk chiffon dress, looked as though it had been dyed to match both the seats and her eyes.

The theater was full of Sally's family, friends, lawyers, accountants, business manager, agent, stylist . . . forty-five of her nearest and dearest. Her peeps.

Nikki and her husband, Jack Trevor, were in the seats directly in front of us. My missing husband and Jack had done some business together—developing a fly-in community—years before.

"Jack, you're too fucking tall. Switch seats with Nikki, so you're in front of Steve," Sally ordered.

As he stood to move, Jack turned to me. "What do you hear from Jamie?" he asked.

I shook my head no.

Jack reached for my hand with both of his and looked me in the eye with those famously beautiful green eyes, "I'm sorry, Cissy."

I nodded. I hate sympathy. I hate to cry in public.

Sally was unusually quiet and subdued. I noticed her make a concerted effort to be "up" as she greeted each of the attendees, but as soon as they walked away, she would return to a totally-out-of-character quiet persona. At the time, I thought maybe she was worried about the rough cut.

The film was good: entertaining, exciting, and Sally looked fabulously sexy even in the shower scene. I wondered if that was her or a body double. Not the kind of thing you ask, I decided. Instead, I offered a compliment, "My God, you look hot."

She barely smiled. What the hell was the matter with her?

The surprise to me was that Steve had a speaking part, albeit minor. He came off as stiff and uncomfortable. It was a stretch, but since he was playing a military policeman, maybe he played it as directed. Maybe it was what he needed to get a SAG card.

Before the lights came up and the applause ended, Sally wanted to leave. "Cissy, will you take me home? I think Steve wants to stay here and bask in the glory."

But before we could leave she had to accept the congratulations of all the people in the room.

"Sally! Oh my God, you looked abso-o-fucking-fabulous!" Her agent engulfed her in his arms and showered her with kisses that didn't quite connect. Mustn't mess the make up.

"Thank you," said Sally.

Was I the only one who noticed how unusually restrained she was?

"Sally!" A hunk of a guy grabbed her from behind, wrapping his arms around her waist and kissing her neck. "This will be a chartbuster."

"Thank you," Sally smiled.

"Sally, darling Sally, OMG, you were hot, hot, hot!"

"Sally, you are one talented woman!"

"Sally, I see Oscar nods in the future."

"Sally, I love you, I adore you!"

"Sally, un-fucking-believable!"

After a few minutes of this adulation, Sally turned to me and whispered, "Let's get the hell out of here." We made a dash for the back door while Steve stepped up to receive the congratulations.

She was strangely quiet all the way back to her house with only an occasional comment and the weakest of efforts to make conversation.

I finally couldn't take it anymore. We had already crossed what I considered to be the line between professional and friend. Besides, I knew Sally never saw such a line.

"Okay, out with it. What's going on? What's up with you?"

Sally stared out the window for the longest time without saying a word. I waited. Then, "Let's go in the house. I need a drink."

Since every member of Sally's household was at the showing, the house was quiet. Even the dogs were quieter than usual. We went into the kitchen, and I helped Sally find the ingredients for martinis. We sat down at the scrubbed pine table in the center of the room. We had only said what was necessary to get the drinks made.

"You're scaring me. What's the matter?"

"I found a gun in the house." She stared at a spot a foot above my head. "I don't know what to do about it. Do you have any idea what kind of gun they think killed the doctor?"

I took a deep breath. Shit.

"No, I don't remember if they ever said. It wouldn't mean anything to me if they had, since I don't know the first thing about guns."

"I don't either. But I have such an awful feeling about this gun. I just have no fucking idea where it came from. Or what the fuck I should do with it." Now Sally's jade eyes, huge with fear, looked into mine.

Gently I said, "I think you should give it to the police."

"Oh fuck, fuck, fuck! I can't do that! The publicity would kill my career."

"How could that be? Isn't any kind of media coverage supposed to be good exposure?"

"Yes. But no. It really depends. On one's circumstances. Mine suck. I mean, the studio is about fed up with all the negative publicity I've gotten in the last couple years. They, the all-fucking-mighty they—per my agent—say I'm getting a reputation for being difficult. Oh, I'm fucked!" Sally lay her head down on the table and mumbled. "First, I made horrible scenes all over town, in every hot spot, when that dumbfuck ex of mine was running after every piece of ass he laid eyes on."

Sally pounded her fist on the pine table top.

"Then I gained about a gazillion fucking pounds and couldn't seem to lose it. Then all those terrible photos of me looking enormous and not even faintly glamorous made the cover of every scandal mag in the grocery store. They even delayed the release of this film 'cause they didn't want me showing up at the premiere, or doing any of the promo, looking like an elephant cow rather than the super sexy glamour puss I played in the movie."

She banged her head on the table.

"Sally, Sally. Let's figure this out together. Please, don't hurt yourself." I grabbed her head between my hands and forced her to look me in the eye. "Where exactly did you find the gun?"

"In the back of the fur vault, shoved under an ermine throw."

"Where is it now?"

"I put it back in the same place."

"Let's go get it. I'll turn it over to Detective Rodriquez. Let's see if it even is the gun that killed the doctor before we get too concerned about this. He doesn't have to know where it came from."

Chapter 28

When I left Sally's for the short drive home, I noticed the Bluetooth was flashing. I checked my phone and saw I'd missed messages. I'd turned off my phone for the film showing and forgot to turn it back on.

"Mom, I'm headed over to Susan's. She's hearing things again."

Shit, I wish she would call the police, not Emma.

The next message was from Susan's phone. "Cissy, Emma and I are goin' over to see who's in the main house. We can see lights flickerin' in the attic."

I hoped they thought to inform the police who were pretending to be security, or at least, they had been. Had they left?

Damn! Returning the calls got me both girls' voice-mails. I tried sending a text message to Emma, but got no response.

I dug Detective Rodriquez's card with his cell number out of my bag, but I got his voicemail.

"You said to call if anything suspicious happened. Emma and Susan left me an alarming voicemail an hour ago. They said they were going over to the main house at the doctor's estate to check out noises, but now neither of them're answering their phones. I'm headed over there."

I called 911 and got in line on hold. Damn!

Meanwhile I raced over to the estate, wishing I'd gone easier on the martinis I'd shared with Sally. I was almost to Martin's when the operator took my information.

There was no one in the guard booth. The gate stood open. No lights were visible anywhere, including the low voltage ones that usually lined the drive.

I slowed down, turned off the headlights and crawled toward the main house. No lights flickered in the attic. I lowered the windows. Driving slowly on electric power, the only sound the car made was the soft whoosh of the tires. All I heard was the far-off noises of the city below. Nothing else. Not the girl's voices. Not security guards.

I stopped the car at the side of the main house and turned off the interior lights before I opened the door. I felt around in the console for the flashlight.

I remembered I had a gun in my purse.

I rummaged for the gun, pinching it between two fingers. When I got a good hold of the butt, I removed the plastic bag, and unwrapped the handkerchief Sally had put around it.

I took the light in my left hand, the gun in my right, and elbowed my way out of the car. I nudged the door closed and crept toward the house.

In the deep dark I clanged into a van parked outside the front entrance.

I froze and listened for a long minute for a reaction to the noise.

Nothing.

I tip-toed to the servants' quarters, eased the exterior door open, hesitated when it creaked, and snuck up the stairs to the master dressing room.

Still no sounds.

I stood at the bottom of the attic stairs and listened, but all I could hear was my heart pounding. Where the hell were they?

I heard a loud thud on the floor above, and almost simultaneously my phone beeped.

I had a text message from Emma.

Bad guys attic knife 911.

Oh my God! Were the girls in the attic?

I had called the police, but there were no sirens. What was taking them so damn long to get here?

I climbed the attic stairs, clinging to the inside wall, hoping to stay invisible in the stairwell as long as possible.

Deep, male voices growled above me:

"Mo fo, don't drop the fucking things!"

"Shut the fuck up, asshole! Some of these fuckers're heavy."

"Try carryin' one at a time, dumbfuck."

"Try handin' me one at a time, you dumbfuck."

I heard footsteps in the billiard room. I eased back down to the stairs. The footsteps stopped, and I imagined they were piling paintings on the billiard table.

"Table's fuckin full. Get out here and help me carry

these to the van."

I eased open a cupboard door, slid inside, and pulled the door closed.

Two sets of heavy footsteps came down the staircase. Once they had passed by the cupboard, I counted to fifty, all the while listening for sounds above and on the stairs.

Slowly I pushed the door open, gingerly stepped out and made my way up to the attic.

Light from the attic safe spilled into the linen closet. Two bodies lay on the floor shoved partially under the shelves.

I freaked, ran across the room without thinking of noise, and knelt next to trussed up Emma, and unconscious Susan.

"Oh, my God, Emma! Oh, my sweet!" I touched her neck. Her eyes flickered open.

"Mom," she whispered, "There're two guys, moving the paintings! Get outta here! Get help!"

"I'm not leaving you."

"Mom, they're big, mean. You can't . . . Get help."

"I've got this." I pulled the flashlight out of my pocket. Emma raised her eyebrows. "Mom. Go!"

I shook my head and fumbled out the gun.

"Where? . . . Mom, point it away! Here give it to me."

"You're tied up."

"You don't know how to use it!"

"And you do?"

With shaking hands, I got a good grip on the pistol. "I can point it."

191

"What are we going to do? They'll be back for another load soon. Hide."

"I'll hide 'til the police get here. Unless they threaten you. Let me untie you."

"There's no time. And they'll notice. I'll keep on pretending they knocked me out."

The sound of voices and footsteps from the stairs ended our debate.

I dove under a pile of linens and tried to hold still. My heart pounded so loudly I was sure it was audible.

"What're we gonna do with those two?"

"Leave'em."

"Ah, fuck, I wanted to have a little fun."

"Keep your mind on the fuckin' job. Buy a ho with the bucks we're makin'."

"Blonde's hot. When would you get another chance to even touch one like that?"

I felt the gun in my hand.

No way that creep was going to touch my daughter. If one of them was about to climb into the vault, I should act now and hold them at gunpoint until the cops arrived.

How hard could it be to shoot a gun?

Wouldn't a gun top a knife?

"Stop thinkin' with your prick."

"Just a little feel."

I heard footsteps move toward Emma. I exploded out of the linen pile, hitting my head on the shelf, but I pointed the gun and yelled, "Hold it right there!"

Trouble was, I was too close and couldn't keep both

men covered at once. I scrambled to back out the door where I was less accessible to them, and where I had what I hoped was a clear shot at either of them.

The one closest to me lunged for the gun.

I twisted it upwards. I barely touched the trigger when it went off, and there was hole in the ceiling.

Bloody hell! That was loud! And the kick nearly had me on my ass.

At least they knew I would shoot. "Hands up. Don't move. Or I'll put the next one right where you'll never care to touch anyone again."

The two ruffians raised their hands above their scruffy heads.

Emma sat up. Her hands were tied behind her back. She nodded towards the bigger man. "He's got a knife." She stared at the scabbard on his belt.

"I see it." I trained my gun on the knife. If he went for it, I doubted I could stop him. I couldn't shoot at his hand without endangering Emma and Susan.

Emma tried to stand.

"Everyone stay where you are. That means you too, Emma. Don't get near them."

Visions of bad guys with hostages in front of them, knives at the hostages' throats played in my head.

My gun hand shook violently. Could I really shoot them?

The sound of sirens growing louder filled me with relief, until I realized this was the moment the bad guys might make a break for it, and I had no idea what to do about it. If I pulled the trigger again, they might take advantage of the moment to jump me.

Or I might fall on my ass this time.

I could see the big guy ready himself for another pounce. I braced my back against the doorframe and shot out the top of the window. That way the cops knew where we were.

I listened to the pounding of heavy footsteps that took forever to find the attic, and finally a SWAT team burst into the attic. Once I was sure that all ten guns had everyone covered, I dropped mine into the linen pile.

Later I realized that dropping loaded guns wasn't smart.

*   *   *

"What the hell do you mean, I don't need to know where it came from?" Detective Rodriquez, his dark brown eyes black with anger, wasn't quite as understanding as I had hoped he would be.

"Please, please, just tell me. Is it the kind of gun that killed Dr. Martin?"

Rodriquez examined the gun that was now encased in a plastic bag. "Yes."

"Please have it tested. If it is definitely the gun, I'll tell you where it came from."

"Mrs. Huntington, you fail to grasp the seriousness of this investigation. I could just as easily have you arrested for obstruction." He scowled, shook his head. "And for tampering with evidence. Fingerprints. Firing the gun."

"Oh, come on. You owe me. You pulled the security off and endangered Emma and Susan."

"I didn't pull 'em off. The plan was to stop having anyone in the security shack, make it look like there was no one on guard, and see if anyone came after the paintings."

"What the hell?"

"A little miscommunication. The guy left the booth a little prematurely."

"I'll say." I sounded calm, but the numbness was wearing off.

"It was only a couple of hours."

"A couple hours that could've gotten my daughter and Susan killed."

"Look, we had the guys ready to sneak onto the property when we got word that you had called 911, so I had to organize a SWAT team. Everyone's okay, right? What're you freaking out about?"

"What am I freaking out about? Are you fucking kidding? I could've killed someone. I've never even touched a gun before. What if I had missed and hit one of the girls?" My teeth chattered. My body shuddered. Screaming let off the tension.

"Are you through?" the detective asked.

I nodded.

"Did you find a gun in your house after all?"

"No."

"So where did it come from?"

"I promised I wouldn't tell you, or anyone, unless it

was the gun that killed the doctor. Wait—oh shit! Did I screw that up?"

"Huh?"

"Since I fired it. Can you still tell if it was the murder weapon?"

"Yeah."

"It was wrapped in a handkerchief before. When you tell me . . . then, I'll get permission to tell you." I sank onto the porch step. "I guess I wiped out any hope of getting fingerprints off it?"

"Yeah."

He leaned against the edge of balustrade. "We arrested the two men. Give me the handkerchief. One of my team will drive you home. Get some rest. We'll talk in the morning."

"Susan?"

"EMT's said she'll be fine, but they are taking her for observation overnight. Concussion protocol. Emma seems fine?"

"She says she is."

Chapter 29

Rest was not easy. The adrenalin was still coursing through my body. I'd sit exhausted, then think about what had happened—and what might have happened—and jump up to pace some more. It was a hell of a night.

The antique clock struck 4:00 in the morning.

I went down to the kitchen for warm milk and found Emma doing the same thing. She gave me a weak smile and took the milk from the microwave, shook cinnamon into it, and handed the mug to me. The warmth felt calming in my hands and down my throat. We sat at the table and went back over the events of the previous evening.

"That was the worst moment of my life! Seeing you lying on the floor of the closet." I took my daughter in my arms and held tight until we both felt the effect of the tryptophan. "Let's both sleep in my room. I want to hear you breathing."

*   *   *

"What the heck's goin' on here?" Addie Mae banged open the door to my bedroom. "There's a police detective downstairs. He's got to talk to you."

I struggled to open my eyes. The clock on the bedside table said eleven. Bright light peeked through the edges of the velvet curtains.

Addie pulled the traverse cord of the pair parallel to the bed. The room was flooded with light evoking a loud moan from Emma. "No-o-o, o-o-h, please, no."

"Coffee, please. I need caffeine." I swung my feet onto the floor and found my quilted robe on the end of the bed.

"Gots plenty of coffee in the kitchen. You get your little fanny down there. What're you two doing? Sleeping late."

"Addie, please."

I stumbled into the bathroom, splashed cold water on my face, and ran my fingers through my hair. I could smell the coffee aroma wafting up the stairs. I followed the scent to the kitchen, poured a mug, and drifted into the living room.

"Did Addie get coffee for you?" I asked Detective Rodriquez.

He held up a cup to evidence Addie's politeness. "You have to tell me where you got the gun."

"Did you test it already?" I sipped the warm liquid.

"This is not optional." He glared at me.

I drank more of my coffee.

"Look, Mr. Karloff is understandably anxious to move the paintings to a safe location and turn them over to the appropriate authorities."

"Do you have any idea who the two men are? Or what

their connection is?"

"Not yet." The detective looked away from me toward Addie Mae who had slipped into the room and waited her chance to speak without interrupting.

"Please excuse me, but Cissy, Carl, the floor guy is on the phone and he insists he has to talk to you right away."

"Excuse me, Detective." Addie handed me the phone.

"Hi Carl. What's up?"

"Mrs. Huntington, you had better get over here!"

"Carl, what's the matter?"

"I just . . . Please come over."

"I have Detective Rodriquez here with me. Shall I bring him?"

"Probably not a bad idea."

Chapter 30

Detective Rodriquez gave me a few minutes to throw on clothes. He seemed reluctant to let me out of his sight, but we took separate cars over to the estate. When we arrived, a Brinkley's truck sat in the driveway in front of the main house. Men in white uniforms with white gloves and white hats were carrying canvasses and crates, loading them into the truck. One man with a clipboard checked items off a list as each painting was loaded.

I caught a glimpse of Beyla Karloff in the vestibule.

After we parked, I asked Detective Rodriquez if he had found out when Susan arrived in LA.

"You were right about her not being on that flight. In fact, I'll trade the flight data for the where you got the gun." He almost broke a smile.

When we arrived at the pool house, Carl and two of his men waited on the pool deck. Carl led us inside without explanation. He pointed to a hole in the floor of the dressing room. "My guys found this floor safe under a layer of flooring. They accidentally opened it."

"Accidentally" was quite a stretch. They must have used crowbars and a hell of a lot of muscle.

"Did they remove anything?" the detective asked.

"They said they didn't."

I took my phone out of my purse, punched in some numbers, and said to Detective Rodriquez, "I think Beyla Karloff is over at the main house supervising the removal of the paintings."

When Karloff answered his cell, I said, "Hi. We—Detective Rodriquez, Carl, and I—are over at the pool house. Would you please come over here? Carl and his guys have found something you might be interested in."

While we waited for Karloff, Carl and his guys decided to call it a day and left. Rodriquez and I stared at the floor safe and the papers sticking out. Rodriquez had obviously decided, as I had, that it would be best to have Karloff remove and look at the papers.

"Hello. How are you?" Karloff shook hands with both the detective and me. "What did they find?"

We walked him into the dressing room and pointed at the floor safe with its lid sitting to one side. He picked up the papers and perused them quickly.

"This is interesting. I didn't draw up this exact agreement, but I recognize a partnership agreement that Dr. Martin had me draw up between Dr. Steinman, a Mr. Heidelman and himself for an import company that they were all going to invest in. I thought they had dropped the idea." Karloff read further. "It looks like the doctors used the document I wrote as a basis for this agreement. I don't know what they hoped to accomplish with this. Obviously, they wouldn't be pursuing a breach of this agreement in court."

I was beside myself with curiosity. "What do you mean?"

Karloff looked through the papers again before answering. "This appears to be an agreement regarding the paintings. It seems that a Mr. Heidelman provided the paintings, Dr. Steinman and Dr. Martin were to locate buyers for them, and the two doctors were to make hefty monthly payments to him."

"Wow, Dr. Steinman!" No wonder he's been curious as to what's going on over here And Susan *has* been hearing prowlers, hasn't she? Oh God, I feel bad about the number of times I ignored her concerns and—"

Karloff interrupted me. "Detective, thank you for letting me know about the arrests made last night. I'll be much more comfortable when we get these paintings into a proper vault, and even more comfortable when we work out a final disposition of them. I was relieved to get the word that they could be removed from the premises."

Karloff was looking at me as he spoke to Rodriquez. "Because we have wanted to keep knowledge of their presence here limited to as few people as possible, namely us and any of the conspirators, I had not yet begun inquiries. This morning I activated the removal and the investigation. These papers will be helpful."

"They'll be helpful to our investigation as well. I'll need the originals as soon as you've had them copied, Karloff."

Detective Rodriquez was writing in a small spiral notebook. "Heidelman. Steinman. We'll speak with Steinman again. Either of you know this Heidelman?"

Karloff flipped through the pages of the agreement. "I don't see much about him in these papers. His full name is Ernest Heidelman. That's about it. I'll have copies made of this and the originals messengered over to you as soon as I return to the office."

Detective Rodriquez looked at me.

"Never heard of him," I said to Rodriquez.

Then I spoke to Karloff. "Susan and I have been planning to come over and talk with you. What with one thing and another, we've never managed to do it, but she doesn't know what to do about the house and neither do I."

"Where is she now?"

"I'm pretty sure she's in the guest house. She left a voicemail saying she'd left the hospital."

"Let's go speak with her. I need to fill her in on the latest developments, and we can discuss our alternatives with the house, as well." Karloff stood up from where he had been crouched over the now empty floor safe.

I smiled and waved to the detective as we left the pool house.

Detective Rodriquez did not return the wave or the smile. "I'll be in touch, Mrs. Huntington."

It was interesting listening to Karloff's explanation to Susan as to what had transpired in the last twenty-four hours regarding the paintings, the arrests, and the agreement. There was only one thing I hadn't heard or known before. The two men arrested had known the location of the "secret" panels in the library and had searched those prior to going into the attic.

If someone had been watching the house from one of the hills above, they would have seen lights in the attic rooms on several different occasions, thus making it obvious some activity—presumably not billiards—had been occurring there. Then again, maybe they already knew where the paintings were hidden. Remembering David Steinman's "casual" peek into the attic closet convinced me he had known all along where the paintings were.

"What are we going to do with the house?" I couldn't work up the energy to deal with the damage that had been done. Or work up the interest in doing anything further with the house, especially since it seemed as though we could be at it forever. And how were we going to pay for it?

"I've seen the damage." Karloff sat on a bar stool at the red jasper counter that divided the living room from the kitchen. "It looks overwhelming to me, but it's definitely not my area of expertise. Mrs. Huntington, what do you think?"

"Please call me, Cissy." I dragged myself onto a stool. "I don't know. It's discouraging to look at. Before the damage, I thought it was best to finish the partially done projects, and then sell it as-is. But now it seems like buyers will see it as a teardown. I hate to see that done to such a lovely old house. Shall I get bids on what it would take to fix it?"

"That would seem the best way to proceed. Susan, do

you have any thoughts on the matter?"

"What's happenin' with the overall picture of the estate?" Susan was in the kitchen making coffee.

"This morning's revelation certainly sheds light on what was draining off his rather large income. He was paying nearly a half million a month to this Mr. Heidelman, or so the agreement states."

Susan whistled.

Beyla continued, "I've been talking to a number of doctors about his practice. Now, it seems to me that it was more lucrative than his records were showing. I don't know who was juggling the books, but that half million had to come from somewhere. I'll look at those records again with this new information in mind." He sipped the coffee Susan had handed him. "If I can realize enough money from his practice, we could use it to fix the damage to the house and complete the construction. We'll auction the furnishings from the office and from the house. I've spoken with Sotheby's. Cissy, could you tag the pieces that should bring enough to be worth sending them to auction?"

"What happened when the art experts went to the office?" I ignored his question hoping not to commit to still another task for which there was no agreed upon payment. Sorting through the furniture that had been piled up in the storage building would not be easy.

"You and Susan found the only piece that was worth anything. That wonderful Vermeer. No doubt it had been part of the trove in the attic."

"Is it smart to spend the money to fix the house?

Would it be better to sell it as-is?" I asked. Even though I had lost my enthusiasm for this undertaking, I hated to see the house destroyed.

"Get the bids, then we'll look at it."

"Mr. Karloff, I'm concerned about having Cissy doing all this work." Susan came to my rescue. "How am I going to pay her? I'm actually working for her now in order to have grocery and gas money. We can't keep asking her to do this stuff when we don't know how we'll pay her."

Karloff looked embarrassed to be chastised by his client. "I'm sorry. I'll try to come up with a workable solution as quickly as possible. If you will just get the bids, we'll have the estate pay you a fee from all proceeds, a percentage that will make it worth your while to sort through the furniture. How soon can you get the bids?"

"Will we have free access to the house now that the paintings are leaving?" I asked.

"I don't see any reason why not." Karloff rubbed his head. "But I'll speak with Detective Rodriquez and let you know what he says."

I turned to Susan, "I owe you an apology. You were hearing prowlers. And I completely ignored your fears, but I think it'll be okay now. Mr. Karloff, what do you think?"

Karloff nodded his agreement.

"Thanks. Well, it's nice to know I haven't been hallucinatin'." Susan glanced at Karloff and then looked at me. "We have lots to talk about when we get this project movin' again."

Chapter 31

Susan and I headed for the office, so I could put her to work getting contractors lined up to bid the work. While we drove, we worked out that she would do as much of the work as possible, with me giving her direction. I suggested she have the Sotheby's staff do the tagging of what they wanted to auction. She had a lot of phone calls to make by the end of business hours.

We arrived back at the house to find Emma with Sally and Nikki lounging on the chaises and drinking iced raspberry tea in the atrium. Sally and Nikki each had a toy terror dog on their spandex clad laps.

"Hi, Mom. Look who I found while I was walking Lulu."

Susan glanced into the atrium and was beside herself with excitement. She ran directly into the office and began puttering with papers on her desk.

I continued through the hall out to the atrium. "Nikki, Sally, welcome! Good to see you here." We exchanged hugs and kisses.

"Emma tells us that the Homicide Detective on

Martin's case was here this morning." Sally gave me a pointed look.

I nodded back.

"She also told us she was attracted to him," Nikki said.

Emma jumped up in protest. "What I actually said was, *if* I was still into dark Latin types, he'd be killer."

"The proverbial 'tall dark and handsome' type?" Nikki asked.

"That's him," Emma confirmed.

"I could go for that, although at the moment, I'd rather not meet him," Sally said.

Nikki and Emma gave her surprised looks. Sally was not known for turning down "tall, dark and handsome."

"Susan, come in here and meet these two," I ordered.

No answer. "Excuse me ladies, I'll be right back."

I walked over to the office, "Susan, come here."

"Really?" Susan whispered.

"Of course. Come on," I coaxed.

She stood stock-still. I took her arm and led her into the atrium. "Nikki, Sally, this is Susan. She's working with us. She's Doctor Martin's heir."

"Nice to meet you, darling," Nikki said.

"Yeah, good to meet you," Sally said.

I dragged the silent Susan over to a cushion on the hearth, pushed her down into a sitting position, and poured her an iced tea. She sat there, mouth agape, and didn't even lift her glass.

"I'm sorry about your uncle," Nikki said.

Susan nodded.

"Are you going to stay in California?" Sally asked.

Again, Susan merely nodded.

"Do you like working with these two?"

Nod.

"Where did you come from?" Sally asked.

Susan stared at Sally.

Emma jumped in, "She's from Kansas."

Nikki steered Sally's attention away from Susan. "When do we get to see what you're going to do with Sally's house?"

"Soon," I said.

"That's good, because I was just over there." Nikki pretended to gag.

"We have to go. I'm supposed to get ten miles in today." Sally pointed to the pedometer on her ankle and dragged herself off the chaise cushion. The two tiny dogs jumped to attention onto the floor.

Emma hugged Sally and Nikki. Then I did. We all turned to look at Susan who was still frozen in place, tea glass in hand.

Nikki walked over to her and gently shook her free hand. "Susan, it was nice to meet you. I'm glad you're here to help Emma and Cissy. Looking forward to seeing you again soon."

Sally followed Nikki's example. "Good-bye, Susan. These two need some help." She winked at Emma and me. "It's a good thing you're here."

Emma showed our guests and the two miniature pinchers to the door.

"You sure have an exciting life." Susan sighed. "Well, I need to get to work on the backlog of paperwork." She hesitated. "Almost forgot—I got so excited. Dr. Steinman called. First, he asked for you, but he asked me what's goin' on at the house. I didn't know what to tell him, but he just kept askin'. I didn't tell him anythin'. He said you have to call him."

I had no intention of calling him.

The after effects of last night's adrenaline rush left me exhausted, but we needed to get to work, too. I picked up the samples we would use to match to new samples at the design showrooms. We needed to collect accent fabrics for each of Sally's rooms to take over to her house to try with the rugs Aga John delivered.

"Emma, we need some mother daughter time. Shall we stop for a late lunch on our way to the Design Center?"

"I would love that, Mama."

"The Newsroom over on Robertson. Is that okay with you?"

"Yeah, good healthy food. I could use a few days of nothing but salads."

"Sweetheart, stop fussing about your weight. Ever since we moved to LA you've been obsessing about it, but you are not one teeny bit heavier than you were when we lived in San Francisco. You never worried about your weight then. You aren't even an ounce overweight. What's with that?"

"Mom, have you looked around here? Everyone is so skinny."

"But you aren't trying to become a movie star. Or is that something you want to tell me?"

Emma laughed. "I'm glad you suggested lunch. I do have something I want to talk over with you. But I'm going to wait until we've ordered."

We took Beverly Blvd. all the way from Western to Robertson, talking about Sally's house and various design elements as we drove. Emma steadfastly refused to talk about anything but business.

Once we had settled into our usual table and ordered salads, I said, "Ok Emma, what's up?"

"Jeff asked me to marry him."

"Wow! And you said?" I wondered if they served a decent Champagne at this trendy restaurant that was basically a health food cafe.

"I said I wanted to think about it."

"Do you love him?"

"Of course, I do, but that's not a reason to get married to someone."

"Whoa, I guess things have changed since I was your age."

"Come on, Mom. Dad wasn't the only guy you ever loved, but he was the only one you married."

"You're right. He was the only one who, when I imagined myself married to him, somehow fit. What's the problem with Jeff?"

"I don't know that there is a problem with Jeff. I think the problem is with me."

"Explain, please." I sipped my iced tea and waited for

her answer.

"I can easily imagine Jeff and I growing old together. He'll be such a cute old man, don't you think?"

"Sure. But?"

"He'll be a great father. You should see him with kids. He's not at all condescending."

"I'm glad to hear that. After all, my grandchildren should have the best of everything."

"He makes a good living as a producer, not like Dad, of course, but maybe more reliable. At least I think so. Between the two of us, we will definitely be able to support a family."

"You said the problem, is you?"

"I'm not sure what the problem is. I guess I was thinking of something more romantic. Some dark handsome prince who would sweep me off my feet. Do you think that's silly?"

"I don't think anyone has the answer to that question, darling. These are definitely the kinds of things you will have to decide for yourself. I'm happy to be a sounding board for you." I smiled at my beautiful daughter. "One thing you might want to keep in mind. You're still young. You don't need to rush into anything."

Our salads had arrived.

"But you were pregnant with me when you were my age." Emma said as she took a bite of rabbit food.

"I was a few years older. And as much as I'm looking forward to those beautiful grandchildren, there's still plenty of time for that."

"I guess you're right. Besides, I can't get married until Dad comes home."

I forced a smile, but my heart sank. What if he never came home?

Chapter 32

In the tired state I was in, I couldn't handle any more conversation about Emma's father. "I'm sorry to say we'd better get to work before the day is shot."

We finished our salads in some haste. I paid the bill while Emma collected the car from the valet.

We headed to the Pacific Design Center and began the process of pulling samples and tear sheets for Sally's house, always keeping in mind the theme, "Biggest Female Movie Star in the World."

We were interrupted twice by phone calls from Steve checking on our progress: first just as we arrived at the building, minutes later as we were sorting out who would look for what. Apparently, he felt we were taking too long to do our work.

"Steve, we'll work more efficiently if we are not constantly interrupted."

"Keep me informed as to your progress, then."

"Reporting to you is not, not, not part of our agreement." Was he harassing me in hopes that I would quit? Whatever his motive, he was really pissing me off. It was all I could do not to tell him to buzz off.

"He hung up on me," I said to Emma.

"Good, maybe he'll leave us alone."

"Let's go to Kravet next. I'll do Laura Ashley, you do Ralph Lauren. Lauren has some really nice cream-colored wools."

We were finally on a roll when my cell rang again.

"Oh pl-e-e-a-se, let this not be him again." I checked the number on the screen. "Thank God. It's the office."

Susan was so excited she could barely get the words out. "Nathan Carrington's office called. They want you to get on a plane today to go see him on location in England!"

"Today? Oh, boy!"

"What's the big fucking hurry?" Emma reacted when I explained to her what was up. "If we're flying in one of his planes, can't we just go when we're ready?"

"Sweetheart, we really aren't in a position to tell him to screw off. We have one broke and dead client, and one other one who is under the influence of a nut case. We need to diversify!"

I sighed at the thought of an overseas trip. "We'd better head for home. I'll call his office, get more details, and work out the financial arrangements." I stuffed fabric samples into a bag and started toward the parking structure.

Emma drove while I worked the phone; making arrangements with Nathan's office, canceling appointments, giving Susan lists of instructions, and trying to get a hold of Sally. I wanted to personally explain to her what I was up to, but every time and every number I called I got

Steve, who insisted that Sally was unavailable. I hated leaving a message with Steve, but what could I do? I sent her a text, but I knew she seldom looked at her phone. And maybe she didn't even know how to access a text.

As soon as we hit the house, Emma and I packed enough warm clothes for a week. I asked Susan to please take a note to Sally's house. I hoped Steve wouldn't intercept that.

We drove to the Avjet terminal next door to the Burbank airport, where a very pleasant man took our bags on board while another young man took charge of the car. "Mrs. Huntington, your car will be parked right over here in our garage."

Emma and I boarded the plane. I never have been too good with the names of these planes. My husband Jamie had a G4, but this one was slightly bigger and newer than that, so it must have been a G5. Regardless, it was all shades of tan and cream with good sized rotating leather chairs and highly polished wood fold out tables.

Once on board, we discovered that we were not the only passengers.

It seemed that the trip had originally been scheduled at the convenience of two passengers who were already ensconced in the bedroom at the rear of the plane. They, a man and a woman, poked their heads out to introduce themselves, but then returned to watching the large screen monitor in that room. I didn't recognize their names or their faces. I raised one eyebrow at Emma who indicated that she didn't know who they were either with a shrug of her shoulders.

A steward asked what we would like to eat and drink, apologizing for the limited selections. "We usually stock up on whatever our guests request, but someone failed to ask you what you would like."

Emma assured him that we were not hard to please. "I think it had more to do with the fact that we were added to the passenger list just a little while ago." Emma pointed to the screen of her phone. "In fact, look, here's a message on my cell asking what we would want. I missed it in the rush to get here."

Emma leaned over to whisper to the steward, "Who are they?" She nodded her head toward the bedroom.

"He was the producer of one of Mr. Carrington's first films. I believe they have a meeting scheduled with him," the steward whispered.

Before that exchange was completed we were in the air.

Even in such comfortable surroundings, it was a long trip. I know I sound spoiled beyond belief, but I couldn't help but be a bit nostalgic about the days when I would have had the bedroom and the hired help would have been riding in the front room. Nevertheless, the steward fed us and made us as comfortable as possible, converting the seats into beds. He handed us sleeping suits, and once we had settled into our beds, he layered fluffy cashmere blankets over the down comforters.

We had a short, restless sleep. The steward woke us with tea and coffee in hand. We sipped our tea and enjoyed the view of the morning light on the multi shades of green landscape below as the plane circled Gatwick. Whenever I arrive in England in the morning the landscape puts me in mind of an enormous feather bed sloppily covered by a green patchwork quilt.

Two cars met us: one for the bedroom passengers, one for Emma and me. Our car took us to Ashdown Park Hotel in the middle of Ashdown Forest.

Jamie and I had actually been to this same hotel once, in the late spring. Even for England, it had been exceptionally beautiful that season with enormous azaleas and rhododendrons in full bloom on the golf course that the dining room, the drawing rooms and the suites overlook. We had enjoyed a lovely week golfing, playing tennis, horseback riding and strolling the forest

Now, in midwinter, the gray stone building and the grounds had a melancholy beauty. Most of the trees and vines were bare, except for the giant cedar in the middle of the main lawn and a brace of similar evergreens that rimmed the border of the pond beyond the cedar.

Roaring fires in the enormous fireplaces in the lobby and the three drawing rooms were welcoming on the crisp morning, but we didn't linger. We were immediately shown to our rooms: a small suite on the 3rd floor. Leaded glass windows on two walls of the corner living room looked out on the croquet lawn. The lawn and the giant cedar were lightly dusted with snow.

A tray of tea appeared on the coffee table while we were using the bathrooms.

We had only started to enjoy the tea when there was a knock on the door. A uniformed driver, cap in hand, said, "Mrs. Huntington, I'm to drive you over to the set. Are you ready to go?"

As he was speaking, the phone rang. Emma answered it. "Yes, just a moment. Here she is." Emma handed me the phone, "Mom, it's Yvonne Carrington."

"Hello, I know you may be tired from traveling, but could you possibly come over to the set and talk to Nathan between takes?"

"Of course. Give us a few minutes to freshen up."

"Good, the driver should be there soon."

"Actually, he is here now"

"Oh."

"It's fine. See you soon."

The driver spoke as soon as I hung up the call. "I'll wait downstairs. I'll be in the covered drive, black town car, outside the lobby."

Emma and I took short showers, got into warm layers, and splashed some make up and lip gloss onto our faces. A quick brush through our hair and we were ready to go.

The set was a few miles away on the estate of a Georgian manor house. The grounds were covered with coaches and tents with huge bundles of cords running between them. A young woman armed with a clipboard and wearing a baseball cap through which she had threaded a blonde ponytail, met us at the drive.

"Yvonne will be right out to show you were to go. By the way, we call him Mr. Carrington."

Considering that he was ten years younger than I, I wasn't about to call him Mister, but I simply nodded.

Yvonne greeted us as though we had never met before. "Hello Mrs. Huntington, Emma. I'm Yvonne Carrington. Please come in."

She showed us into a very plush location coach—the kind that has sections pop out when the coach is parked. "He's on the set. He'll be back here shortly. May I get you coffee or tea?" She motioned to the clipboard girl who went running off to get the tea even though there was a complete kitchen a few feet away in the coach.

The coach was entirely furnished in cream-colored suede and ivory leathers with silver, pewter, and black accents.

As soon as we sat down on the deep, exquisitely soft sofa that filled one of the pop-outs, Yvonne handed each of us a several page legal document. "Please read and sign this for me."

The documents were the ubiquitous Non-Disclosure Agreement, the NDA. The title of the page was *Carrington Family Confidentiality Agreement*. Jeez, this one covered not only Nathan, but his entire family as well.

Emma looked at the papers and then looked to me for direction.

"I'm a little too jet lagged to read this with any guarantee I'll remember it all," I said.

"If you'll just sign it, I'll make copies and have them delivered to your suite," Yvonne said.

We both signed and then Yvonne signed as the

witness.

Nathan hopped into the caravan, filled with enormous energy. In our exhausted state it was hard to handle. Even though we had only the slightest acquaintance, having been introduced on no more than two occasions, he pounced on each of us, gathering us up in enthusiastic hugs. His behavior seemed to be as much of an act as what he had just been doing on the set. He was still "on". I later realized he was nearly always "on."

"Thanks for coming. Did anyone fill you in on what I'm up to?" His famous smile lit his equally famous blue-grey eyes.

When I replied no to that question his smile faded, and he looked at Yvonne with obvious annoyance. I guess she was supposed to have filled us in or seen to it that someone had. But really there had not been the opportunity.

"I bought an estate in LA that I want to get furnished. I'd like to be able to move into it as soon as we wrap this shoot." Nathan instructed. "I want all new furniture, top quality, and the best. You would have about four weeks, maybe five, to get it set up."

My hesitation must have shown. "It's possible to do in that time frame, although the selections will be limited to stock items or those few suppliers who do short lead times. That's not the appropriate schedule if one wants the very best quality, but it can be done."

Obviously, this was before I caught on to the fact that one was expected to enthusiastically agree to any request or idea that he had, no matter how impractical or ludicrous or unworkable.

Stone faced, he pulled Yvonne into the back room of the coach and slid the door closed. We, of course, could still hear the basic gist of what they were saying. He wasn't happy. "I thought you said they could do it. What the hell?"

"You want a classy job. They can do it."

"I fucking want it on fucking time."

"I'll make sure it happens."

"You better. I've 'bout had it with your excuses."

They re-entered the room.

"Look, Nathan, I didn't mean to give you the impression we couldn't do this, I just wanted to make sure you understood the possible difficulties and limitations. Are there photos of the estate? Then, we could have a better idea of what we would be getting into."

He sighed and raked the blonde hair back from his forehead. "Yeah, yeah, there is all that. I had wanted for you to see it before you left LA, but somebody fucked that up." He shot a killer look at his sister. "But there is a website. And a photo album. Yvonne will give you all that. I want you to work out the general direction of what you would do and then go back to LA and do it."

"We'll check out the photos and website. Will you have time available tonight?"

"Yeah, someone will give you a call when we head back to the hotel."

Yvonne rode back to the hotel with us. She brought a photo album full of digital shots to our rooms and gave Emma the web address. Emma set up her laptop in the living room of our suite and pulled up the site.

"Here you go, Mom. It's totally spectacular! Seven buildings in the Spanish Colonial style. On top of a hill in Bel Aire. Holy shit, look at the views!"

I sat down and took a virtual tour of the property. Spectacular was the correct word. And an overwhelming amount of work.

"Let's get some sleep before they get back here." I started toward my bedroom.

"Mom, you usually make us stay up until sunset so we don't get jet lagged and can get on the right time schedule."

"I have to have at least a nap. Or I'm liable to piss him off again."

"You aren't the only one who pisses him off. I'd say Yvonne pissed him off more. If Skip ever had the nerve to treat me like that . . . ."

"I'm sure that Yvonne understands that he's under a lot of pressure."

"Sally's a big star too, and she's nothing like him."

"First of all, we've never been around Sally when she's shooting. And even though she has a production company, she really just acts." I didn't want Emma to be pissed off at Nathan before we even started his project. "Not only does he star in these historical/supernatural/sci-fi movies, he also produces them. And from what I hear; he's very hands on, involved in every aspect. It's got to be exhausting. And frustrating."

In the end, we took a brisk, cold walk, a warm soak in the tub, and then a nap. The phone call, from an assistant to someone's assistant warning us that "he" was headed back to the hotel, was our wake-up call.

We dressed in black velvet and cashmere for dinner and made our way through the lounge that led to the dining room. The stars, the stars' entourages, the director, and some of the production crew had pretty much taken over the entire fifty-room hotel. Nathan, followed by Yvonne, his two daughters and their nanny, his other two sisters, and his personal assistant entered the room seconds after we did. He led us to a peach velvet sofa, around which were grouped several tapestry-covered chairs, and we all sat down. Diet cokes were served to Yvonne and the children, wine to the rest of us. No one was asked what he or she wanted to drink. The wait staff seemed to have the routine down.

"I wanted you to see this place. I like it. It's comfortable." All of a sudden, he jumped to his feet and so did everyone else. Emma and I looked at each other and stood up seconds behind them. Yvonne motioned to us to follow as he took quick, long strides down the hall, with his entourage scurrying after him.

He led us to the drawing room off the lobby. "I like this furniture. I like this arrangement." It was a beautiful, comfortable room with overstuffed lounge chairs upholstered in yellow velvet facing an oversized amber sofa, all flanking an enormous fireplace containing a roaring fire. Donald Sutherland and Keira Knightly stood before the fire, along with several others I didn't recognize. Each person had a drink in hand, and the group was enjoying a good laugh.

Before I could ask what in particular he liked about the room, he hurried off to the exercise facility which required going out into the cold snowy night, but not one hint of an objection was made by anyone. "I want exactly this same equipment, and I even like this set up. I don't like the colors. I like blue and green and purple." His tall, elegantly slender body offered only the slightest suggestion that he used such equipment.

"That should give you what you need to know. Let's have dinner."

I started to ask questions, but Yvonne motioned to me to be quiet.

We all rushed back to the dining room where he headed directly for a large round table that filled a window bay. The group settled into several of the sage green slipper chairs at the table with Emma and I hanging back to see which seats we should take. We had barely sat in the last two places, one of which was next to Nathan, when he jumped up to look out the window at the dancing snow-flakes as they floated past the floodlights.

"Look at this!" he enthused. Everyone jumped up. The window overlooked the same snowy scene as our suite. It was beautiful, but it looked equally good from our seats.

The service was slow, elaborate and deliberate with waiters pulling the covers off of our entrees in carefully orchestrated unison. The conversation was equally forced, as Nathan did most of the talking, but occasionally asked a question of his companions. No one spoke without being addressed or asked a question by Nathan.

To the nanny: "What did they study today?"

"English history. We read about Henry VIII."

"Have you scheduled the trip to the London tower?"

"Yes, for tomorrow."

"Good, good."

To his ten-year-old daughter: "What did you learn at Churchill's house yesterday?"

His daughter's answer was a prepared speech that sounded as though the nanny had scripted it. "That a person can accomplish anything one sets out to do as long as one persists."

I wished I was less jet-lagged, as I was aware that my responses were not well received. For one of the few times in my life, I felt socially uncomfortable, as though I didn't understand the culture and therefore the etiquette of this group. I wasn't sure if it was the jet lag, but there was a lack of reality about the entire set up—as though everyone was acting.

Nathan ate his salad, a few bites of the entrée, and then jumped up again.

This time he headed downstairs to the billiards room below the dining room. We all followed. Emma and I stood to one side while he and his daughters played billiards for a few minutes, then he signaled the nanny, who announced it was time for the children to go up to their rooms. He told Yvonne to get the director to come to talk. As we were now being ignored, Emma and I excused ourselves.

"It's a good thing we weren't actually hungry. How

weird was that?" Emma grumbled as we headed through the maze of hallways back to our rooms.

"Yeah. Remind me to eat before we have a meal with them again."

I called Yvonne as soon as we reached our suite. "We'd like to go into London tomorrow, to the Chelsea Harbor Design Center. In fact, I think we'll spend the night at the Chelsea Harbor Hotel so that we could have a couple days to pull together a few items to show Nathan. Before we head back to LA, I want to have some certainty that we understand what he wants."

"Hold on." I could hear her explaining to Nathan what I'd said. He didn't sound terribly interested.

"Okay," Yvonne said, "good idea."

"Shall we rent a car? Or do you have a driver for us?"

"If you don't mind waiting until late morning, you can use one of our cars and drivers . . . after he gets us to the set."

"Late morning sounds great."

It was nice to be driven into London. Chelsea Harbor being southwest of the Chelsea district, the traffic in the area isn't quite as scary as in the City itself. But the whole driving on the wrong side of the road thing can be a bit unnerving, especially when I am tired. One night's sleep, in a time zone that's eight hours off, doesn't do it for me.

The driver dropped us off at the hotel. January was deep off-season, so we had been able to book a room at the last minute the night before. They even gave us a good room on an upper floor facing the Thames. All of the rooms in the contemporary hotel were small suites with living rooms and one bedroom. Each suite was equipped with flat screen TVs, internet access, spacious marble bathrooms, acrylic desks and coffee tables, charcoal grey flannel upholstered pieces, and grey flannel curtains that covered floor to ceiling, wall to wall windows. The bedroom held a king-size bed with an upholstered, ceiling grazing headboard tufted in one-foot squares. We had them set up a bed for Emma in the living room so that if one of us had trouble sleeping, we wouldn't keep each other awake.

As soon as we had dropped our bags in our suite, we walked across the plaza to the convenient design center. It's a small center in comparison to the PDC, but there are plenty of other showrooms in the vicinity, most within walking distance, including the antique auction houses on Lots Road and the swishy high-end antiques boutiques on Kings Road.

The Chelsea Harbor Design Center itself consists of two connected clear glass round domes, each two stories tall. On the first floor—ground floor in UK—of each of the two domes, the shops open off a central atrium. Overlooking the atrium, a balcony runs the circumference of the second floor.

The first shop we hit was Colefax & Fowler. I wished we had more time. I would have preferred to shop at the original C&F location at 39 Brook Street. Sybil Colefax and John Fowler founded C&F, but it was American Nancy Lancaster who joined the firm after Sybil left and made Colefax & Fowler the most famous designers in England.

The original shop on Brook Street is a quaint English warren with rooms opening off a central quad containing an enormous Ficus tree. Most importantly, this shop is the location of Nancy Lancaster's famous yellow room, the room that provided the first public glimpse of a style Nancy had used to decorate her country houses where she entertained the aristocracy of Europe. Ironically, an American heiress upgrading the shabby, carelessly layered look of the homes of the English aristocracy developed the English country style. Before Nancy, English country homes were furnished with an insouciance available to those aristocrats who had no need to prove their status, and little concern as to whether Aunt Marjorie's chair that had been hauled out of the east wing guest suite to be used by the fire in the drawing room really 'went with' the rest of the furnishings in the room. Mrs. Lancaster managed to maintain the casual manner of those interiors. At the same time she raised the level of aesthetic harmony and comfort mixed with an American insistence that nothing be too terribly shabby. I loved to soak in the ambience of the yellow room periodically for inspiration, but alas, not this trip.

Not only was Nathan impatient, there was still Sally's project, the doctor's house, and the matter of a murder left unsettled. I wondered if Detective Rodriquez had tried to call. From London, avoiding answering his question about the gun was easy.

I had replaced my international cell with a national one as a cost cutting measure some months ago. Emma and I were using pay-as-you-go English phones. Susan had our local numbers. I wondered if she would pass them on to the detective.

We spent the day collecting photos of chairs, sofas, lamps, and other furnishings. We bagged fabric and leather samples in every shade of blue and purple and green we could find. We got small pieces of carpet. We made several trips back to the suite to dump off our bags of samples and then we would set out again.

Emma made a trip to the gastropub on the corner of Lots Road and Chelsea Harbor Drive to pick up sandwiches we could eat on the go. She phoned me in the Kravet showroom, and I joined her on a chilly bench overlooking the Thames.

She handed me my sandwich.

"Mom, you won't believe who I saw in that gastropub." Her wide grin gave away her excitement.

I raised an eyebrow at her without removing the sandwich from my mouth.

"Sienna Miller! OMG! She is so beautiful in person. And she had on the greatest boots. And her belt—so cool. I want to look just like her."

"You do look quite a lot like her."

"What, 'cause we're both blonde? I wish."

We finished our quick lunch and went back to work. We took digital shots of antiques and reproductions. We got wallpaper samples and brochures. We sampled all of the typical English fabrics and papers from Colefax & Fowler, Jane Churchill, and David Linley; upholstered seating from George Smith and Charles David; carpet from

Stark, lighting from Christopher Wray; and a little of everything from Christopher Norman.

Emma brought up the crux of our dilemma. "Mom, we don't know if he meant he liked the English style furniture, or the colors, or the furniture arrangement or what."

"Yes, I know. That's why we are doing this exercise. So, we can show him ideas and get a reaction. We better see if we can get some Spanish colonial things."

We spent the rest of the day searching for Spanish-looking items.

Once the shops closed, we retreated to our suite to put our feet up and order panini sandwiches from room service. Emma searched the Internet for more items to print off while I flipped through catalogues.

"Mom, I don't know if it's the jet lag, or just the hours we're working, but I can't stop thinking about Dr. Martin. His murder is creeping me out more now than ever."

"I know what you mean. I've been having night-mares."

"Me, too."

"As soon as we get this project moving, I'm going to help Detective Rodriquez. I'm starting to understand why people worry about 'closure'."

By noon of the second day we had so much stuff we didn't know if it would fit in the car along with our bags and us.

"How are we going to haul all this home?" Emma asked.

"We'll ship it, but first let's see if he likes it." I replied.

"Mom, do you remember the last time we were in London we tried to go to tea at the Ritz but we didn't have reservations and the wait was too long? We ended up at Liberty's tearoom instead. Which was charming, but not the Ritz. You promised we'd go to the Ritz the next time we were here."

I sighed. "Sweetheart, I never imagined that the next time we were here would be under these circumstances. And remember, they recommend making the reservations six weeks in advance, not six minutes."

"Mama, please. Let me just call and see if they have an opening."

"The maître d' did say they're not usually busy early in the afternoon mid week. That's when we've gotten in there without reservations before." I debated my conscience. "Oh fuck, Nathan Carrington. Call them."

"That's right, fuck Nathan Carrington!" Emma had already dialed the hotel.

While I fussed with straightening stacks of fabrics, Emma sweet-talked the maître d' into saving a table for us. "We'll be there in no more than a half hour."

I did a quick check of Emma's attire for the forbidden jeans or trainers as the Brits call sneakers. She passed.

Emma grabbed the fabric samples out of my hand and put them on to the table. "Come on, Mama. Let's have a teeny bit of fun."

We dashed down the hall, into the elevator, out to the front of the hotel, and jumped into the back of a black London taxi. "The Ritz Hotel, please."

The drive to the Ritz took us through the shopping district of Chelsea and along the banks of the Thames, with a view of the Millennium Wheel. We rode down broad avenues near Hyde Park, and past the houses of Parliament. We giggled at the guards in front of Buckingham Palace. I felt the joy of a child escaping from the prison of school.

The taxi let us out at the side street entrance of the hotel. We dashed through the drizzle and through the elegant golden lobby. Emma raced down the vaulted Long Gallery and slid to a stop in front of the portly maître d' at the entrance to the gilded, arched Palm Court.

He smiled graciously as she identified herself. I could see he was even more charmed by her personal presence than he had been when he agreed to seat her without a reservation. If she had been a young man he probably would have even waved their mandatory jacket and tie rule. But then, I doubt if she had been a boy, her charm would have been quite so effective.

He showed us to a round table for two with a view between the gold marble columns to where the pianist played Debussy's *Clair de lune* in the gallery alcove.

We both sighed, as we relaxed into gold velvet Louis XVI chairs, and contemplated the English cream tea, a favorite treat. We ordered the Ritz Royal English tea, an exquisite blend of Assam and Ceylon. The delicate cups on saucers were soon brimming with the fragrant beverage.

Four footman-style waiters brought tiered trays laden with afternoon tea sandwiches of smoked salmon, egg salad with watercress, deviled ham, curried chicken, and cucumber with cream cheese; followed by a tiered tray loaded with assorted tea pastries and rich spice and dark chocolate cakes. A porcelain basket of warm scones accompanied by Devonshire clotted cream and strawberry preserves was placed between us. The final dish of fruits of the forest compote with English cream topped off the feast.

We spoke only in moans and groans of pleasure while we feasted on both the delicacies and the sight of the spectacular setting. The court consisted of tall, mirrored faux window doors reflecting magnificent bronze chandeliers, arched alcove niches with gilded garlands set against creamy white plaster containing gold statues and palms, all topped by the elaborate green and deep teal ceiling embellished with bronze festoons.

"I love this place. And especially this food." Emma said.

"I do too, but we better get back to Chelsea Harbor. Nathan's driver is going to be there any minute."

Fucking Nathan.

We arrived at Ashdown shortly before dinner. The driver had unceremoniously dumped us and our many bags out of the car, as he had to rush to the shoot location to pick up "him".

Yvonne called us as we were hauling things up to our room to invite us to dinner. Emma was violently shaking her head and waving her arms when I said, "Oh, dinner. You know we have a lot of work to do to organize all we found in order to show it. We'll just grab something in our rooms."

We ate sandwiches and drank tea while we organized our finds into categories. Spanish, English that looked exactly like the drawing room we'd been shown, blue schemes, green schemes, purple schemes, blue green and purple schemes, blue and green schemes, and so on.

We had it all set up when Yvonne came up to our room "Are you ready for him?"

We nodded.

Nathan arrived and opened the door. His entourage crowded into the small room.

"Okay, I like the colors. What are you going to use that fabric for?" he asked.

"It's merely an example of the color. These samples and pieces of furniture aren't assigned to any particular thing," I explained.

He picked up a pamphlet of reproductions from one of the very exclusive London showrooms. "Is this bench a reproduction?"

When I admitted that it was, he dropped the pamphlet. "I don't want any reproductions, only the real thing. I like that table. Not that." He tossed the photo of a gorgeous sofa across the coffee table. He spent a few more minutes rifling through the stacks and shoving papers around occasionally picking one up. And then he abruptly lost interest and walked out the door with his entourage hurrying to keep up with him.

Emma closed the door with a sigh. "Jeez, Mom, does that give you enough to go on?"

"Not really. We'll have to do what we think is

appropriate for the house. I don't know about you, but I will be happy to escape before we somehow get sucked into that entourage. There is something about them that I find terribly depressing."

"H-e-l-l-o, it is so-o beyond depressing." Emma was throwing samples into bags. "I want to get out of here as fast as possible. What are we going to do with this stuff?"

"Package up the things he didn't like into the bags of the places they came from. We'll drop off as many as we can on the way to the airport in the morning. Anything we don't get to we'll have the driver drop off. Pack a box for shipping. They probably have FedEx boxes at the front desk, or the concierge."

Emma picked up the ringing phone. "Hello? Just a moment please. Mom, it's Sally."

"Have you completely abandoned me?" Sally complained in her usual high drama manner. "Steve says you aren't interested in my project, that you've gone off to England to work for Nathan fucking Carrington."

"We'll be home in a couple days," I assured her. "You know I wouldn't abandon you. This is exactly what I was afraid of Steve doing when I made you promise to tell me if he bad-mouthed me."

"Oh yeah," Sally said. "Oh fuck."

"And see? He has! Don't let him get away with this, Sally. Listen to me. You've got to put him in his place. Are you going to do that?"

"Okay." Sally was quiet, then she said, "See you in a couple days."

I was putting my phone down when I noticed a phone on the table next to the sofa. Funny, the number listed as the last call on the phone of unknown origins was the same number now listed on my phone. Sally's home phone number was the last call shown on both screens. I wondered who was calling to or from Sally's house besides me.

"Emma, whose phone is that?"

"What phone? Aren't we leaving in the morning, Mom?" Emma looked up from her laptop where she was booking flights because no plane had been offered to us for the return flight. "Why'd you tell Sally we'd be home in a couple days?"

"Yes, we're leaving tomorrow. But it will be a couple days from today before we are really there. Remember how bad the jetlag and time difference will be going that direction? I didn't want to have to deal with Sally the minute we walked in the door. I don't know about you, but I'm going to need a day or two to recover from this trip."

I answered a knock on our door.

"I forgot my phone," said Yvonne.

She had an iPhone in one hand and a Blackberry in her other. "I use different phones for different hats," she explained as she picked up the phone I had been staring at. "I left my personal phone here."

She went out the door without a good-bye or a thank you.

"Emma, it was Yvonne's phone. That's strange. I thought Sally and Yvonne were barely acquainted. Did

Sally call Yvonne to complain that Nathan and Yvonne were monopolizing our attention? No, she wouldn't do that. Did Yvonne call Sally? What for?"

"Mom. What *are* you talking about?"

"That phone. Yvonne's phone had Sally's home number as the last call on the screen."

"That's strange," Emma said.

"That's what I said."

"You need some sleep."

"You got that right."

Emma and I took hot showers and had a couple of hot toddies brought up to our rooms. We snuggled into our beds where we downed the hot toddies. That did the trick. Both of us passed out and got the first decent sleep we'd had in days.

The fog that hung low over the Ashdown Forest the next morning looked the way the inside of my head felt. The gray day matched my mood.

"Emma, I don't know if I can do this. There seem to be a number of hidden rules. Did you notice how everyone agrees with every little thing he says, like he's spouting great wisdom?"

"Yeah, it sucks." Emma continued to look at her laptop as she spoke. "I'm really uncomfortable with how he treats Yvonne. She is, after all, his sister. I'd kill Skip if he was ever like that with me." Emma looked up from her laptop. "Susan emailed that there have been developments with the paintings. She'll fill us in as soon as we get home."

Chapter 33

Emma and I dragged ourselves into the office the morning after we arrived home. Emma sat at her writing table to set up her laptop. I collapsed into the soft cushion of the window seat.

"I've been dyin' to tell you the latest developments. But first how did it go?" Susan asked.

"Interesting," I said.

Emma shrugged.

"What's 'interesting' designer code for?" Susan caught on fast.

"It's code for we signed a confidentiality agreement," Emma said. "If we don't want to say anything, assume the worse."

"Emma!" I scolded.

"Well, it's true," Emma stage whispered to Susan.

At the very moment it was ten o'clock, both phone lines began to ring. Before I could say, "Don't answer that right now." Emma grabbed one, Susan the other. Both were for me. Each line was someone from Nathan Carrington's office. One wanted to make sure I checked my email. There were several emails from several of Nathan's staff that needed "immediate attention". The other call was to let me know that Nathan would be home that weekend and was expecting to see "something" regarding his house. As soon as each call ended, the phones rang again.

Mr. Carrington's architect wanted to run floor plans by me; he needed my furniture layout plans ASAP. Mr. Carrington's realtor needed to show me the house immediately. Mr. Carrington's chef needed to be sure I understood what he needed in the kitchen. Mr. Carrington's estates manager needed to coordinate the move in of the furnishings. Mr. Carrington's landscape architect needed me to review his plans and discuss furnishings for the terraces, tennis shack, and pool house.

Mr. Carrington's head stylist (*How many did he have?*) needed me to be aware of how much space he needed for the wardrobe room and the various other requirements, such as three-way mirrors and enough space to walk in front of the mirror in order to see how the outfit moves. "It is very important that there be enough room to sit in front of the mirror to see how the outfit sits, and enough room for a proper camera set up necessary to check how each outfit photographs," the stylist informed me.

We were soon bombarded by calls from more of Mr. Carrington's staff: his physical therapist—someone has to put him back together after all those stunts, his make-up artist, his chauffeur and his head of vehicle maintenance, his head pilot—yes, he has several, his hairdresser, his head housekeeper, his audio/visual in charge, his personal assistant, and on it went. They each had requirements for the new residence, requirements that the current set up did not allow for and which made doing their job at a satisfactory level, difficult. The phone calls continued until late that evening. They all seemed to be on a ten in the morning to midnight shift.

I requested that each of them put their requirements in writing. It didn't take Susan and Emma long to catch on and start doing the same, giving out our email address and FAX number repetitively.

Susan and Emma sent out for pizza in a desperate move to get some sustenance.

"Let's ignore the phones while we eat. In fact, it's well after business hours, let's ignore the phones, period. What time is it in England? I need to call Yvonne. This can't go on. It's completely unworkable."

I was beyond exhausted; I felt like a zombie.

After we ate, Emma took Lulu for her walk, and I sent Susan home before I handled more emails. As soon as the clock struck midnight, I decided it was late enough to call Yvonne. I got her voice mail.

"Yvonne, we were literally deluged with phone calls and texts today from various of Nathan's staff, each with their own agenda. This is not workable. While we definitely want to be sure that all of Nathan's needs are met, we cannot personally deal with the amount of phone traffic your staff generates. I would appreciate you letting each of them know that the most effective way to make their needs known to me would be to put them in writing and email them to us. Please organize this."

As I dragged myself up to my bed I realized that we had never finished our conversation about the murder, and that Susan hadn't filled us in on the latest developments. Maybe, tomorrow?

Chapter 34

But the next day was no improvement. Susan, Emma, and I had only a few minutes prior to ten o'clock in the morning for a quick meeting before the calls began. We had decided exactly nothing when the girls began to work the phones.

Evidently that message I left for Yvonne accomplished nothing. I called her again. "Glad I caught you. Listen, we are being deluged with phone calls. Can you do something about it?"

"I'm sorry. I put out the word, and I'll do it again. Can you be ready for a meeting on Friday evening? Oops, sorry, I have to take this other call. See you Friday."

I had had enough.

"Okay, that's it. Leave the phones. Let the answer machines get the calls. Susan, every couple of hours play the voice mail to see if there are any real emergencies other than 'I need room for both a massage table and a facial table.' We have two days to organize a presentation and we haven't even seen the house."

I was intent on getting the job under the control, so I

didn't hear the front door open.

"Susan, run over to the art supply store to pick up mat boards in blue, green and purple. Here, match these fabrics. Emma, bring a digital camera and come with me to check out the house."

"What about me?" Sally poked her head into the front office. "We've been trying to get through on your phones for two days."

"I'm sorry darling. We have to get together a presentation. As soon as we have it organized, we'll get back to yours. I promise."

"I guess I'm not as important as Nathan—fucking—Carrington."

"Sally, please, you know that's not true. It's just that we have a very limited time frame. We need to get him moved, and he is only going to be here this weekend for his kid's soccer game, and I really don't want to have to keep making trips to England to meet with him. It's just too exhausting."

"Yeah, and I'm just around the block. I get it. When do we get back to work on my house?"

"Soon, I promise, very soon. In fact, while I'm at the design center today, I'll pull things for you, too. By Monday, you'll have my full attention."

Chapter 35

For the next two days, we worked nearly round the clock, stopping long enough to grab a few hours sleep and eating while we worked. Emma and I had toured the property, (which was awesome), drawn up furniture lay out plans, rendered two sample rooms, and made presentation boards for those rooms. By Thursday evening, I was more exhausted than I had ever imagined possible.

On Friday the phone calls slowed some, but now Sally's office was calling frequently with various requests.

"Mom," Emma said, "this is not going to work out well. Both of our clients are used to being the center of the universe. We can't deal with them both at once."

A knock at the door startled the three of us. It couldn't be Sally again. She doesn't knock. If the door is locked, she yells.

"I'll get it," Susan said. "I hope it's FedEx with those fabric samples Emma ordered."

"Emma, I think I'll have a talk with—" I started to say, but then I saw Susan backing into the room with her hands in the air. Dr. Steinman walked into view with a shiny silver gun in his hand. His Ralph Lauren ensemble was rumbled. His shaking free hand tried to smooth his comb over back in place, but nothing hid his wild-eyed look. He didn't speak. He waved the gun, motioning us to the window seat.

I backed into the seat without taking my eyes off the gun.

"What do you want?" I asked.

No answer. His head twitched in a ten second rhythm. The hand that held the gun wobbled with each quiver. His dilated pupils obscured his gray eyes with black. He stared at each face in turn. God knows what he saw.

"What?" I asked.

He looked at me and pointed the gun at my face.

Susan whimpered. Emma sat still. I had no idea what to do.

"Do you want something from us?" I waited for an answer. When none was forthcoming, I tried another ploy. "Would you like a cup of tea? Emma, get the man a nice soothing cup of tea."

Emma stood and started for the archway leading to the kitchen. She got less than three feet when he motioned her back to the seat.

"Please tell us what you want," I said.

His gaze fastened on Susan's face. "Where is it?" Dr. Steinman growled.

"Where's what?" Susan squeaked.

He backed to the table where Emma's laptop sat. He shoved the lid closed and slipped the computer under his arm with his free hand. He moved to Susan's desk and rummaged through the papers glancing up at us every few seconds. He cleared the top with one shove of his arm. "Where are my papers?"

"Dr. Steinman—David—we don't have your papers. The police took the papers," I said.

His head shook violently, the gun jumped back and forth.

"Are you looking for the agreement with Heidelman?" I asked.

He stared, directing the gun at me.

"We don't have it."

He moved the gun toward Susan. Her eyes opened wide, she let out a soft squeal.

"She doesn't have it," I said, willing his attention back to me. "Karloff took it and sent a copy to the police."

He fumbled with the drawers in Susan's desk, opened the file drawer, rifled through the labeled folders, all while the gun was trained on us. He pulled the center drawer all the way out and dumped the contents on the floor. When the bottom of the drawer was empty, he tossed it across the room.

He backed away from the desk and stood behind my table. Samples of fabric and carpet flew as he dug. He picked up, glanced at, and dropped each paper he found.

Lighting and furniture catalogues landed with thuds as he yanked binders from the shelves. Stone and tile samples shattered as they were thrown onto the terra cotta tile floor of the sun porch. A few shards slammed into the presentation boards neatly stacked under a window. I prayed the design boards and all three of us would survive.

He slid sideways back to Emma's little writing table, pulled out its one drawer, tossed the contents, and walked to the entry arch. He took a quick look at the hall and living room before he exited, slamming the front door behind him.

Three huge sighs as we began to breathe again.

"What the hell was that?" Emma asked.

Susan released her suppressed sobs, wiped tears and snot from her face, and cried, "Cissy, my God! What if I had been alone in the guesthouse? What if I hadn't been sleeping here?"

I picked up the phone from the floor next to Susan's desk and called Detective Rodriquez. "Steinman just left here. He held a gun on us while he tore apart the office."

"What was he looking for?" asked the detective.

"All he said was, 'Where are my papers?' I could guess what he was looking for."

"I'd probably guess the same thing."

"He took Emma's laptop."

"Humph. Are you okay?"

"We're fine."

Sort of. Susan verged on hysteria. Three bad guys in one week were a bit too much for her. She sobbed as she picked up papers off the floor.

Emma was on the phone with Karloff's office warning him that Steinman could be en route, gun in hand.

"Where did he go?" asked, the detective.

"Maybe to Karloff's office. I told him Karloff had the Heidelman agreement."

"Thanks."

I examined the presentation boards we'd done for Nathan. One cover would have to be replaced. Thank God, it wasn't worse than that because we had minutes before we had to leave for Nathan's place, or be late.

Emma laid the board on my table and cut off the damaged cover while I packed samples with shaking hands.

"You okay, Mom?"

"Scared shitless, but I'm not sure which is scarier, Steinman or Nathan. You?"

"I can deal."

Gleeful laughter replaced Susan's sobs. Emma and I joined in the nervous giggles, and we cracked sarcastic jokes trying to lighten the mood.

Once everything we planned to take with us was organized, Emma and I splashed cold water on our faces and wrists and climbed into Armani and Versace suits, respectively.

We piled the presentation into the back of my Prius, and Emma and I were at the house exactly as requested at 6 p.m. We set up our presentation and then waited twenty minutes for Nathan.

Staff scurried from building to building on the property. Food and sodas were brought to the room where we had set up the presentation.

Then, like the lull before a storm, it got very quiet. I heard the sound of a handheld two-way radio informing someone in the next room, *He* was close to arriving. Five minutes later he walked into the room.

He was in a snit when he arrived. Somehow his sunglasses had gotten lost, and no one had managed to come up with another pair. The poor thing had had to sit all the way through the soccer game wearing his assistant's sunglasses! The assistant was a nervous wreck, hands shaking, and a stiff, forced smile on his pale, ashen face.

Nathan walked in, took a minute, not a second more, to look at our presentation offering three possible design directions, announced, "I hate it!" And left the room as I was about to explain what each board represented. The six-person entourage followed him.

Emma and I were in shock, not sure what we should do next. I called Yvonne's cell. "Is it possible for us to get more specific feed back?"

"Not today. We'll talk in the morning," she answered.

"Mom," Emma said, "Now what do we do?"

"As Sally would phrase it, 'Let's get the fuck out of here.'"

Chapter 36

"At least now we can catch up on the gossip."

I tried to look at the bright side, but unfortunately, it wasn't Susan with gossip, but rather Detective Rodriquez who was waiting for us as soon as we arrived home.

"I should have told you not to leave town," he grumbled. "You suddenly disappeared."

I nodded. I was too damn tired to deal with this. "What do you want?"

"Know that gun you gave me?" Detective Rodriquez stood there looking none too happy. "Where did you get the gun? Did you find it in the house?"

"Is it the gun?

"It's probably one of a pair. It seems very likely that the mate is the gun that killed Dr. Martin."

"Damn."

"Did you find it in the house?"

"No. Believe me, I would not have touched it if I'd found it in the house. But it was from the leather box in the cupboard behind the panel, wasn't it?"

"Oh yeah, thanks for leaving the box exposed for us." The sarcasm dripped off his voice. "You should know we have arrested Dr Steinman. And I know he's a friend of yours."

He whipped out a photo of me on Steinman's arm walking into the Getty. "If you're trying to protect him, you can forget it."

' "You didn't arrest him for murder, did you?" I pointed to the photo. "As you can plainly see in this photo, he is the same height as me." Did I have to remind Detective Rodriquez that the crime scene investigator—that is, the firearms examiner—had said that based on the trajectory of the bullet, I was too short to have been the shooter? I recalled his words, "The angle of entry and the pattern of the forward blood spatter indicate a much taller person."

"He would've hired a killer if he wanted his partner dead."

"And take a chance on the stolen art being discovered in the house?" I asked. "He's not that stupid."

Detective Rodriquez muttered and quickly changed the subject.

He opened a briefcase. "Here's Emma's laptop. We didn't find anything on it that would explain why he took it. Rodriquez laid the computer on the desktop. "Where did you get the gun?" he repeated.

"You knew the doctor owned the kind of gun that killed him." I finally twigged. "That's why you were certain that it wasn't a professional job. A pro would have used a gun he brought with him, a gun that couldn't be traced."

No reaction, not even a twitch.

I continued. "The gun that killed him came from that cupboard and was used by someone who knew the gun was kept in that cupboard. Right?"

Typical of our one-sided conversations, the detective said not a word in response to my question.

"Emma, please call Sally. Tell her we are on our way."

I led Detective Rodriquez down the street and around the corner to Sally's. She met us at the front door.

"Sally, I've got some bad news."

"Emma told me. Please come in."

I introduced Sally to Detective Rodriquez.

She repeated what she had told me about where she found the gun. "There it was. Shoved under the ermine throw. I used a handkerchief to pick it up. Were there fingerprints on it?" Sally didn't wait for an answer. "Oh, I can't fucking believe it was *the* gun! Detective, I would have no reason whatsoever to kill the doctor."

"Ms. Abbey, was he blackmailing you?" Detective Rodriquez studied Sally's jade eyes, not in the slightest bit afraid to ruffle the feathers of the "World's Biggest Female Movie Star."

"Blackmailing me? Why would he do that?"

"For money?" Rodriquez said.

I was way too tired to make any attempt at tact. "Sally, you acted like you didn't know him. Which was strange since both Emma and I had seen you in his office."

"Okay, okay. I was embarrassed to admit I had liposuction. And Steve thought it would be a serious detriment to, you know, selling his weight loss program. But it's not worth killing over, for fuck sakes!"

"Do you have any idea how the gun got in your fur vault?" Detective Rodriquez asked.

"Not a fucking clue."

"Show me the vault."

I trailed along behind Sally and the detective up the stairs, through her bedroom and dressing room, and into the vault. The door of the vault was wide open.

"Don't you lock it?"

"Only if I'm going out of town. Otherwise it's too much hassle to open it up. Fucking thing is hard to open." Sally pointed to the old fashion dial of the lock on the heavy door. "It's left from when Gloria Swanson owned the house."

"Have you been out of town since the murder?"

"I went up to Santa Barbara for a weekend. The weekend right after he died."

"You locked it then, right?"

Sally hesitated and then nodded yes. "I'm pretty sure. Well, fuck, I think so."

"Who has access to the vault?"

"Lots of people: my stylist, my housekeeper, the laundress, my trainer."

"All of those people know the combination?" Detective Rodriquez asked.

Sally partially closed the door and pointed to a paper laminated in plastic that hung on the wall next to the door. There was a combination along with a list of what was kept in the vault.

I looked around. Every shelf, every drawer, and every cupboard had a label listing what was kept there.

"I get frustrated with trying to find things." Sally explained.

I knew from my experience that when staff are putting items away, there must be definite agreements as to where everything is kept.

"Do you have any ideas how the gun could've gotten in there?" Detective Rodriquez asked.

"No."

"For future reference, ladies, picking up a gun with a handkerchief doesn't preserve fingerprints. It only smudges them. Did any of your staff know the doctor?"

"Not that I know of. Except, of course, my trainer, Steve."

"Where were you the afternoon the doctor was murdered?"

"Home. Actually, in the exercise room."

"Show me that," the detective demanded.

Sally led us out to the exercise room that was part of the pool house. The main room of the pool house had a bed, along with a desk, a dresser, and two chairs. The adjoining mirrored exercise room was fully equipped with an elliptical machine, a Stairmaster, a recumbent cycle, a treadmill, weight machines, a Pilates board, a wall-mounted rack filled with weights, a sound system, and a large flat screen TV.

"Can anyone verify that you were here then?"

"Steve, my trainer, was with me. My housekeeper was

here. She would have seen us." Sally pointed out the wall of glass that faced the pool, and directly beyond the pool to the laundry room and kitchen. She led the way across the pool deck and into the laundry room, which was outfitted like a seamstress salon.

"Also, my stylist and the laundress were working in here that day. They were preparing for the things I was going to wear in Montecito that weekend. For Oprah's Legends Party. There was a lot of press expected.

Detective, is there any way you can keep this quiet?" Sally asked. "I asked Cissy to help me with this 'cause I really don't need this kind of publicity right now."

"I can't make any promises, but I won't call a press conference."

With that he left.

Sally turned to me. "I must have misunderstood; I thought you were going to be tied up for a few more days."

"I am gone. It only looks like I'm here. I'm a completely jet lagged, exhausted mess."

I must have looked tired because Sally insisted on driving me the two blocks to my house.

I walked by Emma's room on the way to mine and noticed that she had fallen asleep on top of her bed, fully clothed. Lulu was curled up next to her. I slipped off her shoes and tossed a down quilt over both of them.

I continued down the hall to my room and fell into my bed. Good to be in my own bed.

I passed out.

Chapter 37

A few short hours later, I awoke to the phone ringing incessantly. I glanced at the clock, three in the morning. What the hell? I pulled a pillow over my head and went back to sleep.

Emma called to me from my doorway. "Mom, it's Sally. She says she has to talk to you 'right the fuck now.' She sounds like she's been drinking or something. I told her you were asleep and exhausted but she insisted I tell you she's on the phone. I've told you so now I'm going back to bed."

Emma left my doorway.

I picked up the phone.

"Please come over here."

"Sally, it's the middle of the night. I'm wiped out."

"Please. Please. I'm begging you!"

"You can come over here. I can't possibly come over there."

"I'll be right there."

I pulled on a robe and went down to the kitchen. By the time I pulled a mug of warm milk with cinnamon out of the microwave, I heard the knock at the door.

"What's the matter?" I asked her.

She had thrown a sweatshirt over a nightgown. Her hair was twisted into a sloppy ponytail and she was pale. Despite the fact that Sally's communication was so urgent she couldn't wait until morning to talk to me, she sat down at the scrubbed pine kitchen table and asked for a cup of tea before she answered my question.

I put a tea bag in a mug of water and microwaved it, then handed it to her.

"So?"

"Steve wasn't with me that afternoon." She delivered the line with all the drama one would expect of an actress of her stature. And then she hesitated for a full minute for extra emphasis. "I realized shortly after I told the detective he was with me that day, I had the days confused. I worked out by myself that day. I was also doing fittings, and he hates to wait while I do the fittings."

"Where was he?"

"I suspect, at the doctor's house."

Chapter 38

"Really?" I asked.

My God! But it certainly made sense of a number of things. Certainly, would explain why Sally and I being together made Steve anxious. And why he didn't want to go with us to Dr. Martin's estate when the workmen were there.

"Yeah, I just got through talking to him," Sally said. "Steve claims that, even though he was at the doctor's that day, he only threatened the doctor with the gun. He didn't kill him. He says he left when the workmen left."

"Why did he threaten him?"

"He said the doctor was attempting to blackmail him. He says he wanted to impress on the doctor that he would not stand still for it."

"What was he blackmailing him about?"

"I just realized he never said, but I assumed that it was about the lipo."

"The lipo you had done?" I asked.

"I had just a little bit of liposuction done. Steve was

worried that if the press got a hold of it, they would blow it all out of proportion and make his weight loss program look bad."

"Do you believe him?"

"I don't know what to think. It does line up with the fact that it wasn't that gun that killed the doctor." Sally put her hands on either side of her head and rested her forehead on the honey hued antique table. "There's more," she mumbled.

I sipped my warm milk and waited through her dramatic pause.

"This is the strange part," she continued. "I think Steve is having an affair with Yvonne Carrington. When I picked up the land line to call you, I heard her voice and Steve's. He must've called her as soon as he left me and went to the pool house. I'm really uncomfortable with this. I don't want to stay in that house with him. I thought he was in love with me, and that—not that I reciprocated, but I did think it was only because I had resisted his advances that we weren't at least having sex—if not a relationship—I don't know, I had no idea he even knew her. Other than the most casual of acquaintances."

I remembered seeing Sally's home phone number on Yvonne's phone. "She's been in England. With her brother. With Nathan."

"I don't know where the fuck she is," Sally said. "That's not the point. I listened to their conversation. Steve told Yvonne what he had told me. Then she said, 'Did she believe you?' The way Yvonne said that sent chills down my spine, like she knew that he was lying or something, I'm sure they've got some kind of conspiracy going."

Chapter 39

Sally slept in the guest room. She was asleep when I got up around nine. She still hadn't surfaced when I got through explaining to Emma what had happened with the detective and what Sally had told me in the middle of the night.

"What now, Mom?"

"I think we ought to call Detective Rodriquez. I'm pretty sure Yvonne sent us to England to get us out of here, but I can't figure out why."

Susan arrived at 9:30. "Oh, I'm glad you're up," she said. "I was tempted to sleep all day. I thought you might since you must be even more tired than me. But I could hardly wait to tell you the latest news. Guess who's been arrested?" She didn't wait for us to answer. "Steinman."

"For murder?" asked Emma.

"No. For conspiring to sell looted art, or something like that. I'd have to ask Mr. Karloff exactly what he said, but that's close. I didn't get that part 'cause I didn't start taking notes right away. But look," Susan held out her note pad for me to see, "I took notes when I realized he had a lot to tell me."

I didn't mention that Rodriquez had already told me about Steinman's arrest.

Susan continued, "It turns out that the paintin's came from lots of places in Europe: a castle in Poland, a palace in Belgium, a chateau in France. And Cissy, remember when you asked me about that Martin guy in Zurich?"

"Andre' Martin?" I answered.

"Yeah. One of the paintin's did come from him. But not most of them." Susan paused. "Remember that Mr. Heidelman, the one in the agreement?"

"Yes," I said.

"Well he died recently, and the two doctors, his partners, were worried that he might have left somethin' in writin', like that agreement that Carl found a copy of, or maybe somethin' in his will. They had decided that they needed to get rid of the paintings ASAP. I guess Steinman confessed all this. He even confessed to hirin' the prowlers. He wanted to show how silly it would be to say that he had murdered Martin, because it would have exposed the paintin' plot and cost him millions."

"I've been trying to make that point with the detective myself. There is no logical reason for Steinman to have shot Martin, and no matter what else one might say about the pretentious little bastard, one wouldn't expect that he would endanger that kind of an investment," I said.

"How did they get the paintings?" Emma asked.

"That part's in my notes. Wait 'til you get this," Susan paused for drama, and then read us her notes. "Heidelman was a Nazi. He was a courier for some big shot Nazi, Marshall Goering."

"That's pretty freaking big," Emma said.

"Before the US got into the war, this guy, this Heidelman, he would bring these paintin's to a dealer in New York City to sell to collectors. The paintin's had been looted from the occupied countries," Susan continued, "but after the USA got into the war, none of the collectors wanted to admit they owned paintin's they had bought from Nazis."

"That's understandable," I said. "After all, that would have meant that they had contributed to the Nazi war chest."

"Yeah, but this Heidelman knew where most of the paintin's had ended up, so he went around and collected them from the buyers. If he could get'em for a few cents on the dollar, he did. If the collectors didn't sell to him, he had'em stolen. He was pretty sure no one would report the loss, and he musta been right about that, 'cause it seems like no one did. He was sellin' them to the two doctors."

"Did they—that is the doctors—know the paintings were stolen?" asked Emma.

"Who knows? They definitely knew somethin' was not on the up and up. They made up this story about some family in Switzerland having just discovered these paintin's in a family vault where they'd been locked since before the war." Susan held up her fingers in quotations marks "They were, 'in discussions' as Mr. Karloff put it—with someone at the Getty about purchasin' the collection. Mr. Karloff says that the story they made up was that when Dr. Martin was in Switzerland years ago, when he discovered lipo there, he made friends with this family and they contacted him when they discovered the paintin's in a vault. Steinman and my uncle agreed to say that he—that is my uncle—took the paintin's off their hands."

"How did they intend to explain how they got the paintings here?" I asked.

"I didn't get that part of the story. But I did get that negotiations with the Getty were well under way, and that the last thing in the world that Dr. Steinman would have wanted to do was upset the apple cart with a murder."

I shook my head. "Didn't anybody at the Getty suspect there was something fishy about this story?"

"If they did, they're not admittin' it," Susan said.

"Well, does that let Steinman off the hook for murder?" Emma asked.

A bedraggled Sally was hanging on to the polished but worn wood stair banister with both hands as she carefully made her way down the stairs. "Who's off the hook?" she demanded.

She walked through the entry and into the library-turned-office. "What's going on?"

We explained about Steinman.

"Cissy, what are we going to do?" was her response to our explanation.

"We need to tell Detective Rodriquez everything we know." I looked at Susan. "We all do."

Susan looked appropriately uncomfortable. "What do

you mean?"

"We all need to come clean on this. Do you want to discuss this in private?"

"Discuss what in private?"

"Susan, I've been waiting for you to tell somebody—if not me—then Detective Rodriquez," I said. "Last chance, do you want to discuss this in private?

"I don't have any secrets from you guys."

My patience had run out. I was too tired, too annoyed to wait any longer for her to offer up an explanation. "How long have you known that Dr. Martin was your father?"

"What the hell, Mom!" Emma said,

Susan stared at me. "Wha-a . . . How did you know?"

"Well, there was the photo of your mother. The one you have in the bedroom of the guesthouse. You look very much like the doctor, but your mother looked nothing like him. She didn't look like she could possibly be his sister."

All three of the women were staring at me now.

"Then there's fact that you were already in California when Karloff reached you on your cell but you pretended to arrive at LAX the day I picked you up there."

Susan covered her blush with her hands.

"Oh, and how about the fact that you were born in San Francisco, not Kansas. Interesting that Dr. Robert Martin, not your mother, had possession of your birth certificate. The day I saw that in his office, I knew my suspicions were correct."

Susan finally spoke, "Uncle Robert . . . I mean Dr. Martin." She took a deep breath. "I mean my father told me when he came to her funeral. I was pissed at him and emotionally a mess. I didn't want to talk to him about it at the time, but later I got curious. I called him and he sent me a ticket to come out here, I was even more pissed when I saw how he lived. You can't imagine how hand-to-mouth my mom and I were at times, and while I appreciated an 'uncle' that sporadically helped us out financially, a father who neglected us like that royally pissed me off."

"When did you actually arrive in LA?"

"The day before. Same flight. And when I got to the house, the police were there. There were emergency vehicles and police cars. I saw a coroner's wagon enter the gate. So, I had the taxi take me back to the airport. I was at a hotel near the airport waitin' for a flight out the next day when Karloff called my cell." She paused again. "I don't know why I didn't want to say I'd been there, I was confused as hell." Susan seemed to be lost in thought for a minute. Then she rubbed her face, shook her head and continued.

"But right before we got to the entrance of the estate, I saw Yvonne Carrington sittin' in a car next to the wall. At least I think it was her. It was someone who looked almost exactly like Nathan. In fact, I got all excited when I saw this person wearin' a baseball cap and a black sweat shirt because I thought I had just spotted my first celebrity. But when I took a closer look I realized it was a woman. After that I got distracted by all the excitement at the gate."

"Susan." I walked over to her and held her arms, so that she had to look me in the face. "You must tell Detective Rodriquez everything that could possibly help him. And that's an order."

The office phone ringing interrupted us.

"Susan! Don't pick up that phone! Go in the kitchen and call the detective now."

I turned to Sally. "You go with her. Tell him everything."

Chapter 40

After they left the room, Emma shook her head. "What now, Mama?"

"Let's get back to work. We don't have time to waste."

Emma and I stacked fabric samples to one side of my table/desk and pulled three chairs up to it. Emma placed a notepad in front of each chair.

"Did you call him?" I asked Susan when she re-entered the office.

"He's coming over."

"Let's do our meeting before he arrives."

"We have some time," Susan said. "He's going to Sally's first. She left to go over to her house to meet him there."

"Good. Have a seat."

We all sat down and smiled at each other.

"I don't think it is feasible to work for more than one of these big names at a time," I announced. I had gotten some sleep and had some time to think over the events of the past few days. "Even if it is feasible, I don't want to do it. Susan, please add up the hours we spent on Nathan

Carrington's project and see if we've used up the retainer he paid us. If not, please write a refund check for me to sign."

"Really?" Susan asked, her eyes wide with surprise. Perhaps the concept of firing a big-name movie star astonished her.

I nodded. "Yes, really."

Susan smiled and returned my nod.

"I'll write a letter explaining that we're not in a position to take on such an all-consuming project with these time demands at this time, thanking all of them for blah, blah, blah . . . ." I smiled with satisfaction. I had to admit I liked the idea of firing a pain-in-the-ass client.

"Emma, please organize the work we did."

Emma grinned. "Gladly!"

"At least his next designer will know what not to do! Let's package it all up and get it out of here."

I breathed a huge sigh of relief thinking about how nice it would be not to have to deal with the intensity of that group.

"I need to talk to Sally and see if I can repair the damage I did by ignoring her. Steve's last phone call was rather nasty, but fortunately, Sally and I can work things out."

First, I needed to write the letter. Surely, I was not the first person to fire Nathan Carrington as a client, but I enjoyed the idea he might notice not everyone was willing to put up with his arrogance.

The office phone rang again.

"Ignore that." I told Susan. "Just get the hours and

expenses figured out please."

Chiming computers announced the arrival of emails. The Fax machine spit out a note from Yvonne wanting me to call her.

Susan got the hours totaled, and I signed the refund check.

"Messenger all this stuff over to his production company. I want to be officially free of that project ASAP."

Susan called the messenger service. Emma attached the envelope addressed to Nathan's production company with the check, accounting, and letter to the outside of the box she had packaged. She carried the box to the front door just as the bell rang.

A smiling, uniformed deliveryman held an enormous floral arrangement from the upscale florist, Mark's Garden. "For Mrs. and Ms. Huntington."

"Oh, it is beautiful," Emma called to me. "Mom, should I send it back?"

I went to the door in time to hear the deliveryman say, "*Please* don't do that. It will make it look like it wasn't nice enough."

Christ, even the florist delivery was intimidated by that asshole.

The arrangement was in a large basket filled with tulips, roses, and irises, with branches of spring blossoms interwoven into a tall curved handle.

"It is spectacular." I grabbed my purse off the hall table and dug out cash to tip the worried man. "Thank you, we will enjoy it as a farewell gift."

271

Emma carried the arrangement to the mantle in the library.

"Wow! Are you sure you want to send that box? Looks like an apology," Susan asked.

"Yes. I definitely want to send it. And we have other things to deal with."

Susan looked at me with a frown.

"We also have to confront that elephant in the room: the murder!" I smiled at Susan and waited for her to speak.

She hung her head.

"Little Miss Susan, I know you didn't murder anyone."

Susan couldn't have been the shooter. The CSI had said I wasn't tall enough to be the shooter, and Susan was three inches shorter than I. And she wouldn't have gotten someone else to do it.

"And I seriously doubt that you did anything really wrong. Maybe a few minor infractions, but you are making yourself look very suspicious by guarding your secrets closely. And as long as you guard those secrets, the police are going to have difficulty catching the real killer."

Susan protested, "You already know my secrets! All of them."

"Susan, you not only lied about arriving on the flight that Karloff had booked for you, but you also planned an elaborate ruse to cover up your actual arrival. Now why would you do that?"

"What would you have done? I told you, when I arrived at the house, there were police everywhere."

"What were you hiding?"

"I freaked. It was all just too much. I'd had these murderous thoughts. I wanted to kill him myself—not that I would have, but I sure wanted to get back at him somehow. I guess I had a guilty conscience. I guess I figured that the police would figure I had a reason to kill him."

"What *had* you done?" I asked.

"From the airport, I took a taxi to his office. The night before I left to come here, I'd called and told him what time my flight arrived. I thought maybe he would pick me up at the airport, but he told me to take a taxi to his office. When I got to his office, his receptionist showed me into the room with his desk." She sighed, then sat quiet.

"And?" I prompted.

"The receptionist said he was expectin' me, and he told her if I got there before he did to have me wait in his office. She gave me a stack of magazines and closed the door. There was a lot of commotion in the office. Upset patients who were pissed off, I guess about waitin' too long for the doctor to arrive. No one paid attention to me. After awhile I got pretty bored. Then I noticed his laptop sittin' there. It was beckonin' to me. I couldn't help myself. I had to look. I opened it up and started openin' up documents. I was curious to see if he ever wrote anything about me."

"Did you find anything?"

"Nothing at all about me."

"Then what did you do?" I asked.

"I was looking at the screen when I heard someone outside the door to the room. I was embarrassed to be caught lookin' at it, so I slipped it into my carry on that was on the floor next to the chair. A nurse opened the door and said she didn't think the doctor was comin' into the office. She said that she and the rest of the staff were going to be leavin' and would I please come back tomorrow or call for another appointment. She stood there waitin' for me to leave, so I couldn't very well take the laptop out of my bag. I took it with me."

Susan sighed. "I thought about takin' it back to the office, but I never figured out how to do it without anyone noticin'. I was embarrassed to admit to anyone that I had in essence stolen it. That day that you took me to the office, I really didn't want to go for two reasons. One, I didn't know if the staff would say somethin' about me havin' been there before, and two, I wanted to go when I had the computer with me. 'Cause I didn't have it with me that day."

"That's why you were worried about the fingerprints in the office?" I asked.

Susan nodded.

"I wondered what that was about."

"That was weird that day, the day you and I went, 'cause the receptionist and the nurses didn't seem to even remember me. I've been carryin' the damn thing around with me ever since tryin' to think of some place I could put it where it would be found."

"You have it here?"

"Yeah, sure."

"You need to give it to Detective Rodriquez, but let's see it first. What have you learned from it?"

"I haven't looked at it since the day I got it." Susan

pulled a MacBook Air out of her bag and opened it up. She clicked on a file on the screen. "Here's the agreement you found in the pool house. It looks pretty much the same to me."

Emma, who had been quietly listening to us, piped up, "How much charge do you have on that thing?" She looked over Susan's shoulder. "Luckily I've got that same computer, I'll get you a charge cord."

Emma scampered out of the room and up the stairs.

Now I knew why Steinman took Emma's computer. He thought it was Dr. Martin's.

Susan continued to open files. "Look at this one. It's pretty interestin'. There are some email exchanges with a Betsy Brumley. She's a director at the Getty. Look what he wrote."

I took the laptop and read the email:

"I was in Switzerland for several months in 1979. I was staying with friends in Zurich. My friends' family also had a house in Geneva. While I was there, the patriarch of the family became ill. As a visiting doctor, I was asked to take a look at him while they waited for the family physician to arrive.

"I found him to be in a fevered state and he seemed to be suffering hallucinations. He kept muttering about a vault and paintings. I thought the mutterings to be nothing more than ramblings symptomatic of the onset of dementia, but some twenty-two years later, my friends from Zurich contacted me with a very interesting story. Their ninety-four-year-old grandfather had died and once they read his

will, they finally understood what he had been muttering about for all those years.

"There was a vault below the Geneva house that contained more than 70 paintings of major significance. The paintings had been bought over the period of a lifetime. Many of them had been purchased at a price not based on their value, but rather based on what the previous owners needed in order to escape war torn Europe, or later to quietly settle estates. There are appropriate bills of sale for each piece.

"The family wants to keep enough of the paintings so that each family member can select one to keep as a memento. The remainder are to be sold in order to equitably divide the estate. The family requests that utmost discretion be observed; they do not want there to be any unnecessary publicity until such time as an agreement has been reached. They prefer to sell the paintings privately, not at auction. They have no interest in their family's finances becoming public knowledge.

"They have asked me to act as intermediary and to discreetly inquire as to the possibility that your institution would be interested. I assume that they have similar intermediaries in discussions with other institutions, but I did request that if I were to take an interest in this matter, I would be allowed to convey to you first right of refusal."

I scrolled down to her answer. "Wow! She was going for it, I wonder what she thinks now." I pushed the laptop back to Susan. "The last email is dated the day before he was killed. He was to present the first samples for authentication that next Friday." I sighed. "I think this will pretty much kill once and for all any idea that Steinman had anything to do with the murder. Murdering his partner, particularly the partner who had possession and was negotiating the sale of their investment, would be completely illogical."

Emma returned with the charge cord, which she plugged into the computer. "Okay, okay Mom, we got it. You don't think Steinman did it. But don't you agree that murder can be illogical?"

"Not for Steinman. He's much too interested in money and spending it to impress. I bet this is what he was looking for."

"This is so cool. What else is in there?" Emma asked.

"A surprising amount of stuff that makes no sense unless you have been tracking the entire thread of email exchanges."

Emma and Susan continued to look at the laptop. Occasionally they exclaimed at something they found entertaining, but they didn't find anything else that shed light on the case.

"Susan, tell me what the other thing is?"

I'd lost interest in the laptop and felt it was time to get on with it.

"The other thing?" Susan asked.

"Yes, the other thing you haven't told me about. The thing that brought you out here."

Susan sighed. "I guess I'm really transparent. Okay, when my uncle, um, father was in Kansas for my mother's funeral, he told me that he had some jewelry he wanted me to have. He had brought one piece with him, and he gave it to me that day. It looked like a diamond and pearl brooch. Very pretty, very antique lookin'. He said, 'I noticed all the girls are wearin' these again.' I honestly assumed that it was not particularly valuable, but I recently got around to havin' it looked at because one of the pearls looked like it was coming loose. I was shocked to find out that not only are all the stones real, but they're very high quality as well." Susan's eyes filled with tears. "I couldn't believe he had actually given me somethin' that was valuable and that I had a family heirloom."

She stopped to use a tissue from the box I handed her.

"Go on," I prompted.

"I called him last week. He told me to come out here. He said he wanted me to have his mother's jewelry, and that the piece he had given me was just one of a dozen. You know what happened after that. When I got here, he was dead, so I have no idea where the jewelry is. Maybe it never existed." Susan's sentences were broken by sobs. "Maybe it was just another of his lies."

Now Susan's speech was difficult to decipher as her sobs became more frequent.

"What I expected, sob, . . . to find when we searched the house, sob, was the jewelry. I had asked the police to tell me if they found any jewelry in the safes. But they didn't."

"Should have been in either the safes or the cupboards hidden behind the panels. We did find cases." I mused.

"Did you check the safes at the office?"

"Mr. Karloff did."

"You did tell him about this, right?"

"Yes, and he said that it would be good if the jewelry were to be found, because I might be allowed to keep items given to me prior to his death. Or at least an argument could be made for that. He said since a certain amount of heirloom jewelry is usually exempt from being taken in a bankruptcy, I could probably, you know, have my family's jewelry." Susan blew her nose and wiped her eyes.

"Mr. Karloff has been terribly kind," she continued, "doin' all this work when the situation is so very different than one would have expected when your client is a highly successful Beverly Hills surgeon. I have picked up a few things while I've been here. I mean, I noticed his other clients are people like Kecks, and Hopes, and Spreckels, and I understand who they are now—people who will never run out of money."

"Don't count on it." I'd gotten to be terribly pessimistic about money.

Chapter 41

Emma continued to look at the laptop.

An idea occurred to me that might resolve this murder mystery. I called Sally. "Hi Sally. I have a request to make of you."

"Sure, anything," she replied.

"Can I put a nanny cam or baby monitor in your pool house?"

"Sure! Of course, you can. You are going to tell me why we are doing this, right?"

"I want to find the other gun. I'm hoping to catch Steve in the act of moving it."

"Gotcha. Do you have one?"

"No, but I know where to get one." I looked at Emma. "Emma would you please handle that? Remember where we saw those things? While you're over there, Sally, can you please help Emma search for the other gun to that pair?"

I hung up and punched in another number.

"Yvonne, are you in England?"

"No, I didn't go back with him," she answered. "We

were shocked to receive your check. Are you sure you want to do this?"

"Yes, I'm sure. But listen, I want to talk with you in person. Do you have some time today?"

"I'm just getting onto the elliptical. Do you want to come over and work out with me?"

"I'll come over and talk while you work out. Be right over."

I took a nice brisk walk over to Yvonne's relatively modest Cape Cod style gray clapboard house. A charming white picket fence enclosing the front yard matched the white trim on the house. Masses of white Shasta daisies filled the flowerbed running the length of the fence and another bed in front of the house. An arbor trellis covered in Lady Banks yellow roses sheltered the curved top of the front gate.

Yvonne's assistant met me at the gate and showed me to the building that had been converted to an exercise facility by replacing garage doors with a double set of French doors. The floor was covered with sisal matting and the walls with mirrors.

Yvonne was still in her warm up mode just finishing up on the elliptical machine when I entered the room. We made greeting small talk while she moved to the Pilates Reformer.

She was hitting her rhythm when I wondered out loud, "Is it safe to do that when you are pregnant?"

She looked startled but ignored my question. "We were stunned to receive your letter and your check. Are you sure?"

"Very sure."

"I haven't told Nathan yet. You could still change your mind," she managed to spit out the words despite the heavy exertion required by the equipment.

"Yvonne, tell me why you want me to do this project."

"Well, I've heard that you are very good, and Nathan wanted to do this new estate very quickly." She took several deep breaths. "And I knew that you would be discreet. All of those things are important to him."

"But the designer he has been using is very good, very discreet, and wouldn't have to take the time to come up to speed on what he likes. Seems like that would be a much quicker solution." I sat down on the bicycle seat and my feet fiddled with the pedals.

"Honestly, the designer we used for the last project won't even take my calls."

"Oh."

That surprised me for a minute, but then I thought about the few days when we were officially the designers for the mega movie star. It was reassuring to know that I wasn't the only one who thought it wasn't worth it.

"I think you need a very large design firm to service the large organization that makes up his household. Don't you agree?"

"You could be right about that." She wiped her face with a small towel. "But Nathan prefers to keep it more personal than that."

"Yvonne, I'm still hung up on why you would hire us.

Who recommended us to you?"

"Steve Able."

"Really." Pieces started to fall into place.

"Is Steve the father of your baby?" As soon as I said it, her face told me that I had gotten it wrong. She ignored my question.

"Yvonne, both Susan and I saw you outside the gate of Dr. Martin's place the day of the murder. We haven't spoken to the police about it yet. I'm trying to get a grip on the big picture here without any unnecessary publicity for anyone."

Again, my communication was met with silence.

"Look, I don't think you murdered Dr. Martin, but I think the police are definitely going to want to question you."

Yvonne was tall for a woman, but not much taller than I am in my stiletto Jimmy Choo sandals. And she always wore "sensible" shoes. She wasn't tall enough to be the shooter. But she could be an accomplice.

"Maybe I could ask Detective Rodriquez to meet you at my house? That might avoid any publicity for the time being." I gave her the same spiel about how keeping secrets was making it hard for the police to catch the killer, but she failed to respond quite as well as Susan and Sally.

Yvonne abruptly stopped using the machine. "I think it is time for you to leave." Without uttering another word, she stepped off the elliptical, opened the door to the exercise studio, and motioned me out. She slammed the door shut behind me.

283

I stood in the quiet garden for a few seconds to regain my composure, and then walked the few blocks back to my house.

"How did that go?" asked Emma who was in the entry hall when I arrived. I motioned to her to be quiet with Susan in the next room and walked up to my bedroom. Emma followed me.

"Not well." I collapsed into one of the cushions in the window bay. "She's pretty determined not to talk to me. I'll have to fill in Detective Rodriquez on what we know. But you know, I think first I'm going to get with Sally. All of us really need to get this murder resolved and get on with our lives. It's just a matter of time before the tabloids get wind of Sally's involvement with this. Clearly the murderer is still messing with us in ways we haven't understood. But I have the beginning of an idea."

"What?"

"I'll let you know when I have it fully developed. How did you and Sally do?"

"We didn't find anything, but we put the nanny cams all over the place. Sally has made arrangements with the bodyguard she uses when she travels to stay at her place for a while. He's going to keep an eye on the cameras, and, honestly, he was the one who installed the cameras while Sally and I searched. With all those exercise machines, there are just so many places he could have hidden a gun. And Mom, we really don't have any reason to believe that he is the murderer. The story he told Sally is feasible. Sally repeated it all to Detective Rodriquez, and he didn't arrest

Steve or anything."

I picked up my phone. "On the other hand, Sally is nervous enough to have her bodyguard living in her house." I called her and asked, "Sally, want to go for a walk?"

I met her in the circular drive in front of her house.

"I want to apologize for getting so caught up in this Carrington project that I ignored you. It was really stupid of me. I've fired him as a client, although honestly, it may have been just a pre-emptive firing."

"I appreciate you telling me. But I don't want you to think that I expect exclusive rights to your time."

"I know you don't. I realize it's a matter of being able to keep all the balls in the air at a time."

"Yeah, and that means not having a client with so many damn balls that they monopolize your attention. And Nathan has plenty of fucking balls!"

"You got that right!" We exchanged chuckles.

"As soon as we clear up this murder, we'll get back to work on your house. In the meantime, I have an idea," I explained what I needed Sally to do. "Will you talk to Nikki for me?"

"Oh, this is going to be fun. I'm in! And Nikki'll love it, too." Sally laughed.

Chapter 42

Sally organized a cocktail party for Thursday night. She had her assistants apologize to all of the guests who were emailed and then called, for the last-minute invite, but she had a big announcement for which she wanted all of her friends present.

Thursday night we all donned our finery and headed for Sally's loggia. Massive flower arrangements and soft candlelight ameliorated the purple furniture as guests passed through the living room. A roaring fire blazed in the outdoor fireplace. Pillar candles six inches in diameter and three feet tall sat on staggered pedestals in groups of three in between each arch. The row of arches framed the view of the garden lit by hurricane lanterns. To insure a festive mood, waiters circulated with trays of champagne.

Yvonne, clad in a somber gray pantsuit, leaned against the inside of an arch. A waiter offered a tray filled with champagne flutes to her. "No thanks. Please get me a Pellegrino."

I smiled at her when she caught me watching her. She looked away abruptly.

Nikki Howe arrived without her famous husband. This being the second social occasion in as many weeks she had attended without him, undoubtedly the rumors would fly by morning. Her petite, but curvy figure was encased in a pale blue crystal beaded gown that perfectly matched her eyes. Her blonde hair fell in soft curls on her bare shoulders.

Nikki grabbed a flute of champagne, as she made straight for Steve. She greeted him with even more lavish affection than was the usual Hollywood custom. Emma and I watched in fascination as Nikki used every one of her formidable flirtation skills to distract Steve from any other woman's attention he might receive that evening.

He did receive a great deal of attention as Sally's announcement was that his diet and exercise program book, *Steve Able's Secret Weight Loss Program of the Stars*, was to be released shortly. A mock-up of the book cover was displayed on the mantel.

An infomercial promoting a DVD of exercises showing Sally before and after, and Steve discussing the merits of his program was looping on every monitor in sight, including a large flat screen that had been hung above the fireplace.

Steve was clearly enjoying the attention. He preened like a peacock in his black Armani suit and light blue open collared shirt with Nikki decorating his arm. I could almost see his thoughts like a cartoon character's in a bubble above his head. "Look at me, I've got one of the sexiest, most beautiful women in Hollywood clinging to my arm and my every word. And, when my book sits on the

287

bestseller list for years longer than Dr. Atkin's, I'll own this town."

In fact, I heard him say to starlet Cassie Green, "Oh, the low carb, high fat and protein diet is so-o over. You are going to love my program. Look at how great Sally looks."

I took Sally aside. "I'm impressed; you put this together very fast."

"It was nothing." She smiled. "The independent publishing thing was already in the works, I just lit a fire under them and had my publicist do the book cover. Delegate, delegate, that's my motto."

The evening flew by. Yvonne was the first guest to leave; she wasn't looking too happy when she thanked Sally. I had watched her reaction to the affection between Nikki and Steve. No, she wasn't happy, but at least on her way out the door, she returned my smile.

She was halfway down the front walk when she returned to murmur to me, "I'll call you tomorrow. You were right; we should talk."

I squeezed her hand reassuringly. "Good," I said.

Before I returned to the loggia, I stopped in at the temporary set up in one of the extra garages where Sally's bodyguard was monitoring cameras around the perimeter of the property. "Be sure to record the nanny cams tonight."

"No problem, miss, we're all set."

Back on the loggia, the party was winding down. In order to encourage the departures, Emma and I made a show of leaving. We went part way down the street and then cut back in the side entrance and made our way to the kitchen. From the kitchen window, we saw Nikki and Steve enter the pool house.

Sally joined us for peppermint tea as soon as she had said goodbye to the last guest. "That went well, don't you think?"

"It had the desired effect on Yvonne. She's agreed to talk to me tomorrow. Now let's see how Nikki does with Steve. Doesn't she have any worries about the rumors that are going to fly?"

"Nikki's nowhere near as stuffy as you might think. Besides her marriage is solid. Let's go watch the nanny cam and see what she's up to. This is the most fun I've had in ages." Sally rubbed her hands together.

Chapter 43

Sally and I soon got bored with watching Nikki skillfully fend off of Steve's advances at the same time as she encouraged him to think he stood a chance with her, but Emma was mesmerized.

"I could learn a lot from her!"

As we watched, Nikki complained to Steve that even though her husband was one of the most successful stars in Hollywood, he was stingy with the jewelry. "He spends all of his money on planes and real estate. He never buys me really fantastic pieces. I really like the antique ones, don't you? I always have to buy my own jewelry. I think jewelry is the most romantic gift, don't you?" All in her breathless, Marilyn Monroe voice. If that didn't get him, nothing would.

"I can't watch anymore. I'm going to get some sleep so that I can be alert tomorrow. See you two in the morning," I announced after a few more minutes.

Emma, glued to the monitor, mumbled, "Bye," without moving her eyes. Sally smiled, said goodnight and blew a kiss.

I was so anxious to speak with Yvonne that I was tempted to go see her right then. I was afraid she would change her mind by morning, but I didn't know which would be worse: waiting too long to see her or going prematurely. In the end, I went home and fell asleep.

Chapter 44

The next morning, I wasted no time with elaborate dressing. I threw on sweats and rushed over to Yvonne's house where, to my great relief, she welcomed me warmly. She opened the red front door and walked me through the living room. Simple Shaker furniture on rag rugs fit the house and her personality.

"I decided you're right. I need to talk to someone about all of this, and since you've already signed a confidentiality agreement regarding the entire Carrington family, I pick you."

"I appreciate that, but I think I should say if you tell me anything that could be seen as me withholding information vital to the ongoing investigation, I'm not excused by virtue of that confidentiality agreement."

Fair's fair. I couldn't let her think that the designer-to-client relationship had some kind of privileged communication protection. "Having now signed a number of those things, I checked with my attorney."

Yvonne's eyes widened as she studied my face.

"On the other hand," I continued, "even if you should

tell me something that is vital, I can help you to figure out how best to let the information be known only to those necessary."

"I understand. Come and have a cup of tea."

We walked out to the used brick patio overlooking the pool. A round table under the white trellis was already set with a delicate, white porcelain tea service for two and a plate of scones. A bowl of red strawberries provided the perfect accent to the table-scape.

I guess I wasn't too early.

Once we had our cups in hand, I asked, "Well?"

"You're right, I am pregnant. I guess it's starting to show."

"It's not that so much as I noticed you never drink alcohol, even when every other adult is doing it. And you get really sleepy looking and yawn a lot in the afternoon. An inch of your light brown roots is showing, leaving me to assume that you're aware that dark brown hair coloring isn't a good idea right now. And if you haven't had your breasts done lately, well you know. And you excuse yourself to go to the bathroom frequently. I've been pregnant; I recognize the signs."

"Well, you seem to be the most observant person I know. The only other person who knows is Steve Able, and I had to tell him."

"It's not his?"

"No. It's Robert Martin's."

"Dr. Martin's?"

"That's the one."

"Uh, . . . so, . . . well." I hadn't seen that coming, but now I wondered how I could've been that dense. "What's the deal now?"

"I thought that Steve and I were falling in love. I thought it would only be fair to tell him. How ironic that I wanted to be fair to him, huh? You saw him with Nikki last night, didn't you? Now that he's becoming successful, he's going to fall for every slut who comes on to him, isn't he?"

"How long ago did you tell Steve?"

"Six weeks."

"And what about Dr. Martin? Robert? Did he know?"

"Oh yes, he did. Not that it mattered. He offered to give me money for an abortion."

"I gather that you didn't take him up on it."

"Not a chance," Yvonne said. "It was too late for a simple abortion by the time I realized that I wasn't just starting menopause. That's what I thought until I went to the gynecologist to get some hormones for my symptoms."

Recalling how easily I recognized the symptoms of my second pregnancy, I realized she had obviously not been pregnant before.

"Anyway, it turned out I was more than four months gone."

"What did Dr. Martin, um, Robert say to that?"

"He started questioning whether or not it was actually his. That was when I broke it off with him. Not that we had any kind of a formal arrangement. Ours was a very loose relationship, strictly one of convenience. I think he was using me to get close to Nathan, and I was using him to have someone to be with." Yvonne played it tough.

"I didn't expect him to marry me, although I knew there would be hell to pay with Nathan if I had a baby out of wedlock. Which, obviously, I will. This is my last chance. But the tabloids are cruel." Yvonne groaned. "Then Steve and I started getting to know each other better. We would see each other around the neighborhood, especially when he would be out walking those monsters of Sally's. At first, I thought Steve and Sally had something going, but he started coming on to me. I figured I'd been wrong."

"You started seeing each other?"

"Not officially. Once I told Steve about the baby, he said I should sue Robert for child support. He said I could get so much that it wouldn't matter that Nathan is going to fire me. He thought we should be careful not to be seen together so that there wouldn't be any complications with the lawsuit. After Robert died, Steve told me I should be hiring a lawyer to get part of the estate." She sighed and took a sip of her tea.

"Did you hire a lawyer?" This story was so absorbing that I forgot to eat the scones and I really like them.

"Yes. And last night I planned to tell Steve that there was no reason for us to keep our relationship a secret anymore, because my lawyer found out from Robert's lawyer that there really isn't any money in his estate. How's them apples?"

"I'm sorry that things have been going badly."

"It's the men in my life, they all suck!"

"You do have a point there." All three of the men in

her life, Dr. Robert Martin, her brother Nathan Carrington, and Steve Able, were jerks, and had managed to make my life complicated too. "Does Nathan know you're pregnant?"

Yvonne hesitated for a moment. "I haven't told him."

"Could someone else have told him?"

"I think a few of his staff may have guessed."

"Any possibility he knows who the father is, um, was?"

"My assistant knew I was seeing Robert. No one on his staff would dream of keeping a secret from Nathan. If he asked."

"How would he react to you being pregnant?"

"He'd be pissed at me. He hates giving the tabloids anything to write about."

"Would he be angry with Robert?"

"Oh, yeah."

"Angry enough to kill him?"

Yvonne stared at me. "No, that's impossible."

"Why? Was he in town the day of the murder?"

"Don't you get it? Nathan doesn't have that kind of personal freedom. He always has someone, an assistant or a bodyguard, or somebody with him. Even if he got rid of them, he can't go anywhere without being recognized. Sometimes he goes out on his motorcycle and the full-face helmet gives him some anonymity. But the paparazzi have learned to recognize all of his bikes, so even that's pretty unsuccessful."

"What about hiring someone?" But I knew what an unlikely idea that was as soon as I said it.

"He's not stupid enough to give anyone reason to blackmail him."

"I saw someone who looked like him near Robert's house the day of the murder. That was you, right?"

"Oh my God, I've done some stupid stuff." Yvonne got up from the table and paced the patio. "What am I going to do?"

"Tell me what you've done."

"I told Steve about the secret panels in Robert's house. I even made a drawing so that he could find them. I told him about the guns in there. He said he was going to use a gun to try to scare Robert into being more sensible about the baby. That was a crock, wasn't it? Oh God, what a fool I've been! Saying all this out loud is putting it into a new perspective. Steve asked me about the workmen's schedule, about Robert's schedule, and the day of the murder, Steve asked me pick him up from Robert's house. I waited just down the street for him to call me. There was a lot of traffic in and out of the estate that day. A taxi kept cruising the place, and you arrived, too.

He said he only tried to reason with Robert and then, when that didn't work, he tried to scare him. He swore he hadn't shot Robert. He even had me smell the gun he had with him to show me it hadn't been fired."

"Do you happen to know a good criminal lawyer?"

"No."

"I'll make some phone calls. I think that's who you should speak with next."

"What? Do you think I'm, like, an accessory, or something?"

"I don't know. Hopefully, it's not anything too serious. And maybe, if you help the police to catch the killer, they'll go easy on you. But before you talk to the police, talk to a lawyer."

Yvonne nodded and sat back down at the table.

"Don't tell Steve we've talked. In fact, I suggest you don't even let on that you're upset with him over the way he behaved last night. You could tell him you went home early because you were tired."

"Yeah, and I'm definitely not going to tell him about the lawyer."

"Did Steve say anything to you about some jewelry?"

"No. What are you talking about?"

"There are some jewels missing, jewelry that belonged to Robert's mother. Did Robert mention anything about it?"

"Let me think."

"Susan would like to have her grandmother's jewelry. Your baby might like to have a piece, too."

"There were some velvet bags and cases in that cupboard when I opened it. Did they have jewelry in them?"

"Maybe."

I stayed quiet while Yvonne thought for a minute. When Steve got the gun out of the cupboard, he could have easily gotten the jewelry too. "Did Steve take the jewelry?"

"When I picked him up, he wasn't carrying anything. He had on a big jacket, one of those with lots of pockets, a fishing/hunting jacket. He pulled the gun out of one of the larger pockets. He could've had stuff in the other pockets. But nothing big."

"I am curious about one thing: did Steve just walk out the front gate and meet you?"

"Not in the end. I was waiting for him across the street and down the road a bit. But he didn't come out. Even when I saw truckloads of workmen leaving. Then he called me and had me come to one of those places where you pick up day laborers."

"After you talk to a lawyer, I have an idea how you can help the police."

Chapter 45

I found Nikki, and Sally in the courtyard when I returned to my house.

"Nikki, you were brilliant last night! What a performance!" I said.

"I did okay, didn't I?" Nikki dangled her feet in the spa. "I think he's going to give me a piece of the jewelry this afternoon. We're meeting at the beach house for cocktails at sunset."

"Oh, how romantic!" teased Sally as she lounged on the chaise.

"But that means that somebody better be watching him to see where he has the jewelry hidden," said Nikki.

"Don't worry, we have nanny cams all over the pool house, and my security guys are keeping watch on the monitors. They'll follow him if he leaves to go anywhere at all." Sally was really into this detecting thing.

"Did he do anything, like get some jewelry out last night?" Nikki asked.

"No."

"This morning?"

"No."

"He didn't pull out any jewelry," Nikki said. "Shit, this better work." Nikki pounded her right fist into her left palm.

I interjected, "Who is a really good criminal lawyer? Do either of you know?"

Nikki and Sally both shook their heads.

"Haven't had a lot of dealings with that, thank God," Nikki said.

"Well excuse me, I've got to make some calls." I retired to my office.

I called my lawyers, and a judge that I'd met, even Beyla Karloff, and there was one name I heard from most of them, Don Hager. I got the phone number for his Century City office and walked back to Yvonne's house with the information.

"Here's the guy you should call."

"Did your lawyer recommend him?"

"Actually, several people recommended him, including a judge. You know what they say, 'A good lawyer knows the law; a great lawyer knows the judge.' This guy seems to know everyone, and speaking from experience, that makes a huge difference. Call me as soon as you've seen him."

When I got back to the house, Emma and Susan had joined Sally and Nikki.

"Well everything seems to be in place," I said to the girls. "As soon as Yvonne let's me know that she's spoken with Hager, I'll give Rodriquez a call and let him know what we're up to."

High fives all around.

Nikki excused herself. "I've gotta get ready for my big date. He better come through with the rocks!"

Chapter 46

"Detective Rodriquez, would you please come by my place sometime this afternoon? I need to fill you in on what we girls have been up to."

"What've you been up to now?"

"I'd rather explain in person. You're gonna like it."

"Ok. I'll be over, but first I have to go to this lawyer's office in Century City. He says his client has something to tell me in connection to Martin's murder. You happen to have any clues as to what he is talking about?"

"I really couldn't say." I was getting good at this discretion, NDA thing.

"I'll call you when I'm leaving there," he said.

Now that I had all the balls in the air, I found myself unable to concentrate on anything I was supposed to be working on. Emma and Susan seemed to be suffering from the same malady.

"What shall we do?" Emma asked.

"Clean the office," Susan said.

"Boring," Emma answered.

We all three looked out to the courtyard where Sally, still on the chaise lounge, dozed in the sun.

"Hey, *she's* a movie star. *We* have to work. I can sort samples for returns, that's a nice mindless job," I said as I picked up the first piece of fabric and folded it with the label out. I started a pile in the appropriate design showroom bag.

"Somebody, go online and check on the latest about Steinman. There must be some news about him," I suggested.

Emma volunteered for that duty.

Susan said, "I'm goin' to read some more of the stuff in Robert's laptop. Maybe even more emails." She typed as she spoke. "It seems like he didn't know how to empty his trash. There's a lot in there."

"Mom, here's that photo of you on Steinman's arm, going into the Getty again. It's on Facebook, and now in the articles about him."

"Why would anyone give a shit about that?" I said.

"Well, because he's the center of a big scandal now. It says not only was he involved in the art laundering scheme, but he was also allegedly the front man for a Ponzi scheme that bilked a number of celebrities."

"What? That boring man? Hard to believe." I doubted he acted on his own.

"There are hundreds of millions of dollars involved. The so-called broker involved just surrendered to the FBI for lengthy interrogation. They locked him up so he's convenient to be questioned each day! Anyway, Steinman's on the list of his known associates. Seems they suspect he had something to do with this. Appears that he recommended this guy to several of his patients. There is this whole long list of 'investors'." Emma read through the list. "Ah, Mom. Uhm, we know some of these people. Look!"

I looked over Emma's shoulder at her screen. There was a long list, nearly three hundred names.

"Who's on that list that we know?"

"Try Sally Abbey! How about Dr. Robert Martin? Uh, oh, Nathan Carrington. Even Steve Able. I wonder how many of them were Steinman's patients."

"Interesting. Very interesting." I wondered if this connected with the doctor's murder.

"Here's the really bad news for these so-called investors: if they gained, they have to return that gain to the trustees to redistribute the funds in a more equitable fashion. Dr. Steinman is on the list of those who came out ahead. Oh look, Carrie Snodgrass has already repaid her gain. So, has Gretchen Van Vleck. Gretchen returned $230,000."

"I suppose Uncle Robert was also one of those who gained?" Susan piped up.

"Yeah, how ever did you guess?"

"God, that man screwed up every way possible."

"Trying to get something for nothing. I figure the liposuction thing came so easy, he thought money was always going to fall in his lap," I commented.

"Don't you think that's why many of the people on that list were fool enough to think they were going to make money that easy? I mean look at that list."

Susan and I both looked over Emma's shoulder.

"Everyone on that list has lots of money that they got fairly easily," said Emma.

"Interesting theory." I thought about it for a minute. "I agree. I think you're right."

"How much does Robert owe? God, am I going to spend the rest of my life paying his debts?"

"Thank God, it doesn't work that way. You won't be held responsible for this," I assured Susan.

"The estate will," said Emma.

"The estate. That's a laugh. It's not an estate; it's a money pit. Speakin' of which, the prices on fixin' the house arrived. Your copy is on your desk and, as you instructed, I forwarded them to Mr. Karloff. He's figurin' out if we should just liquidate as-is or what. I'm just gonna leave it to him, but I wonder if he knows about this. I'm gonna call him right now."

Susan returned to her desk and picked up the phone. "Mr. Karloff, please. This is Susan Wallerski Martin calling. Yeah, I'll hold."

Emma and I both looked over to where Susan was sitting at her desk.

Susan put her hand over the receiver. "Well, Wallerski is such a stupid name, nobody can ever figure out how to spell it, I don't even know where my mother got the name. So, I'm switching to Martin. Mr. Karloff said it would be no big deal to do it."

Into the receiver, "Mr. Karloff, did you know about this Ponzi scheme Robert was involved in?" There was a minute or two of silence. "Oh, good. Okay." Susan listened for a few seconds more. "Well yeah, I guess so. If you think it's the right thin' to do. Thanks. Bye."

"Yeah, he knew. In fact, Uncle Robert, seems to have been a procurer of investors," Susan relayed to Emma and me.

I wondered if any of the so-called "investors" were pissed off enough to hire a hit man when they learned they had been scammed.

"He says the news media wants permission to go onto the estate to photograph the scene of the crime. He figures the exposure might be good in terms of sellin' the property. He also said there isn't enough cash or equity to do any further work. We need to sell everything as-is." Susan sighed. "I guess I'll be lookin' for a place to live."

"Oh, boy. Once the media gets onto the property, the whole story is going to come out. We better warn Sally." I looked out to the courtyard. "She's not there. When did she sneak out?"

I picked up my phone. "Oh, and Susan, I think Yvonne is going to want to tell you something."

The words were no more than out of my mouth when both of the other phone lines started to ring. One was Detective Rodriquez saying he was just leaving Century City. The other was Yvonne with the same news.

They both ended up on my doorstep thirty minutes later.

"I should have known you were in on this," said Rodriquez by way of a greeting.

"Come in, please."

Sally jogged up the front walk.

"All of you," I said, stepping back to let them by.

Sally and I paused in the entry.

"You think the media is going to have this story soon? I really want to have this murder resolved before they start speculating as to which of us did it. They start printing all that shit, and it never goes away. Some reporter will be asking me what the true story was fifty years from now." Sally wrung her shaking hands.

I didn't know how to re-assure her. I put my arm around her and took her into the living room

Yvonne stood in the corner talking softly with Susan. I heard Susan say, "Can I tell?"

Addie Mae had entered the room on the pretense of taking drink orders that she passed on to her helper, and then she quietly sat down in the burgundy red wing chair in the corner of the room. Detective Rodriquez was in one of the two indigo chairs flanking the fireplace. I took the other one. Sally and Emma shared the claret red sofa. Susan and Yvonne left the corner and sat on the opposite matching sofa.

I cringed at having these clients and potential clients in this room that had benefited from so little of our design attention. True, the magnificent Persian rug patterned in indigo and claret floral arabesques, the one that my great, great grandparents must have had delivered to California via clipper ship, sat on handsome dark pegged-and-grooved hardwood floors. Thankfully, the skirts of the fully upholstered indigo chairs covered the worn and burnt spots near the fireplace. But the windows were bare. The curtains that had been there when we took possession of the house had been shredded beyond rescue. We had simply removed them and placed two large Kentia palms in front of the French windows that faced the street.

Susan was grinning from ear to ear. "I have good news. I'm gonna have a family! I'm gonna have a sibling! Well, a half one anyway." She looked at Yvonne, "Do we know what it is? I mean, boy or girl?"

"We learned it's a girl from the blood test. I'll know everything after the amniocentesis that I have to do because of my age."

"Wow! I'm gonna have a sister."

"Holy shit!" "Un-fucking-believable!" A chorus of surprise from Emma and Sally.

Detective Rodriquez was smart enough to wait for everyone to settle down again before he spoke.

"Any of the rest of you have anything you haven't managed to tell me yet?" He looked around the room, but his eyes landed on me and stayed there.

"Let's see, now you know about Yvonne being pregnant with the victim's baby. At the attorney's, you must have learned that Yvonne picked up Steve from the temporary workers station the afternoon of the murder. You know about Susan arriving the day of the murder and taking the laptop from the office. You know about Sally finding the gun. Hmm, do you know about Dr. Martin and Dr. Steinman being involved in a Ponzi scheme?"

"Yes. I also know that Sally and Steve were into that

too."

"I was? What the fuck are we talking about?" Sally looked baffled.

"You don't know?"

We all looked at Sally.

"No, I don't fucking know!" Sally was losing patience. "Somebody better start explaining."

Everyone started talking at once.

"Wait a fucking minute! One at a time," Sally said.

In tandem, Emma and Susan explained the story of the Ponzi scheme.

"I had no idea. Do you suppose Steve used my name? Somebody did. Oh fuck! I need to start paying better attention to these things—start taking responsibility for my own life. I've gotten carried away with the delegating. How much did you say I owe?"

"Per the list, you were one of the losers," said Emma.

"Well, that's a relief." Sally laughed.

"Just what was it that you ladies wanted to tell me?" Detective Rodriquez looked like he had had about enough estrogen for one day.

"We are after two things. You see, we think—that is—we are pretty sure that Steve Able killed Dr. Martin, but we don't really have any proof. We know he was there, in the house at the right time. I figure he could have shot the doctor right before the men quit work for the day. The sound of the shot would have easily been mistaken for the shot of a nail gun. Then he left with the load of day workers and was driven to the temporary workers' station. He's got to be the big guy who could handle the floor sanders, the guy Carl mentioned. Remember? Carl said that guy never showed up again after the murder?"

Detective Rodriquez nodded. "Yeah, I remember."

I continued, "Steve showed Yvonne a gun he had in his pocket when she picked him up. He even had her smell it to prove that he hadn't fired it, but I figure he had the other gun, the mate, in another pocket. The one he had actually used.

"There's another thing. Susan is missing jewelry, family heirlooms, that, as you know, were not found in the safes in the house, or in the office. I think Steve found the jewelry in the same hidden cupboard as the guns and took it as well. Thus, the empty jewelry cases. We know from Yvonne that he had on a jacket with lots of pockets. Then, I figure Steve hid the gun—the one that didn't kill the doctor—in Sally's fur vault. I don't know why he did that. Maybe just to cause trouble for Sally."

"I think I know why. Maybe he thought the police would think I had something to do with the murder and get sidetracked. Or maybe just 'cause he's an asshole," said Sally.

"But didn't he know they would test the gun?" Emma said.

"He must have," Sally said.

"Here's the stupid explanation: he got the guns mixed up. He thought that was the one he used to shoot the doctor," As soon as I said it, I realized that my theory was probably accurate. Steve wasn't the brightest light in the room; he just thought he was. "As to why, maybe he was thinking publicity?"

"What did he do with the other one?" asked Detective Rodriquez.

"Well, that's what we wanted to talk to you about," I said. "I was going to have one of the girls, probably Yvonne, tell him that Sally had found a second gun and turned it over to the police. I figured if Yvonne told him, she could say she didn't know where Sally found it. Then he'll go look where he hid it to see if it's gone. We hooked up nanny cams all over his room and the exercise room. Sally's security guys are watching the monitors."

"And you waited to tell me after the fact?" Rodriquez barked.

He sighed. "Ok. That could work. Let's do it, but with my guys watching the monitors," the detective said.

"Yvonne, has he called you today?" I asked.

"Let me check." Yvonne pulled out her phone and listened to a message. "Yep, he has. He wants to come by. He sounds a little nervous. Wonder why? Ha. Be quiet and I'll call him back now."

"Hi!" A few seconds elapsed. "No, I'm fine. I got tired last night, so I left kind of early. Sorry to have missed part of your big night. How did it go?"

Yvonne did a good job of sounding casual.

"Good, yes, very good. Congratulations. Listen, there's something I heard today that I thought you ought to know," she hesitated for just a moment to set up the full drama. "It seems that Sally has turned a second gun over to the police.

One that looks just like the first one she gave them."
Yvonne winked at us but managed to sound serious. "No, I
don't know where she found it. I didn't talk to her. Emma
told me when she was walking the dog past my house—No,
I'm not home. I had a couple of errands to run."

"Emma, please go quickly and move Yvonne's car into
the garage," I whispered.

Emma picked up Yvonne's keys from where she had
dropped them on top of her bag.

Yvonne said goodbye and sighed with relief when she
ended the phone call.

"Good job," I thanked Yvonne.

She looked at Detective Rodriquez who nodded back
at her.

"Now what do we do?" Susan asked.

Detective Rodriquez turned to me. "You have a plan?"

"Sally and Yvonne, I think you should both stay here
until Steve leaves the area. Hopefully he'll check on the
gun right away." I looked to Rodriquez. He nodded again.

Sally was already on the phone with her security,
"Dave, be on the alert. He might go for the gun now—
Okay, let me know. Dave says that Steve was just getting
out of the shower when the phone rang, and now he keeps
checking his watch. He's probably afraid to be late to meet
Nikki."

"Did they see him with the jewelry?" I asked.

"Not that they could tell for sure. He was screwing
around with the equipment in the gym, but they never saw
him actually take anything out."

"Let's have Nikki call him and tell him she's going to be late. Then he'll have time to look for the gun," I directed Sally.

The detective was full on scowling at me.

Sally called her. Sally grimaced as she listened. "She'll call him, but she's getting a bit nervous about meeting him at the beach house. What do we do now?"

"Meeting him where?" the detective said, "No, you need to tell me the whole plan."

I too had some misgivings about Nikki being alone with a killer. "Let me think, maybe there's another way."

"She'll have to go with it. Fuck. She can handle him," Sally said, "She can have a shit fit if he doesn't bring the jewelry and make him get it."

"Do I need to remind you ladies, this isn't a movie?" Detective Rodriquez was looking pissed off. "Bullets in real guns are liable to actually hurt!"

Sally glared at him. "Oh, for fuck sake."

"I don't know, Sally, you're not thinking with how dangerous Steve is. He's already killed one person. Why wouldn't he kill again?" I was worried. Had I started something I would regret?

The detective nodded his agreement. "Have her put him off. She needs to tell him she'll call him when she is close to the beach house. I've got a team in place near Sally's that will follow Steve, but I'm going to send some officers out to Malibu. Do you have the address of the beach house?" asked Detective Rodriquez.

I grabbed the phone from Sally. "Nikki, what's the address of the beach house? Detective Rodriquez is going to send some men out there so they will be nearby just in case you get scared. We'll let you know when they are in place."

Sally turned to me. "Cissy, she fucking has to call him now!" Sally stomped her foot and snatched the phone out of my hand. "There's no time. We don't want to blow this."

I hated to let this end without getting the jewelry, but Nikki's health and life were definitely not worth some stones.

"Nikki says she's sending one of her security guys out to be visible when Steve arrives. Here's the phone number for her security so that you can coordinate with him. His name is Mike." Sally scribbled a number and the address on a scrap of paper and handed it to the detective.

Into the phone Sally said, "Call me back after you call Steve."

Sally dialed her security. "Dave, what's he doing now? Answering the phone? Good." Sally relayed his answers to us. "He's gone back into the exercise room. He's looking at the elliptical machine. He's moving over to it. He stopped. He turned around. He's gone to the drawer in the cabinet. He took out a screwdriver. He's unscrewing the attached tv screen, he's reaching into the pipe thing, he's pulled out something wrapped in cloth, and he's unwrapping it—it's a gun."

Detective Rodriquez pushed a button on his phone. "Okay, move in—" He was interrupted by screams. "Hold on a minute."

"NO! NO! NO! NO! NO! NO!" Five women screamed

at once. Addie May shook her head.

"We don't have the jewelry yet."

"He'll never tell where he hid them."

"Please, please, wait. Please wait!"

"You have to give him a chance to go for the jewelry," Susan pleaded.

"What, and give him a chance to ditch the gun? No way!" Detective Rodriquez shook his head.

"You'll be watching him the whole time. It'll be okay. I just know it will," I said. What was I thinking? Caught up in the moment, I'd put Nikki's life in danger with one of my harebrained schemes.

"Please, please!" Susan begged.

He spoke into the phone, "Hold off. Watch for him to come out. Don't lose him! He should be headed for Malibu colony. You got the text? That's the address. There's a security guy named Mike who will be in place there. Make sure the subject doesn't ditch that gun on the way. If he looks like he's going to throw it away, like in the river, grab him fast." He listened for a minute. "Yeah, yeah. I know. We're waiting to see what he has done with some jewelry."

Rodriquez listened for another moment. "Yeah, I know, but it's some important jewelry, heirloom pieces and the ladies—the owners—are concerned that he'll never tell where he's hidden them if we don't get them now."

Sally kept abreast of Steve's movements on the phone with her security. "Has he left yet? What's he doing now? Putting on makeup? Ugh, I had no idea. He has the gun in the left bottom pocket of his black leather jacket. He's putting things like wallet and keys in his pockets. He's smiling at his reflection in the mirror, checking his teeth. Now he's out the door. Shit! Stay away from the windows everybody. He'll be driving by here soon." Sally motioned to the girls to move away from the street side of the room.

"My men have him in sight. He's in a black Beemer. Putting the top up."

"Wouldn't want to mess up his hair!" Emma said.

"He's turned onto Los Feliz Blvd. He's probably headed for the I-5 to the 10." Detective Rodriquez updated us.

"Nikki, he's headed for the beach house. Where are you?" Sally had Nikki on her cell on speaker.

"Still in Brentwood. I'll call him now and tell him I'll leave now."

"If the traffic isn't too bad, he'll be there in forty-five minutes. He has the gun."

"Oh, that's reassuring! Does Mike know that?"

"I'll make sure he's told. Call back when you are close."

"Will do."

"Yeah, yeah, we'll tell him. I'm going to leave now. How much trouble are you ladies going to get into once I leave?" Detective Rodriquez looked at his feet in an unsuccessful attempt to hide his grin.

"What could we possibly do?" I asked with a smile.

"Somehow I'm sure you'll think of something!"

Chapter 47

As soon as he was out the door, I said, "Hey let's go take that pool house apart. That jewelry might be in there. Ladies, grab your cells. Let's go."

Five of us speed walked to Sally's. Addie Mae had opted out of this part of the action.

We started taking apart equipment the minute we hit the door.

"Wait, wait," Emma said, "let's organize this better. If we scatter these pieces all over the place, we'll never get them back together. Let's pair up and do one at a time." Emma kept her head as usual.

Sally and Emma attacked the Stairmaster. Susan went to Sally's housekeeper to ask for empty boxes to put the pieces in.

Yvonne and I went for the treadmill. "The bottom of this thing looks like it could hold a lot of stuff." Yvonne grinned at me as she sat on a stool with the box in her lap. I handed her screws from where I sat on the indoor/outdoor carpet. "Sally, we really need to get rid of this carpet," I said. "A good faux sisal would be nice."

Sally was intent on her task and didn't even comment. Once Susan had rounded up several boxes, she helped me with the heavy pieces of the treadmill.

Two crime scene investigators, one of whom I recognized from the afternoon I spent at Dr. Martin's place, knocked on the glass pane of the door. "Miss Abbey, do we have your permission to look at the bedroom in this building?" He held his credentials and ID out for her perusal.

"Abso-fucking-lutely. Come on in."

I left the treadmill to Susan and Yvonne and watched the investigators from the door to Steve's room.

The two CSIs headed straight for the shoes in the bottom of Steve's closet. They found a pair of new looking work boots in the back of the closet. I saw the ink and paper come out of their bag and knew from my own experience that they were transferring sole and tread patterns onto the paper.

Next, they dug through the clothing in the closet, the drawers and the hamper. I assumed they were looking for bloodstained clothing. I found it hard to believe that Steve would be stupid enough to have kept the clothes he wore that day. And I also suspected he had more than one pair of work boots, as the ones they were handling had not a speck of dirt or a sign of wear on them.

"Gentlemen, there are some bags of clothes to be given to Goodwill in the garage. You may want to check them. They were supposed to be taken last week, but I noticed that two bags must've been overlooked. They're behind the green garbage dumpster," Sally volunteered. "And you can ask my laundress—she's over there in the laundry—if she's seen anything suspicious. She does all of the laundry for the entire household."

The CSI's thanked her. One of them continued to look through Steve's room while the other went over to the laundry.

We continued to take apart exercise equipment. We got so into our search, we were startled when Sally's cell rang.

"Nikki, are you close? Oh, you're there. Good. Do you see anyone around?"

Sally put her cell on speaker so we could all hear Nikki, "Mike's out front. There are a couple of guys out on the sand that I haven't seen around here before. Steve hasn't been here other than that one 4th of July with you, so he wouldn't know they are not residents. I haven't seen that detective friend of Cissy's yet."

I wondered what Detective Rodriquez would think of that description of him.

"Nikki," I said, "put your cell on speaker and leave it on. Sally, as soon as Nikki gets her cell all set up, put yours on mute so that Steve won't hear any noise from this end. Nikki, do you have a pocket you could hide it in?"

"Yes, I do. Good thing I wore these baggy menswear style trousers because my lace cami top certainly doesn't have any hiding places." A few seconds of rustling fabric noises preceded Nikki saying. "Can you hear me now?"

"Loud and clear."

"Cool, I'll feel much better knowing you guys are

listening. If things get too scary, you'll call the police, right?"

"Abso-o-fucking-lutely," Sally assured Nikki.

"Yes, we will. I'm putting Detective Rodriquez on my speed dial right now," I said. "And Sally, you know how to record this too, right.

"Fuck yes."

"Oops, I hear his car in the drive," Nikki said, "Wish me luck and turn on your mute."

We heard the doorbell ring and the soft clip clop of Nikki's sandals as she headed for the door.

"Hi! Good timing. The sun is just starting to get low."

We could easily hear Nikki greeting Steve. His answer to her was a bit harder to make out. We all stopped what we were doing and sat still so that we could hear.

"What do you want to drink? My new fave is mixing pomegranate juice with prosecco. The pomegranate juice has lots of antioxidants, you know."

"I'll try that."

That was very clear, he must be right next to her. Oh whoa. We could hear the sound of him kissing what? Her neck?

"Hey, buddy, slow down. Let me mix these drinks. I'll make a pitcher we can take out on the deck."

We could hear the clink of bottles and the ring of crystal as Nikki prepared the tray to take outside.

"Here, let me get that!" Steve's voice.

"I'll get the door," Nikki's voice.

We heard the door close.

"It's going to be a perfect sunset. It's always better when there are a few clouds to catch the light. Look, it's already starting to turn the underneath of those clouds bright pink," Nikki said.

"Beautiful, but not anywhere near as beautiful as you," Steve said.

"Oh, ugh," said Sally.

"Yuck," Emma added.

"I don't know if I can take this," said Yvonne.

"Hey, shush guys. I want to hear," I said.

"Cheers." We heard the chime of crystal glasses touching.

"Your weight loss program is pretty exciting. I bet you're getting a great response."

"Yes, I am. Pretty soon I'm going to get the good tables even if I'm not with Sally." Steve's voice was as loud and clear as Nikki's which meant he was back to being all over her. We could hear him groaning with desire.

"My God, you are so beautiful."

"Steve, are you teasing me? Let me see what you have in your pockets. What did you bring me?" Her hands slapped his clothing.

I held my breath. Nikki, you don't want to find the gun.

"What do you mean? Bring you." His voice was still coming through loud and clear and his groans were intensifying. "I'll bring you to the height of ecstasy."

"You're such a tease. I want the jewelry you promised to bring. Let's see it."

"I didn't have time to pick it up, but don't worry, I'll get it. I'll go get it for you a little later. After."

"Alright, that's it. I don't get involved with men who don't keep their promises. Get the hell out of my face. No, I mean it. Back off!" Nikki sounded furious.

"Don't get so fucking excited. What's your problem? I said I'd get it."

"Don't get rough! I told you what my problem is. I don't like men who don't keep their promises."

My finger was poised on the dial button of my cell with Detective Rodriquez's number on the screen. I wasn't sure how this killer was going to take this reject from Nikki. He had a loaded gun in his pocket. Had she forgotten this creep was a killer?

But Nikki was there. She was the one looking into his eyes, and she was reading his reactions. I've observed her handle even the most temperamental men, so I hoped for the best. But that didn't keep my heart from racing.

"Okay, let's go for a drive." Steve's voice was gruff, but he didn't sound too pissed.

"Where are we going?" Nikki was back to her usual breathless voice.

Nice try, Nik, I thought.

But he answered, "You'll see. Let's go."

"Hey, take it easy with my arm! That hurts."

Chapter 48

I pushed the button on my cell. "They're leaving!" I said as soon as Detective Rodriquez answered.

"Where are they going?" Detective Rodriquez asked.

"She asked, but he wouldn't say."

"How do you know?"

"Nikki's got her phone on speaker in her pocket. Sally's got her on the line."

"Clever. But you don't know where they're headed?"

"No. But if I had to take a guess, I'd say Dr. Martin's house. I think maybe he hid the jewelry there."

"What makes you think that?"

"It seems unlikely that it is here in the pool house as we've nearly taken everything apart without finding a thing. We'll have to go through Sally's house next. After all, he planted that one gun in her fur vault. Possibly, he hid jewelry somewhere in her house. But I think it's even more likely he hid the jewelry before he left the estate, don't you?"

"But we've ripped that place to shreds. The only sign of the jewelry we found were the empty cases," the detective answered.

"I'm only too aware of the fact that you ripped the place to shreds. Hold on, I want to hear what Nikki's saying now."

"Steve, shall I drive? Take a separate car? If we're headed into town, I may not want to drive back here tonight."

The sound of footsteps on gravel was clear, but not Steve's muffled voice.

"We can't make out what Steve is saying now. He must be too far away from her," I told the detective.

"Shit. Be careful with my arm, will you?" Nikki's voice was loud and clear.

"I can see them," Detective Rodriquez informed me. "They just got into his car. He's driving. We'll follow them. Call me if you get any clue as to where they are headed. You sure she's okay? He's being a bit rough with her."

"She'll let us know if she gets scared."

I hoped I wasn't kidding myself as well as the detective.

Chapter 49

Sally got up from where she had been taking apart the weight stand while she listened. "I'm not fucking doing this anymore."

"Mom, listen to this. Nikki's un-freaking-believable."

"Steve, I like the way you operate. I admire a man who doesn't let anything get in the way of getting what he wants."

I could just see Nikki leaning over the car console and putting her head on Steve's shoulder, so that her pocket was right under his chin. His voice was clearly audible.

"You think that's good. You know that Steinman guy? The cash from that art deal would be mine if he hadn't fucked the deal."

What art?" Nikki asked.

"When Heidelman died, Steinman started freaking."

"Wait, wait," Nikki said, "I don't get it. What art? Who is Heidelman"?"

"Heidelman was this old Nazi guy who put us onto the paintings. He was a courier for a bunch of Nazi bigwigs. Brought paintings to NYC and sold them to various collectors. The money went into financing the Nazi war effort."

"Nazis?" Nikki squealed. "Was that before we got into the war? So, it was still legal. Right?"

"Yeah. Sure. But most of the collectors were too embarrassed to ever admit they had paid into to the Nazi war chest. Pretty simple to get the paintings cheap. He knew who had most of them, and most of those fuckers still had'em."

"What happened when Heidelman died?"

"Nothing really, but Steinman was sure that Heidelman had left evidence, written agreements or some shit that his kids were going to find, and then we would all be fucked. The stupid shit, all freaking out over nothing. We bought the paintings, so what was the big deal?"

"Yeah, BFD," Nikki said. "You really are an unbelievably good businessman."

"Steinman, that stupid shit, panicked. He wanted to dump the paintings as fast as possible. Martin had a good thing going with the Getty. Steinman was gonna fuck it up."

"Wow, bad huh?" Nikki asked. "But I don't understand what Steinman was worried about?"

"Deal with the Getty wasn't strictly on the up and up. Heidelman's involvement mighta squelched the whole thing."

"What kind of money are we talking?"

"Hundreds of millions."

"Wow!" Nikki exclaimed. "I suppose the two doctors put up the bucks to buy the paintings from Heidelman?"

"Those two dumb shits? Not a chance. They both spend every penny they make."

"Who came up with the money?"

"I did."

"I'm impressed," Nikki purred. "But aren't we still talking a considerable amount even if you got'em cheap?"

"I handled that with an investment scheme. But Steinman is a fucking chicken shit. I put him on to a great investment, but he blew it big time and the bottom fell out."

"That's where the money came from? From an investment scheme?"

"Yeah. Yeah. We were doing great. I took his patient list and Martin's and we'd just gotten started signing them all up when Steinman chickened. He threatened to blow the whistle on both schemes. Martin said he could handle him, but he wasn't doing it. He fucking blew it. Then Heidelman died."

"So, what did Steinman do?"

"The worst thing he did was to pull all of what he claimed was his share out of the investment scheme. Made the whole pyramid come tumbling down. Then the so-called broker we brought in got indicted. Turned into a complete cluster fuck."

"Sounds terrible," Nikki said.

Wow, did Steve really never understand his so-called "investment scheme" was a Ponzi scam?

"The only good thing was some other stupid dickhead, this stupid shit broker we used as a front man, got blamed for most of it."

Steve was bragging himself into several criminal charges.

"Feds thought that we were just victims, too. The only problem we had was that some stupid trustees are trying to get the money back from us. Never guessed that it was all my idea in the first place. Thanks to both Martin and Steinman—those stupid fuckers—the whole house of cards came down."

Wow. I really had this wrong. Here I had been thinking it was Sally's lipo he had been covering up. He was involved in every one of these schemes.

Pretty interesting how between the three of them, the doctor, the dentist, and the trainer, they had all the physical aspects of a body covered: cosmetic surgery, cosmetic dentistry, and weight loss. All of these were very lucrative activities, especially in LA, but evidently, not lucrative enough for the super greedy. They formed a triumvirate and were running illegal "get rich quick schemes."

Steve continued to brag to Nikki about what a brilliant businessman he was. He seemed to be completely unaware that most of the activities—the fraudulent laundering of art, the Ponzi scam, and even the fraud of claiming that Sally's weight loss was due to his program—were fraught with illegalities. In his world, he had just been slightly bending the rules, and as a "smart businessman," that was within his moral code.

But where was he taking Nikki? Martin's estate had been completely torn apart looking for the gun. Surely the jewelry would have been discovered if it had been on the property. But that sure seemed to be where they were headed.

"Are we going to Martin's place?" Nikki asked, but Steve didn't answer. "I've always been curious about that estate. Look at this one. It has a half mile of frontage on Alpine. Do you know who lives there?"

Nikki let us know where they were.

Steve was not to be distracted from his bragging. "I thought up this investment scheme, you know. Both of the doctors had patient lists of the richest people, people with more money than they know what to do with. I thought we should capitalize on that, so to speak."

"Wow, Steve, I had no idea that you are such a genius business man. Honestly, I thought you were just a good looking, charming hunk. But you've got brains, too. Did you figure out how to set up the art thing too?"

"Yeah, sure," he said. "See we had this one director at the Getty who was an investor in our fund. She wasn't too concerned with exactly how the money was made, as long as she got her dividends. I could tell she was a player, so when Martin started talking about this old German guy he knew, he said the guy had contacted him because he, the German, knew that Martin had some money, at least he thought he did. Martin's dad knew this German. Everybody always thought that Martin was loaded from the lipo. He held the American rights to it, but he blew money like it was water. Guy always needed more."

"You'd never do that." Nikki laid it on.

"Anyway, I realized we could sell the paintings to the

Getty. I knew this director would help us authenticate whatever we needed as long as she got a cut. You know, I even built that room in the attic. Those two doctors couldn't even hammer a nail between them. We didn't want any workmen to know about it, so I picked up day laborers, different ones each day. Did you ever see it?"

"No. Sounds very professionally done."

"Damn straight, it was. I did a damn good job on it. Got fucked by that Cissy Huntington and those two girls, though. I knew the minute that Martin hired that Huntington bitch that she was going to be trouble. I didn't want her in that house, but Martin got real stubborn. He thought she was his ticket into the old money club."

"Did she design all the work in the house?"

"Nah, only the recent stuff. He had to have all that English antique shit. Had all this crap shipped over from England. The fireplace was one thing; he had to have the ceiling raised, and a wall knocked out in order to get it into the room. Then whole rooms of paneling! Whatta stupid motherfucker he was! Thought he was the guy from that "Citizen Kane" movie!"

"I heard that the fireplace has some really ornate carving on it."

When I heard Nikki say that, I finally remembered that the bear's head in the center of a medallion on the fireplace could be screwed off to reveal a hollow space behind it. Shit!

I called Rodriquez. "I know where they're going. It's Martin's place. There's a huge, dark wood mantel and fireplace surround in the living room that was brought over from Scotland. The head of the bear unscrews, and there's a cavity behind it. I'm going over there, but Steve and Nikki are going to get there first."

"Got it. I remember that fireplace. Amazing thing. I looked to see if there were any trick panels, but we couldn't bring ourselves to cut into it."

"Thank God, for small favors."

Detective Rodriquez ignored my comment and said, "Look I can get there ahead of them. Don't you try to get over there! I've got it covered."

"Sure." I hung up.

"Come on girls. We've got to hurry or we'll miss all the excitement."

Chapter 50

Emma, Sally, Yvonne, and Susan had no idea what I was talking about since they had been listening to, and even trying to record, Steve and Nikki's conversation, not mine. But they jumped up and followed me to the car without a moment's hesitation. I used every backroad route in my arsenal of missing-traffic-jams tricks to get to the doctor's as fast as possible.

Rodriquez called me back. "I unscrew the head of the bear? Is that what you said?"

"Yeah, counter-clockwise."

"Well, well, what do you know. Looks like you were right. There's a large velvet bag in here—the kind used for jewelry. I have to hang up, it's going to take two hands to get this pouch out without damaging anything."

*　　*　　*

As I drove, the girl's continued to monitor Nikki's cell transmission.

"So, this is Martin's place. Good grief, there must be

hundreds—no make that thousands of blood red roses," Nikki said. "What's going to happen to this place anyway?"

"How should I know? I don't give a flying fuck." We could hear the sound of tires on the crushed rock parking area. They had arrived at the house.

"Hey, lighten up! That hurt!" Nikki screamed, "Not in the damn car! Get off. Jewelry first!"

We heard Steve curse, then a car door slam, followed by the front door banging shut.

Their voices echoed as they walked across the huge vacant living room.

"Wow, this place is a mess. But that fireplace is amazing. Hey what are you doing? Don't break it!" Nikki said.

"I'm not breaking it. This head unscrews and there's a hole behind it."

"How cool is that?" Nikki sounded enthralled.

"What the fuck? It's empty!" Steve's bragging tone had completely disappeared. "How the fuck?"

"Are you sure you put'em there?" Nikki asked.

"Somebody would have mentioned if they had found these jewels. Did any of those stupid bitches say anything about it to you?"

"I have no idea what you are talking about." Nikki's sandals slapped the hardwood floor, she must have moved away from Steve. His voice was fading.

"Maybe the jewelry is some place else. Aren't there more hidden places in this house?" Nikki asked.

"Yeah." Heavy footsteps, a couple of deep grunts.

"Come here you. Where do you think you're going'?"

I could make out the sound of Nikki's sandals hitting the floor and echoing through the empty rooms.

"I'm going through there, into the library," Nikki said.

A sharp cry from Nikki, then "Isn't this where they found the doctor's body?"

"You're one weird bitch."

"Come on, baby, that's not very nice. I'm being nice," Nikki cooed. "Whoa, look at the color of the walls! What would you call that color? Blood red? And where are those secret panels?" Nikki asked.

"Oh, you know about those?"

"Yeah, well, I think someone mentioned something about files behind secret panels."

"Just what is the story with you bitch?"

A thud that sounded like a body hitting a wall.

Where the hell was Detective Rodriquez? If he was in the house, I didn't want to call him and give him away by having his cell ring. If only Nikki could get him to say something really incriminating while Rodriquez was listening. I figured that was what he was holding out for.

Nikki ignored the sudden change in Steve's tone of voice. "Steve, you don't know where the secret panels are, do you?" she challenged him.

That's right Nikki. Get him showing off again.

"Sure, I do. That's where Martin hid files he brought home from the office. Files of patients that he would recommend our investment fund to, and depending on who they were, Martin gave them the phone number for

335

whichever one of us whose voice they wouldn't recognize. They would call me, or Steinman. The investors thought they were talking to the CFO of our fund. Later we got that broker."

"We started out with a bunch of files he already had here. He had thought he'd use them to blackmail these stupid bitches who really thought nobody would realize they had had cosmetic surgery. Like any stupid dickhead can't tell, huh?"

"What happened to his blackmail scheme?"

"Well, the first stupid bitch he tried it on told her lawyer husband. They threatened to go to the police if he contacted them again. But then he leaked the info to the *National Star* and they printed that she had had some work done. Martin thought that would show the others that he could, and would, give the press the info."

"Let me get this straight: first he tried to blackmail them, and when that didn't workout, he had them invest money in some fund he was recommending and they did it!"

"Well, not all of them, but some. We'd take a bit of money from them, say ten G's, and then we'd pay them back twenty G's. Then we'd take the twenty and give'em back forty. Pretty soon they'd be wanting to give us hundreds of thousands, if not millions.

"People gave you millions!"

"Yeah. One guy put in fourteen mil. And another put in eight, but four to five was about average."

"What happened to all that money?"

"We used some of it to buy the art with. See, we thought if we made a huge profit on the art, then we could pay out these huge dividends and then really clean up, 'cause every time we paid out money, we'd get ten times as much back. You know, 'cause the suckers not only want to double up their money, but they'd brag to all their friends 'bout how much they were making, and we'd have a whole new batch of investors."

"Too bad he had to get himself killed here. Kind of blew the art thing huh?"

"No! Those stupid bitches blew it! We coulda got the paintings out of here and still sold them. Steinman also had a line to the director. It was that fucking Martin. He was messing up the whole thing doing all this work on the house. We had to get Cissy out of here and he wouldn't fire her."

A loud thump sounded like Steve had slammed a fist into the wall. I wondered if my beautiful blood red walls would have a fist sized hole in one.

"I spent two fucking days as a day laborer so I could get in here to figure how to get the art outa that house with all the workmen and security. Couldn't fucking be done.

"I tried to reason with him, but he just couldn't see that if he kept it up, he was going to blow the whole damn scheme." Steve was on a roll reliving how stupid the doctor was. "Acting all superior. Thought he was smarter than me 'cause he had degrees. That motherfucker pissed me off so fucking much! But I showed him who was the better man."

"So, . . . you shot him?"

We didn't hear Steve say a word. No denial, nothing. Just silence.

Then what sounded like a gasp from Nikki. "What are you doing with that gun?"

"Get in there." Steve's voice was gruff, pissed off. No hint of seduction. "Now!"

We heard Nikki's cell bleep that the battery was getting low.

"What the hell, bitch?" Steve roared.

Chapter 51

I was sure the thud I heard next was Nikki's body hitting the library wall. Oh God, please don't let the next blood in that room be Nikki's! My heart stopped. My stomach lurched. I couldn't breathe.

"You're under arrest for the murder of Dr. Robert Martin. Anything you say, can and will be used against you, . . ." Detective Rodriquez said.

We all came tumbling out of the car in front of the house and ran into the library just in time to see Steve held against the paneled wall while Rodriquez's assistant closed the handcuffs on his wrists.

Detective Rodriquez stuck a pen in the barrel of the gun and put it in an evidence bag.

"Congratulations ladies! You got your man!"

Nikki fell into Sally's arms laughing but the laughter quickly turned to tears.

"Shi-i-it!" Nikki collapsed. "I tried so hard not to think about the fact that this was real. I just kept pretending it was a role, a part in a movie, an improvisation, anything but real life. But when he took that gun out of his pocket and pointed it at me, I think I peed my pants!"

All of us girls hugged, laughing and crying at once.

The police were trying to get past us and out the library door. And Steve was definitely not laughing.

"Fuck, this blood red leather-like shit sure is cool." Sally rubbed her free hand over the waxed red wall while she held Nikki with her other arm.

From the entry hall we saw Carl, the flooring man, pull into the driveway as Steve was being led to a police car. Carl jumped out of his truck, hurried over to the car, and looked over Detective Rodriquez's shoulder. "That's him, that's the big guy!" he said.

Emma, Nikki, Sally, Yvonne, Susan, and I, went into the living room where I showed the girls the secret compartment behind the bear's head. Of course, the detective had taken the jewelry with him.

"It's probably evidence, but you'll get it back eventually," I told Susan.

"I caught a glance of it hanging out of his coat pocket. A nice, good-sized bag," said Nikki.

"It would have been nice to have at least seen them." Susan looked dejected but only momentarily. "Hey, we did it! Mystery solved."

"Nikki, you did an amazing job. It was great how you managed to clear up many of the questions. Like that Steve pushed Yvonne into hiring us to work on Nathan's house so that he could get us out of the country. He must have been terribly disappointed when we came back so soon," I said.

"He did everything he could to get me to fire you. He

was constantly complaining about you. I guess he just didn't want you around," Sally said. "He couldn't believe it when you fucking fired Nathan Carrington as a client. Who fires a huge star? You and Sumner Redstone, huh?"

"He didn't want us working on the house because they needed to move the paintings," I said, "At first, I thought he was just jealous of our friendship, but now I think he didn't want Emma and me around you because we were also involved in the doctor's house. He must have worried that we might eventually start putting two and two together. God, when Susan started working with us, he must have been really worried."

"If Steve and Steinman knew all a long where the paintings were, who were the prowlers I kept hearing?" asked Susan.

"This is what I think: Steinman was at least smart enough to realize how at risk they were. There was the agreement that we found in the pool house. That incriminated Steinman and would have led us to the paintings if we hadn't already found them. Steinman hired those guys to find anything that might have implicated him. And to move the paintings so he could cut Steve out of the deal. No honor among thieves."

"Then how 'bout Dr. Martin's laptop? That must have really freaked them out when that was missing," Emma added.

"That was why Dr. Steinman went to Robert's office." I looked at Susan. "Remember the receptionist told both of us that he had been there right before us the day we went to the office to look at the painting?"

Susan nodded at me.

I continued. "The small painting did turn out to be a Vermeer—a long lost Vermeer."

"Susan, they probably never thought to look in your carry-on for the laptop," Emma said.

"Well, after the one time when I missed my chance to return it to the office because I had left it at your house, I kept it with me all the time. They really didn't have much of a chance to find it."

"Mom, what made you certain it was Steve?"

"It had to be a tall man."

"And that was why?"

"The only way on to the property was through security. Truckloads of day labors were brought in each day, but they were all men. And that was the only way to get in, or out. There were only three men that appeared to have a motive. That pretty much narrowed it down to Steve Able, David Steinman, or Nathan Carrington. Steinman and Carrington are both too short to have been the actual shooter." I looked at Yvonne. "Also, it was you, Yvonne, not Nathan, Susan and I saw outside the house that day."

Yvonne winced and nodded.

"Did you figure that Steve was more likely to pass for a day laborer than Dr. Steinman?" surmised Emma.

"There was that. I've explained many times that even though he—that is Steinman—was a pompous ass, and now, it seems, also a greedy criminal, I just didn't see Steinman as stupid enough to commit murder in close proximity to where he was hiding several hundred million dollars worth of possibly stolen paintings. Not to mention that Steinman isn't taller than me. But Steve is."

Nikki commented, "Steve seems to be so stupid that he didn't even get that what he was doing was illegal, let alone wrong."

"Yes, so I noticed. He also has such a self-importance button that he can't see past his nose. It was pretty obvious that he wouldn't be able to stomach living in Sally's shadow for long. It was obvious that he was tired of depending on her pull to get him parts in movies or tables in restaurants."

Nikki nodded her agreement.

"Excuse my frankness, Sally." I smiled at my friend as I spoke, "This last slump in your career must have scared him enough to realize he had to find a way to be independent of you. The weight loss program was his key to fame. The lipo had worked great, and the means to Sally's dramatic slimming had been kept secret, but he couldn't trust Dr. Martin. Martin must have threatened Steve like he had everyone else whose files were in that cupboard."

"Oh yeah, totally. I remember you saw Sally's medical file in the cupboard," Emma pointed out.

I continued, "Steve wasn't going stand for still another person he had to kowtow to. There was another thing, the security guard told me that the cameras around the house were messed up the day of the murder because of work the electricians were doing. It wasn't a coincidence. The wires had been cut to the cameras that would have showed Steve going in and out of the house. He was somewhat disguised, but he wasn't taking any chances that someone might catch a glimpse of him."

"That also explains why Steve would never return to the estate when Carl or any of the other workmen might be there," Sally said. "No wonder he took an Uber home from the PDC that day. He must've fucking freaked when we said we were going over there to see Carl."

"Yeah, Steve was the big guy who didn't show up for work the next day. The one Carl mentioned. We'll have to make sure that Detective Rodriquez knows about all of this. Not just Carl, but also the other workmen will be able to place him at the scene."

"I imagine he got the idea of going in and out with the day laborers from when he hired day laborers to build the room for the paintings," said Susan.

"Agreed," I said. I turned to Sally. "Your independence was just too much for him. He thought the weight loss system would make him wealthy and famous. He could get his own tables, his own entrée to the hot spots. But you wouldn't stick to the program. You were impossible to control. It's lucky he didn't try to kill you!"

I thought about what I had just said for about two seconds. "Maybe that's why he hid the gun in your fur vault! If you were tried for the murder there would be tons of publicity, including for his weight loss program, and you wouldn't be a threat to his plans. You would be out of the way!"

"It's a good thing for me that he is such a fuck up that he planted the wrong gun!" Sally engulfed me in one of her huge hugs.

Chapter 52

The next week, Sally and I had a fantastic shopping day. We were having so much fun doing her house I often forgot I was getting paid to do it. We found this beautiful ivory colored silk to use for her bedroom curtains and to drape the bed. The transparency was just enough that back lighting created a soft warm glow. Sally's skin would look incredible in that room.

The very best find of the day was a spectacular 1935 Jansen chinoiserie dressing table with mirrored corners. Sally was over the moon about it, and the glass tile we'd selected for her bathroom. Finally, I had a happy client!

I had just come in the front door and dumped my bags in my office when I heard Emma call to me as she descended the front stairs.

"Oh, Mama. It was like a dream! Come sit with me so I can tell you about it."

I followed her to the patio.

"Jeff came by for me yesterday. He grabbed a bag that Addie Mae had miraculously packed with all the things I would need for a romantic interlude, and he whisked me off to where he had a bonfire, a thermos of cosmos, and a candlelit dinner, together with chaise cushions set up on a very private beach."

Emma was grinning from ear to ear and sighing with delight. "It was so romantic," she cooed. "We had a wonderful evening. Then, he silently took my hand and led me to the room he had reserved at the hotel just above the beach. We walked through a magically-lit garden, down a private path that ended at French doors. He opened the doors to a room with the creamy linen covered bed turned down, a glowing fire, and dozens of candles lit all around the room. He was just the right amount of forceful . . . and gentle and . . . romantic. He kissed my neck, nibbled my ears, and—"

"Not too much information," I held up my hand, "But it sounds wonderful, and I'm glad to see you looking so, shall we say, satisfied."

"I haven't gotten to the good part. I think you are going to like this part." Emma grinned at me. "I told Jeff I would marry him as soon as Daddy comes home to give me away!"

"Oh, my darling girl! I do like that part." I enveloped Emma in a bear hug. Joyous tears streamed down our faces. We held each other for several minutes and then ran for the tissues.

"The only part that worries me a bit is the part about Daddy. I really don't know how to find him."

I blew my nose and screwed up my courage. I could do it. I could find him. I had to. "I guess we start by running personal ads in every major newspaper, offering rewards for information about him, posting requests for information on the Internet. Aren't there websites for that? Those 'people search' sites."

"Mama, I know you'll find him. You've got plenty of time. We won't start real, finalized planning until you find him. In the meantime, I can just be engaged and spend hours day dreaming about weddings, days shopping for the perfect dress, and months finding the perfect location."

I do my best not to interfere in my children's lives, but sometimes there's just no helping it. I confess: I had one or two conversations with Jeff. After all, he is a sweetheart, and until now, Emma hasn't always demonstrated the best taste in men.

Oh hell, now I have to find her father. Maybe Karloff can recommend a P.I.

Chapter 53

"Isn't anybody going to answer that door? I hurried toward the incessant ringing. I opened the door with the martini shaker in one hand.

Detective Rodriquez stood there looking none too happy. "What else have you failed to tell me?"

"Well, I don't know. I'm a little confused as to who I've told what," I mused. Then I spotted a good-sized red velvet pouch in his hand. "What's that?"

"Is Susan here?" He, as usual, ignored my question.

"Yes, as a matter of fact, she is. Why?"

He held up the pouch. "I thought she might like to have this back.

"Oh, is that the jewelry? I thought it had to be evidence until the trial is over." I moved aside and motioned for him to enter the hall.

"It's been recorded, and it isn't really vital to the murder case. I thought she could use the dough." He hesitated in the doorway.

"Please come in. Would you like a drink?"

"Yes, I would." He stepped into the entry hall.

"Oh, you're not on duty." I smiled.

"That's just one of those things they say on TV. Or maybe you would call it an urban legend. But no, I'm not on duty. Just thought I would drop this off on my way home. Are we drinking martinis?"

"Apple martinis. I make them with a touch of fresh squeezed apple juice. They're delicious. We're celebrating the sale of Martin's estate."

I steered Detective Rodriquez to the courtyard where the gang, Nikki, Sally, Emma, Susan, Yvonne, Addie Mae and Beyla Karloff Jr. had gathered in front of the roaring blaze in the outdoor fireplace. The day had a slight chill that kept them all close to the cushioned hearth.

I introduced Detective Rodriquez to Nikki; they really hadn't had much of a chance to be properly introduced the day of the arrest.

"Nikki, this is Detective Rodriquez."

"Detective, this is Nikki Howe."

"My name is Manuel," said the detective, "Manny to my friends. I'm delighted to meet you Ms. Howe."

They shook hands, while Nikki bestowed one of her magnificent smiles on Manny.

I turned to where Yvonne sat in one of the cushioned wicker chairs. "And this is Yvonne Carrington."

"Yvonne, Manuel Rodriquez."

I remembered the meeting at the attorney's office. "Oh yes, you've met."

"Detective, I think you know all the rest of my guests."

"Ms. Carrington, delighted to see you under more

pleasant circumstances. And hello to the rest of you."

"Can we call you Manny?" asked Emma.

"Absolutely, everybody but Mrs. Huntington. That is, Cissy."

"Oh, she has other things she calls you anyway!" Emma laughed.

Manny sat next to Susan on the hearth and gave her the pouch full of jewelry. "Ms. Wallerski, I've arranged to return these to you."

"Please call me Ms. Martin. Or Susan. Oh, my God, that pouch is huge!"

Susan looked at Beyla before she carefully poured the contents of the bag onto the coffee table in front of the outdoor fireplace. The blaze of the flames flashed off the startling mound of brilliance. Susan and Sally immediately began to sort the pieces by types of stones: a diamond choker, a diamond tennis bracelet, diamond stud earrings and diamond pendant earrings made the first pile.

The second heap consisted of a pearl choker with a sapphire and diamond clasp, a single strand of pearls, a double strand of pearls, a sapphire and pearl brooch, pearl studs, pearl cufflinks, pearl clasp earrings and a black pearl necklace.

The third was the rubies: a pair of pearl and ruby earrings, a ruby and diamond necklace and a delicate gold chain with a ruby pendant.

Yvonne had learned the day before that the baby was healthy and a girl. "Susan, I'm going to buy some of those pieces from you for my baby. I want her to have some heirlooms from her father's family, even if she doesn't have a father."

"Yvonne, your baby—my sister—is going to have me. If you let me be a part of her life, I would very much like to be part of a family. Which piece do you think she will like? I'm going to give her some of these. You aren't paying me for them."

"I know you need the money. It's my way of helping you out."

"Yvonne," I interjected before the discussion of the jewelry of questionable origin continued, "here's some sparking apple cider for you. Now, everyone has a glass, we are ready for a toast. Susan would you care to do the honors?"

"Yes, I would. We're here to celebrate the sale of the estate. Mr. Karloff," Susan nodded towards Beyla, "you were brilliant to realize that publicity would sell the property quickly—and for a good price! And you sold the practice. You worked it out, so that I didn't end up in a hole, financially speakin'. In fact, I even have a nice little nest egg, so I won't have to sell all this family jewelry. Here's to Mr. Karloff. Cheers!"

"Cheers!" we all echoed as. A buzz of conversations filled the room.

"Wait, wait, I have more," Susan continued. "I also want to thank Cissy and Emma for befriendin' me and becomin' my employers. And thank Cissy for her persistence in clearin' up the murder. Here's to ya!"

"Here, Here!" Another sip for all.

"I have more! Nikki, thanks for your bravery! Here's to Nikki!"

"To Nikki!" we chorused.

"Here's to Sally for takin' me in. I love the pool house and having the exercise room next door ought to make it easy to get myself on the equipment. Before you know it, I'll look as good as all the starlets around here. Here's to Sally."

"To Sally!" said all. I refilled everyone's glasses.

"Here's to Detective Rodriquez, Manny, for doin' his job well, and for being at least somewhat understandin' about some of us not being entirely forthcomin' with some of our secrets."

"Here's to Detective Rodriquez. Here's to Manny!"

"And finally, here is to my new baby sister, and to her mother. To my new family." Susan used the back of her free hand to wipe tears of joy from her cheeks. With her other hand she raised her glass up high in Yvonne's direction.

"Cheers!"

Acknowledgements

I was lucky to begin my interior design career with work I loved and people I admired. Many of those who encouraged me are still with us and I'm grateful to them all. But three who were special to me, Carl Marias, Buff Secor, and Tony Heinsbergen are gone now—I miss them, their stories, and all the material they provided for my writing.

I owe thanks to numerous people who helped me to write this novel. First, Jerrilyn Farmer accepted me into the mystery writing class she taught at UCLA Extension. I was intimidated when I realized I was the only novice writer in the class but Jerrilyn and the class members were gracious and encouraging.

Sharon Doyle, Mark Hosack, Shari Shattuck and I formed a writers' group. Once again, I lucked out big time! All three were skilled, experienced writers who gently critiqued my work. And what fun we had!

I got lucky still again when Candy Somoza, a retired English and Creative Writing university professor, agreed to edit this series. And the fun continues!

Thank you to all of the above writers, editors, and teachers as well as fellow members of Mystery Writers of America and Sisters in Crime. The mystery writing community is generous, welcoming, and yes, fun.

Most of all thanks goes to my husband, Michael, for not just edits and support, but for his understanding of my need to write.

Turn the page for an exciting early look at:

ICED BLUE

Sherri Leigh James

A Cissy Huntington Mystery
Interior Designer to the Rich and Famous

Coming Summer 2019

Prologue

The woman struggled to sit upright on the slippery blonde leather seat of the limousine as her driver navigated the streets of West Hollywood gliding past the Robertson Boulevard boutiques and the Ivy Restaurant.

Pull yourself together, you silly old broad, she scolded herself. What is the matter with you?

"Madame, are you alright?"

How many times had she asked Thomas to call her by her first name? She lacked the energy to remind him again. She nodded.

Apparently, he missed her motion.

He asked again, "Are you okay?"

He turned the corner onto Melrose.

Did she look as bad as she felt?

"I'm fine," but her voice was no louder than a whisper. What had happened to her strength? Was this a stroke? Was it her heart? She pleaded with God, "Don't let me die until I set things right."

"Madame, do you want me to help you in? I could park instead of using the drop off."

"No." Worry had sharpened her voice. "Thank you, Thomas." Softer. Better. "I'll be fine." She sank into the leather for a quick rest while Thomas walked around the car to her door.

He opened the door and offered his sturdy brown hand. Covering her frail, trembling hand with his, he drew her from the car and on to her feet. "You are very pale. I don't think I should leave you here."

She waved him off, smoothed her auburn hair, concentrated on putting one foot in front of the other, and walked to the entrance. She had to fix the stupid, selfish things she'd done. She had to speak to her.

Chapter One

"Who is that woman in the front row?" I leaned over to whisper in the ear of my fellow panelist, Alexa Hampton. We sat in pale blue Eames chairs pulled up to a white Saarinen tulip table on the stage of the Silver Screen Theater in LA's Pacific Design Center.

"The one in the ice blue jacket? The one who's staring at you?" Alexa gave an imperceptible nod toward the woman who had fixed her pale blue-eyed gaze on my face.

"Yes," I said. "Does she look familiar to you?" She definitely did to me, but I wasn't certain if it was another instance of my mistaking an actress from the last movie I saw for an acquaintance. Whoever she was, her stare was creeping me out.

Alexa grabbed the chrome frame of her chair and scooted it closer to mine. "I think maybe she's an actress, but I don't remember her name. She sure looks familiar. I wonder why she's so-o intent on you?" she murmured, her face turned away from the audience.

Good question. But the moderator, Linda Desante had begun to speak. My curiosity would have to wait.

"First, this lovely lady on my left is Cissy Huntington, designer to the stars.

I nodded and smiled at Linda.

"I'd like to, somewhat belatedly, welcome her back to LA. As many of you know, she had been retired in San Francisco raising her family until last fall. Now that her youngest is a freshman at UC Berkeley, she has returned to both our city and the business. I don't imagine any of you missed the Architectural Digest cover featuring her project last month. And Cissy and her charming daughter, Emma, are currently working on a residence for super star Sally Abbey. Cissy will give you the inside scoop of what it's like to work for the super stars."

I was roped into this panel at the last minute, when fellow interior designer Rose Tarlow came down with a severe case of laryngitis. What a great excuse! Too bad I hadn't thought of it. Although Rose was probably disappointed: she had a new book to promote.

I had no idea that Linda, the moderator, was looking for a replacement panelist when she called the evening before. I set myself up by telling her that I was fine and planning to attend the discussion of LA design.

It wasn't that I minded being on a panel, but I was in no way prepared. I would normally have done some research, and, of course, there was the what-shall-I-wear issue.

Emma, my daughter and design assistant, insisted I had to wear something more hip than my two-year-old black Armani suit, now that I was to be on the stage. So, we spent what felt like hours last night with me trying on outfits and Emma critiquing. I'd ended up in my usual black slacks and one of Emma's white ruffled shirts.

Ironically, Alexa, daughter of recently deceased designer Mark Hampton and closer to Emma's age than mine, was dressed in a grey suit that looked suspiciously similar to my Armani.

"Next is Alexa Hampton. Alexa has just completed the re-do of the décor for Blair House in D.C., and she also has a beautiful new furniture line for Baker. She has some very nice slides of her pieces to show you. The actual pieces are on display upstairs in the Baker showroom. Alexa will address how best to use her furnishings in LA."

Alexa tossed back her chestnut hair and smiled sweetly in response to the applause.

"On Alexa's right is Buff Drake. Buff has some slides he would like to show you of his unique interior designs that make use of intense, bold color palettes. He also has a beautiful book that he will be happy to sign for you after our discussion. And he will recommend how to use his book in designing LA interiors."

Buff was dressed in his usual flamboyant style: a hot pink suit, a pale pink shirt, and a lavender tie. Where in the world had he found those spectator shoes in shades of pink?

Having seen him, certainly no one was surprised to learn that Buff is known for his unusual use of showy furnishings as well as bright colors in interior design.

I looked past Buff's new book, covered in purple faux ostrich skin displayed at the front of the white tulip table and noticed that the pale woman was still staring at me. I returned her gaze and smiled. My smile was not returned.

The moderator had begun without our fourth member, but he needed no introduction.

Frank Gehry entered the room shouting as he stormed down the aisle to the stage swinging his cane.

Every head in the auditorium but one turned to watch him. The auburn-haired head of the elderly woman remained forward, and her eyes remained fixed on my face. What was the deal with her?

Frank wore blue jeans, and a gray sweater with a black cashmere sackcloth blazer and black Doc Marten's all of which contrasted with his full head of snowy-white hair. Frank's the guy who does those way-out-there sculptural metal buildings: Bilbao's Guggenheim Museum, Seattle's Rock 'n' Roll museum, and our very own L.A. Disney Concert Hall.

The LA Times had to pick that particular morning to print a story about the park that was to be built around the Disney concert hall. "This is just bullshit." He roared at us all. "The city never even had the decency to reject our submission of over a year ago. Not one damn word. And then, out of the blue, this announcement of their selection of a new landscape architect. They're going to ruin my building! The setting is vital!" He was evidently oblivious to the fact that the moderator was attempting to talk. He stomped down the aisle, walked up to the microphone and continued to rant.

The thing about Frank is he's charming as hell, even when he's pissed off. And he's that rare phenomenon: a genius artist—in this case architect—who is popular in his own time.

I needn't have worried about what I was going to say. Frank's rage pre-empted most of my time, and I yielded much of what was left to Alexa. Between Alexa's delightful presentation of her new furniture line, Buff's proud showcasing of his new book on design, and Frank's blistering anger with the city management of LA, there was really no opportunity for me to say much more than that designing for the stars is a delightful, occasionally demanding, challenge.

The moderator barely got the words out that it was time for questions from the audience when several hands shot up. I was surprised that some of the younger guests yelled out their questions without bothering to raise their hands. "What is the hardest part of designing for the superstars?" one young lady shouted from the back of the auditorium.

"Cissy, I believe that question is for you," said the moderator.

"The bad news, for those of you aspiring to be designers to the stars, is that you must be on call 24/7," I explained to the audience. "Movie stars tend to keep odd hours. Three a.m. phone calls from clients are standard. One way of avoiding paparazzi or over-eager fans is to go out in the middle of the night. I once dropped off a mega star at a gym at one o'clock in the morning . . . after our meeting. It was the one time of the day he and his personal trainer could use the facilities in peace."

Several people hollered, "Who was that?" at once.

I smiled. "Of course, I won't be telling you who that was. Which leads me to the next bit of news: you won't be entertaining your friends with tidbits of gossip about your clients. In fact, keeping quiet will soon become such a habit that you'll find yourself out of the gossip loop entirely as you have nothing to exchange. Because, you see, you will inevitably be asked to sign a confidentiality agreement, the ubiquitous NDA."

The moderator said, "Thank you," as she pointed to a young woman in the second row with her hand raised.

"Is there anything good about designing for the stars?" asked the young woman whose head-to-toe black ensemble was punctuated with a pale pink statement necklace.

My fellow panelists smiled at me as I took the question. "There are some perks: traveling via private jet at someone else's expense is great. And a few of my clients have become good friends. On the rare occasions that you take your celeb client out shopping, it's fun to watch the reactions, as long as you avoid being caught in the crush."

"Do you have any advice for us wannabe designers to the stars?" asked a black-clad lad.

"Here's a tip: avoid the valet parking stand at the Ivy. I'm sure you've noticed the tourists hanging around there waiting to get a photo of a celeb. I walked by there with John Travolta once and was nearly trampled by the stampeding herd of tourists trying to get a shot of John." I ended on the gratifying laughter that story elicited from the audience. The only one who wasn't at least smiling was the woman in the front row who stared stone faced at me. She looked too delicate to be dangerous. But what if she had a gun?

I shook off my discomfort.

"Have you slept with any of your clients?" That was shouted anonymously from the back of the hall.

"Have I mentioned those confidentiality agreements?" I winked. Alexa was squirming in her seat. Frank was scowling at me. "That's enough questions for me. Ask Frank about his new project."

But apparently no one wanted to chance Frank ranting again. Even the Gehry groupies in the left section of the auditorium were quiet.

A sweet young man in the center section asked Buff if any of his clients ever resisted Buff's bright color palette.

"Why would they call me?" he answered. "Actually, I sometimes have clients who want such intense color and shocking combos, they're too over the top for me . . . if you can imagine such a thing."

There were a few more questions before the moderator announced, "That's all folks," and we were free to mingle with the audience briefly. I shook a few hands. Buff and Alexa both had agendas. Buff had a book to sell and Alexa a furniture line to promote.

My only agenda was to get out of there as fast as possible. I glanced around the auditorium. Despite the thinning crowd, I didn't locate the woman from the front row.

I had a lunch date in Beverly Hills with two of my movie star clients/friends. I had made the date when I knew I would already be at the PDC and could easily hop over to the restaurant right after the panel. Of course, at the point when I made that plan, I had no idea I was to be part of the panel and therefore possibly trapped.

I pushed through the crowd of BevHills matrons, design and architecture students, and Frank Gehry groupies that had rushed toward the stage, and flew up the aisle past the ceiling height maple doors. I dashed through the grey flannel anteroom and down the stairs past the round security and info desk. Planning to exit the parking tollbooths before the bulk of the crowd, I hurried to my car on the second floor of the garage structure.

The line for the valet had been long when I arrived, so I'd self-parked. Having learned a while back where the parking lot filled up last, I usually park there unless I have clients with me. I dashed up the stairs rather than wait for the elevator.

My gray Prius was parked behind the bank of elevators. As I turned the corner of the building, I saw an ice blue jacket on the hood of my car. What the hell?

I got closer. It wasn't just a jacket. It was the upper part of a person. Whoa, I recognized that auburn hair. Christ, it was the woman from the front row, what the hell? Draped over my car. Had she fainted?

Now I could find out who she was. Her Jimmy Choo-clad feet grazed the ground while most of her body rested on the hood of my car.

"Hello." I tapped her on the shoulder. No response.

"Hey!" I shook her. Still no response.

I bent down to look at her face. Her once pale blue eyes were now black and had that nobody's-home-look of the dead.

Oh, damn! Shit, shit, shit!

I searched for a pulse with one hand while I dialed 9-1-1 on my cell. I felt her wrists and her neck. She was limp. I couldn't find any sign of life.

911 put me on hold—why the hell do they do that? I really hate that shit!

I have got to learn CPR. This was the second body I'd found.

Reader Praise For

GIRL WITH A PAST

by Sherri Leigh James

"I couldn't put this book down. Read it in one day. I loved the characters, setting, the times and the detail. Each chapter took me deeper into the mystery. Ms. James knows how to tell a story."

"I really loved this book. The author sucks you right in with an infamous unsolved murder mystery—and descripttions of Berkeley tumultuous days that could've only been written by someone who lived it. Great read!"

"Girl with a Past has it all. There is authenticity in her portrait of San Francisco and the lives of the wealthy—as well as her evocation of Berkeley in the sixties. The heroine keeps plowing fearlessly into the past—unlocking family and police secrets. Lots of surprises and imaginative storytelling."

"This was a fun read and a great first novel by Sherri Leigh James. I picked up the book and within a chapter or two knew I would finish it quickly as it was hard to put down."

"It was engaging and fun and kept my interest level up. Brought back lots of memories of Berkeley in the 60's and 70's."

Made in the USA
Monee, IL
31 July 2021

74685055R00225